Jane Austen: Blood Persuasion

Also by Janet Mullany

JANE AND THE DAMNED
THE RULES OF GENTILITY

Jane Austen: Blood Persuasion

JANET MULLANY

WM

WILLIAM MORROW

An Imprint of HarperCollins*Publishers*

JANE AUSTEN: BLOOD PERSUASION. Copyright © 2011 by Janet Mullany. All rights reserved. Printed in the United States of America. No part of this book may be used or reproduced in any manner whatsoever without written permission except in the case of brief quotations embodied in critical articles and reviews. For information address HarperCollins Publishers, 10 East 53rd Street, New York, NY 10022.

HarperCollins books may be purchased for educational, business, or sales promotional use. For information please write: Special Markets Department, HarperCollins Publishers, 10 East 53rd Street, New York, NY 10022.

FIRST EDITION

Library of Congress Cataloging-in-Publication Data has been applied for.

ISBN 978-0-06-195831-1

11 12 13 14 15   OV/RRD   10 9 8 7 6 5 4 3 2 1

To Jane Austen and all those who love her

Acknowledgments

Thanks to Su and Keith Blakey for a wonderful visit to Steventon and Chawton in 2010; my agent, Lucienne Diver, and editor, May Chen, for their patience and help in making this a better book; Alison Hill, beta reader (is Jane nicer now?); Steve, for making coffee and performing other services; the staff at Jane Austen's House Museum and Chawton House; and everyone for listening when I complained about the book that refused to write itself.

Jane Austen: Blood Persuasion

Chapter 1

Chawton, Hants, 1810

"She's an extraordinarily troublesome girl," the Reverend James Austen said.

Jane watched in fascination as the girl in question, her niece Anna, pulled a hideous face at her father, an expression that lasted only a second before her pretty face resumed its normal sweetness.

"Come, brother, you'd rather have her commit folly at twenty-seven than seventeen?"

"I was sixteen when it started, Aunt Jane," Anna said.

"Indeed, a whole year of foolishness." James stood as his mother entered the drawing room. "How goes the garden, ma'am? I have brought you some cuttings; your garden boy has them."

"You did? Heavens, he'll probably kill them by looking at them. What possessed your brother to send me that boy I cannot imagine. He's all thumbs and none of them green. Come now, James, give your old mother a kiss. And you, too, Miss Anna, you must help me in the garden."

James frowned at the display of affection between Mrs. Austen and her granddaughter. "She is here to reflect upon her foolishness and inconstancy, ma'am, not to enjoy herself."

"Oh, of course," Jane murmured. "But you hate gardening, do you not, Anna? And going for walks, and playing upon the pianoforte, and talking nonsense, and reading novels, for that is all we do here, I fear."

"Hmm." As James spoke Jane saw a quick glance of affection between father and daughter, quickly masked. "I had in mind some improving literature and early nights."

"Naturally. Bread and water we can supply too, James. Never fear. We shall be the consummate gaolers."

"Oh, stop talking nonsense and make tea for us, Jane." Mrs. Austen removed the wide-brimmed, unfashionable straw hat she wore for gardening. "We shall keep Anna busy, you may be assured, and fortunately there are no eligible bachelors in Chawton."

"Indeed, yes," Jane said, measuring tea into the teapot. "For Mr. Papillon is destined for me, you know. If you set your cap for him, I shall be most displeased, Anna, and send you packing off home to Steventon again."

"Really? You have a beau, Aunt Jane?"

"Your aunt is funning you." James, softening a little, winked at his sister. "How goes the scribbling, Jenny?"

"Fair enough. Gallons of ink, acres of paper, and every morning my sister and mother and Martha have to wade through my torn-out hair a foot deep on the dining room floor. I thank you for asking, brother."

"I'm not so sure it wasn't novels that caused all this trouble in the first place," James said. "They contain much romantic silliness."

"Oh, heaven forbid we should act as rational creatures," Jane said. "Do you think we do not know the difference between fact and fiction, James? That all we read in novels is but a fantasy of the life we lead, and we such poor creatures we cannot tell the difference? And," she added, "mine don't contain romantic silliness. Silliness, possibly. Romance, possibly. But the two together? Impossible."

"Hush, Jane, or he'll take dear Anna away again." Mrs. Austen squeezed her granddaughter's hand. "I assure you she shall return to your house a sober and chastened creature. You will scarce recognize her. Jane will be in charge of her practice upon the instrument—the gentleman who comes to tune, by the way, is quite ugly and married with five children—Cassandra and Martha will teach her to bake and brew; and I shall make her pull weeds all summer."

"Very well." James accepted a cup of tea from his sister. "Where are Cassandra and Martha Lloyd? I should have liked to see them."

"I believe Cassandra is engaged in visiting one of the women in the village who is taken ill; we must add such calls to the list of suitable occupations for Anna," Jane said. "And the last time I saw Martha she was plucking a fowl and was all over feathers. You'll stay to dine, James?"

"No, I thank you. I must return home and write a sermon and cover my own floor with my hair." He reached into his coat. "Here's a London newspaper which Frank brought down."

"Oh, excellent." Mrs. Austen handed the newspaper to Jane. "You may read it, for I have no idea where my spectacles are. Now, tell me, James, do you know anything of Edward's new tenants in the Great House? We know they have moved in, for Edward wrote to tell us so but said little enough about them, and of course it is not proper for we ladies to call upon them . . ."

As mother and son engaged in gossip and exchanged news,

Jane leafed through the newspaper, with Anna looking over her shoulder.

"Aunt Jane, do you think I could remake this gown to match the one in the picture there?"

"I don't think so," Jane said. "We intend you to wear sackcloth and ashes to atone for your sins. Besides—" She stopped as a headline caught her eyes. "Oh!"

"What is it, my dear? Navy news?" Mrs. Austen asked.

Jane wondered at her mother's ability to carry on one conversation while keeping track of another. "No, ma'am, merely that the Prince of Wales has banished the Damned from Brighton and from the court."

"I should think so, too," Mrs. Austen said. "They are wicked and ungodly creatures."

"You forget, ma'am, that we sit here at liberty and talk English and not French because of their heroism some thirteen years ago," Jane said.

"Oh, that." Mrs. Austen flapped a dismissive hand. "As though our militia and Navy had nothing to do with it."

"The writer of this newspaper article would certainly agree with you, ma'am. There is no mention made of our debt to them."

"I believe it was greatly exaggerated at the time," James said. "Certainly I never saw anything of the sort. Indeed, I don't remember seeing a single French soldier."

"I assure you that you are mistaken, brother. I was there. I—"

"Well, that's all past," James said with a male heartiness that made his sister want to shake him. "As for the Damned now, we all know that they are depraved and dissolute, and . . . ah, well, up to no good," he trailed off, aware of Anna's interest. "Certainly very wicked and blasphemous. It is not the sort of topic that should be discussed among ladies in the drawing room." He sprang to his feet as Martha and Cassandra entered the room. "Sister! Miss Martha! Why, you look well, both of you. I've brought your errant niece as we agreed."

"*Where* were you, Aunt Jane?" Anna asked in a whisper after more tea had been poured and passed, and the Steventon gossip and relaying of family news resumed once more. "What did happen then?"

"I shall tell you of it later," Jane said. Sometimes the urge to speak of those times was overwhelming; sometimes she wished she could forget. She wasn't even sure that she would tell Anna anything of substance, for, as James said, it was not fit conversation for the drawing room. Much of it was certainly not suitable for a naive seventeen-year-old, whose worst indiscretion so far was to jilt a clergyman twice her age after throwing a year's worth of tantrums until her father agreed to the engagement.

Like it or not, it was Jane's duty to play the role of the respectable and responsible spinster aunt.

Later that night, Jane tapped at her niece's bedchamber door.

A sleepy voice bade her enter.

"I came to see if you were comfortable," Jane said, opening the door a little, "and I see you are, so I'll bid you good night."

"Oh, no!" Anna sat up in bed. "That is, I am most comfortable and not at all sleepy. Pray come in, Aunt Jane."

"Only for a moment. No late nights, remember." Jane came and sat on the bed, placing the candlestick she carried on a small table nearby.

Anna twisted a long curl of brown hair that escaped her nightcap. She had the delicate prettiness of her mother, with the bright hazel eyes so typical of the Austens.

"You don't have to talk about it to me unless you wish to,"

Jane said. "But your aunt Cassandra will almost certainly wish to know every detail, so consider this practice."

"Oh." Anna gave a dramatic, mortified groan. "I daresay you know more than I."

"True, all of our family are terrible gossips, and what we do not know in our letters to each other we invent. So tell me what happened with your Mr. Terry. I know you were mad for him all this last year."

"Papa said I was too young to marry."

"He is twice your age, but that is not necessarily an impediment to happiness, although your father considered you too young to marry anyone. So I admit I was surprised when your papa agreed to the engagement in the new year."

"I wore Papa down," Anna said. "I endured an exile at Godmersham—"

"Now, your uncle Edward's house and the pleasant land of Kent is hardly the equivalent of imprisonment in a sinister Italian castle."

"I feel foolish." Anna hung her head. "I spent three days with Mr. Terry's family only a few weeks ago. And, oh, Aunt Jane, he was a different person at his home. His mother ordered him around and made slighting comments on her neighbors and on me; she told me she expected me to have children but not too many—as though that is any of her business! And she talked continually of the cupboards in his house and how he should order them. Cupboards! The rest of the time she complained of her nerves and my—I mean, Mr. Terry—agreed with her all the time."

"Possibly he had learned a tactful agreement was the only way to deal with her."

"She made me put away my novel and read sermons to her. Michael—Mr. Terry, that is—even took her part in that!"

"Well, you know what I think of people who do not like novels. I am biased in that regard."

"And he made noises when he drank his soup," Anna said with an air of finality.

"A serious offense indeed." Poor little Anna. Jane patted her hand. "Pray try not to fall madly in love with a neighbor next time, Anna. It is so very awkward when things go wrong and respectable families are forced to behave like the Montagues and Capulets of Hampshire."

"Is—is Papa really angry with me? I cannot tell."

"More embarrassed than angry, I think. He looks stern, but beneath it all he loves you. He reminds me so much of my own dear papa, your grandfather Austen. He looks very much like him, too."

Anna nodded, but now there was a gleam in her eye. "Now it is your turn, Aunt Jane. Who is this Mr. Papillon?"

"Our clergyman, a most respectable bachelor whose sister keeps house for him in the village. It is a family joke, that is all."

"I don't see why it is a joke. You are still quite handsome, Aunt Jane. Or at least you would be if you did not wear that hideous cap."

"This cap befits my station as a respectable spinster of a certain age," Jane replied.

"Oh, you are being satirical. Really, Aunt, that cap is most unbecoming, and I shall make it my duty to force you to wear something prettier. But tell me about what no one would talk of, about the Damned."

Jane hesitated. "Briefly, then. I doubt you remember any of this for you were a tiny child. The French invaded and we thought all was lost, but the Damned were instrumental in protecting the Royal Family and leading the fight against the enemy. Your grandmother and grandfather, and Cassandra and I, were in Bath when it happened. And . . ." She fell silent. The golden candle flame wavered, and Jane flapped away a moth, awoken early, that sought to destroy itself in the seductive glow.

Anna looked at her expectantly.

"And now no one speaks of it. It was a shameful time for us, you understand, and many wish to erase it from their memories. Some respectable and wellborn people behaved dishonorably, treasonably even. The Prince of Wales now rejects those who saved his head and his crown. It is unjust."

"You speak so passionately, Aunt Jane."

Jane bent to kiss her niece. "It's time for you to go to sleep. Did you say your prayers?"

"I did, but maybe I should pray that the Prince of Wales behaves better. And that the Damned be granted divine forgiveness and not sent to hell."

"I fear both are impossible." Jane picked up her candlestick. "Good night, Anna."

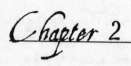 Chapter 2

The night called to her.

She lay in bed, trying not to fidget, for Cassandra slept lightly and Jane did not want to disturb her. But the night, its velvet shadows and the thin gleam of moonlight, beckoned to her. She remembered the embrace of darkness, of slipping through the shadows, strong and dangerous and graceful.

Jane punched her pillow and tried to compose her mind to sleep. In her mind she recited verses from the Bible, poems, the dates of the kings and queens of England, old familiar friends that she had long relied on to lull her into drowsiness. She counted the chimes of the clock in the house and the church clock. But the restlessness prevailed. Memories of power and strength and swiftness came and went.

Memories of being Damned.

More than a decade ago she had accepted such occasional phantasms as part of her being—for she had no word for what she experienced; for certain, she was sure no one else could understand these sensations. She had tried once, timidly, to ask Cassandra for advice, and her sister, blushing furiously, had thought

Jane admitted to some solitary sensual temptation. Prayer, Cassandra advised, and keeping busy, and (blushing even deeper) Jane should keep her hands above the bedclothes.

Oh, if only Cassandra knew.

But Cassandra didn't want to know or even remember. And apparently neither did the Prince of Wales—*oh, George, you are such a fat, foolish thing. And to think you were once my friend. If only I could speak to you and make you see sense.*

We have tried.

Jane sat bolt upright in bed. The reply to her thoughts had come through as clean and sharp as though someone—only she wasn't sure who—had spoken into her ear.

Who are you? Where are you? she asked, fearful, but no reply came.

She slipped from her bed and onto her knees, shivering a little in the chilly air of the spring night (of course the fire was not lit; what a dreadful extravagance that would be!). She clasped her hands and prayed fervently. *Father, if Thou be willing, remove this cup from me: nevertheless not my will, but Thine, be done.*

She rested her forehead on her joined hands, and her thoughts, if not her actual prayer, shifted to her father. Dear James, he'd looked so like him today, with his strong wavy hair and handsome profile, trying hard to be stern with his troublesome daughter.

Her knees ached at the contact with the cold wooden floor, but before she slid back into bed, she whispered one final short, urgent prayer. *Dear Lord, do whatever You will, but please let me write. And let Cassandra love me still.*

The next morning the Austen ladies sat in their drawing room, hands busy at their work. Jane looked at her sister and wondered if the two of them were in some secret, unspoken competition as to who should produce the most unbecoming cap. Even Cassandra, pretty Cassandra—if a woman of her age could be described as pretty—looked rather like a handsome sheep in hers, her chestnut hair covered. Jane might be the only one who knew that a slender streak of gray adorned her sister's rich hair.

Jane dipped her needle into the piece of fabric she had chosen from among the pile of scraps on the table, proud of her small, neat stitches. This gown, she remembered this gown, worn at Godmersham a few years ago, when she had sported a flattering, dashing cap and allowed herself the pleasure of a lot of wine and a little flirtation. And now it was to be part of a handsome quilt, its memories captured and tamed.

"I do not think anyone will come to call," Mrs. Austen pronounced, laying her work aside. "A little nuncheon, I believe, and then—"

But someone hammered at the front door.

"Heavens, it sounds as though the Watch is come to arrest us," Cassandra said.

"Doubtless to arrest my aunts for their dreadful caps," Anna said.

Jane listened as their maidservant opened the door and announced that, yes, the ladies were home. She didn't recognize the voices—or did she? But there was something she did recognize, even without seeing or even hearing the visitors, a knowledge of who they truly were. Certainly she had encountered members of the Damned a few times since 1797, strangers she identified as such by their beauty and pallor and grace. Always she had looked away, fearing that those long, painful days of the Cure, the poison of the Bath waters weakening her and returning her to a mortal state, might be undone. But to have the Damned come to call—and so early in the day!—surely they could not be her brother Edward's tenants?

"Mrs. Kettering, ma'am, from the Great House."

Two ladies entered the room, the second, from her plainer dress and the large basket she carried, an upper servant. But the first . . . she swooped to take Mrs. Austen's hand, all charm and seduction, making the simplicity of the parlor appear drab and provincial, and Jane was powerless to stop her. She introduced herself as Dorcas Kettering.

"Mrs. Austen! I have taken the liberty of coming to call without a letter of introduction, but dear Mr. and Mrs. Knight assured us it would be perfectly correct. Why, you must be Miss Austen and Miss Jane, and who is this charming young lady? Will you not introduce me?"

Power sizzled up Jane's arm as she took the woman's hand. Their eyes met, Mrs. Kettering's mischievous and knowing. With as much composure as she could muster, Jane introduced Anna.

Jane stared in horror as Mrs. Kettering took both of Anna's hands in hers and smiled upon her. "Why, what a pretty child you are."

"Anna is my niece," Jane said in a panic. "She visits us in Chawton. Her father is a clergyman. Quite nearby." As though that would make any difference.

Mrs. Kettering was dowdily dressed, although it did little to hide her beauty, with a bonnet in a shape that had been fashionable a few years ago and an elaborate tucked and embroidered cotton gown. Despite the dry weather she wore a pair of pattens over incongruous jeweled dancing slippers. The woman who accompanied her, plainly dressed and with a chatelaine hanging from her bosom, sat quietly in a corner, the basket on her lap.

"And how do you get on in the Great House?" Mrs. Austen asked. "It is a shockingly old-fashioned place, but my son Edward plans many improvements."

"We are very comfortable, ma'am," Mrs. Kettering replied.

"The other ladies and gentlemen of our party all agree it is a most handsome and pleasant house. But you must see for yourself, for I have come here with the express purpose of inviting you to dine."

To *dine!* Jane interrupted her hastily. "I regret we do not—"

"Now, Jane," her mother interrupted, "here is Martha with some more hot water. You'll take tea, Mrs. Kettering. This is Miss Lloyd, our particular friend who looks after us all. And how do you like our little village, ma'am?"

"It is altogether charming!" she cried. "And this house is so delightful, so snug and . . . rural. Do you know, Mrs. Austen, we have seen some cows this morning!"

"How extraordinary," Jane said. She handed Mrs. Kettering a cup of tea, wishing she could dash it into her face.

"So, you will dine with us tomorrow," Mrs. Kettering said. "My brother-in-law Fitzpatrick insists you must, and he begs to be remembered to you."

"Fitzpatrick?" Mrs. Austen's brow creased. "I don't believe we know . . ."

"He met you in Bath some dozen years ago, ma'am, and was kind enough to help you find some lodgings."

"Oh! I remember now—although at first I did not recognize the name. I could have sworn his name was Fitzwilliam. He was most kind to us during that unsettled time."

"It is the same gentleman, ma'am, and he begs to be remembered to you all. Pressing business prevented him from accompanying me this morning, or so he says, but you know how gentlemen are about morning calls. They are so easily bored with our feminine chatter."

Jane almost choked on her tea in anxiety. William, who had introduced himself to her parents and sister as Fitzwilliam, was now here in Chawton! No wonder she had been so unsettled, and surely it was William who had spoken in her mind last night.

Cassandra patted Jane on the back as she spluttered and dabbed at her lips with her handkerchief. "We no longer go out in society—" Jane began, but she was interrupted by her mother and Cassandra and Martha, who accepted the invitation with great excitement.

"Oh, it will be a very quiet affair," Mrs. Kettering said. "But three or four families, although we can promise Miss Anna dancing and some very handsome partners after dinner. You do like to dance, do you not, Miss Anna? Ah, I thought so."

"You are most kind, Mrs. Kettering," Mrs. Austen cried.

"We are supposed to be keeping Anna out of trouble. She is here for punishment," Jane hissed to Cassandra. "She—"

Cassandra raised her eyebrows.

"Nonsense, look how excited the child is," Mrs. Austen said. "Why, it will do her good to have a little pleasure. And as Mrs. Kettering says, it will be a very quiet affair."

"So, it is settled," Mrs. Kettering said, beaming and showing a lot of teeth. "We shall send our carriage for you at eight."

"Eight, ma'am?" Jane asked.

"Oh, of course. Yes. This is the country. At four, then. Now, maybe you can advise me, Mrs. Austen. My housekeeper, Mrs. Chapple, and I intend to visit the sick and the poor of the village. Whom would you recommend we visit?"

"No!" The word burst out before Jane could prevent herself, accompanied by a jolt of pain in her canines. Her teacup rolled from her lap onto the floor, scattering tea leaves onto the carpet.

"Why, Jane, whatever is the matter?"

"I beg your pardon, ma'am. Toothache," Jane mumbled, on her knees to retrieve the teacup. She swabbed at the carpet with her handkerchief.

"Oh, do not do that, Jane," Martha said. "It will stain the linen. Let me fetch you a clean cloth and some oil of cloves for your poor tooth. Excuse me, Mrs. Kettering."

"Let me think," Mrs. Austen said as Martha left the room. "There is always Miss Benn, of course, but she is a gentlewoman in distress."

"I beg of you, Mrs. Kettering, do not visit Miss Benn. She will not accept charity," Jane said.

"And poor Betty Cooper is quite ill," Cassandra said. "She swooned while walking out—we do not know why she ventured from home—but now lies pale and exhausted and feeble. Martha and I saw her yesterday. I hope she has improved."

"She sounds just the thing!" Mrs. Kettering cried. "So, ladies, Mrs. Austen and Miss Austen and Miss Jane and Miss Anna, we shall be on our way. Where can we find this unfortunate Betty?"

"I shall show you the way," Jane said. "Allow me to fetch my bonnet, ma'am."

She dashed into the vestibule where a row of pegs held the family's bonnets and cloaks and joined Mrs. Kettering and the housekeeper, escorting them from the house with a sigh of relief.

"I know what you are," Jane said when they were a few steps away. "Pray never come to my house again."

Mrs. Kettering smiled. "And I know what you are, dear Jane. No, do not deny it. The Cure is rarely successful—well, sometimes it kills, so I suppose it is successful, for the afflicted then goes to heaven, having repented—but in most cases the signs of your true nature come and go for the rest of your mortal life. But let us not stand on formality. You must call me Dorcas."

"I would prefer not to. And I will certainly persuade my family that you are not fit company, even if you live in Edward's house."

"Oh, foolish Jane." Dorcas took her hands and once again Jane felt the surge of power and awareness, of aching familiarity. "You wish to see William, your Creator. It is natural."

"Stop it!" Jane wrenched her hands away. "Neither shall I allow you to visit poor Betty or anyone else in the village. Doubtless you wish to dine upon her."

Dorcas's canines extended a little: a warning. "You mistake me, my dear. We are country people now. We do our duty to those less fortunate than ourselves. Of course," she added thoughtfully, "that is almost everyone else, but we must do our best."

They stepped back as a coach rattled down the street, Dorcas's housekeeper placing her basket on the ground with a sigh of relief.

"What on earth do you have in your basket?" Jane asked. "It looks very heavy."

"Oh, some nourishing foods," Dorcas said. "Some lemon tarts and a turkey."

"For the sick and the poor?" Jane shook her head. "You are much mistaken."

"Indeed?" Dorcas no longer looked offended; now her expression was one of perplexity.

"How would a poor family cook a turkey? Their hearth is not big enough. And lemon tarts are certainly not suitable for an invalid. You should provide gruel or a jelly. Martha can give your housekeeper a recipe—" Jane stopped herself. She would certainly prevent any contact between the Austen household and the inhabitants of the Great House.

Dorcas beamed. "Oh, how very kind of you. But tell me, do I look the part?"

"Not at all." Jane felt a certain pleasure as Dorcas's face fell.

"Your bonnet is too gaudy, your gown unbecoming and ostentatious, and you need to buy a pair of half boots like mine. The dancing slippers and pattens are ridiculous."

"We have so much to learn, dear Jane."

"But not from me or my household, I regret. I'll bid you good day, Mrs. Kettering. Pray do not call upon us again."

"Oh, here comes my brother!" Dorcas waved as a rider approached.

As man and horse came nearer, Jane could see that the mount was in distress, flecked with foam and showing the whites of its eyes; no wonder, with one of the Damned astride it. The rider struggled to control the horse, which whinnied and shied as it caught sight of Dorcas (Jane refused to consider that she, too, might be a cause of fear), and the gentleman fell from the saddle, landing with a loud thump on the dusty road.

The horse kicked up its heels and galloped back along the road, stirrups swinging.

"Damnation," the gentleman said, and rose to his feet, brushing mud from his coat and reaching for his hat. "Miss Jane Austen, I presume." He bowed. "Your servant, ma'am. Tom Fuller."

"You are riding! Why?" Jane burst out. Everyone knew of animals' dislike of the Damned.

"I am a country squire," Mr. Fuller replied. "Country squires ride. So must I, although, devil take it, this hat is ruined. The wretched beast trod upon it." He smacked at a hoofprint denting the smooth surface of his beaver hat. "I shall talk with William about increasing the dosage. We give them a little of our blood with their feed, Jane, to accustom them to our presence, but apparently not enough. William is most anxious to see you, by the by."

"I regret that is unlikely, Mr. Fuller. I have no intention of renewing our acquaintance. In fact, I suggest you all return to town where you and your favored activities so obviously belong."

"Favored activities?" Mr. Fuller revealed himself *en sanglant*. "Do not deceive yourself, Jane. You are one of us. And we have every intention of staying here."

"Jane has been so very helpful and neighborly already!" Dorcas cried. "Why, country living will suit us so extremely well, particularly with the Austens as our friends. They are to dine with us tomorrow, Tom."

"Excellent. Until tomorrow, Jane. I must make sure my errant horse has returned safely to the stables." He bowed and strolled away, the battered hat replaced on his head.

"I shall accompany you," Dorcas called after him. *"Au revoir,* Jane."

Jane went back into the house where already Anna had brought her best gown into the drawing room and was deep in conversation with Cassandra about how it might be altered, for both of them agreed that Mrs. Kettering's day dress was so very smart the Austens feared they would be put to shame.

Jane glanced out the window. Mrs. Austen had retired to the garden, where clad in her usual green smock, straw hat, and serviceable thick gloves, she was engaged in planting the cuttings James had brought over the day before.

Frowning, Jane retired to the dining room and drew a chair up to the table by the window. She opened her writing slope and removed a creased and stained bundle of papers, along with the clean copy she was making. Yes, it made sense, but for how long? When she had been Damned before, her words had appeared like a mystifying code, a tale told by an idiot, merely words on the page with no sense or coherence.

Or, Jane thought, maybe she had just written badly. She read through the first page in her hand. Some of it was smeared and illegible, but the rest made sense, even if the writing was somewhat clumsy. She smiled and reached for her quill, drawing her fingers down the feather.

A great bird, wings outspread, hissing through an orange beak; green grass, the glimmer of steel gray water beyond, the scent of grass and mud and rank river—she dropped the quill. Queasily she glanced around the room, knowing that any object she touched might communicate through her skin into her mind, and that she must once again learn to control and push aside the immediate, disturbing sensations.

With great care she leaned to pick up the quill and laid it on the small table next to the manuscript.

The door creaked open and Jane turned, annoyed at the interruption.

"Oh, Aunt Jane, I am sorry to disturb you, for Aunt Cassandra said I should do so only on a very urgent matter."

"What is it, my dear?"

"Aunt Cassandra said I must ask you if you knew where her pink ribbon has gone. She is sure we have it somewhere, but if we cannot find it we must go into Alton to buy more."

"Pink ribbon?" Jane echoed.

Anna moved closer, leaning on her chair, her arm brushing against Jane's. *Aunt Jane is so pretty and lively still, I wonder why she did not marry. Oh and maybe tomorrow I shall meet some handsome young gentlemen and I hope my hair curls and . . .*

Jane shifted to break the contact and avoid the intrusion into Anna's thoughts. "My dear, I am afraid I have no idea. Is it absolutely necessary?"

"It is a matter of life and death," Anna said with a self-satirizing air that Jane appreciated. She leaned over her aunt's shoulder. "Is this your book?"

"One of them."

"It looks as though something spilled all over it. What a shame. But you can see some of the words. Do you make a fair copy? Did you spill tea onto it?"

"Something of that sort," Jane said.

Even now, aided by the extraordinarily sensitive sense of smell the Damned possessed, she could pick up the scent of those faded brown stains. Repulsion and longing stirred within her.

Thirteen years ago the pages had been soaked in blood.

Chapter 3

The day consisted of dressmaking frippery that even Mrs. Austen joined, abandoning her garden and scrubbing her nails clean, and even going so far as to retrim her best turban with some feathers that had once graced one of Cassandra's bonnets. Jane, meanwhile, retreated to her table in the dining room and glared ferociously at anyone who might dare disturb her.

"Don't growl at me!" Cassandra said. "I wanted to tell you only that I had borrowed a pair of your silk stockings."

Her hand over her mouth, Jane nodded. Her canines ached and stung, and she wanted to rise and pace around the room. Outside, the sun had passed its brightest and highest point of the day, and in a few hours it would be dark.

"You had best get ready," Cassandra said. "We expect the carriage in twenty minutes, and your hands are covered with ink. How did those papers get in such a state with all those horrid stains?"

"You don't remember?" Jane said.

"They look as though they're fit only to start a fire." She reached a hand out.

"No!" Jane said. "That is—see, I twist each into a spill when I have finished with it." She looked at Cassandra's placid, pretty face and wondered how long it would be before her sister's composure was destroyed.

Do you not remember, Cassandra? I killed a man in front of you, ripped out his throat before he could shoot you, and you lay on the floor among these bloody papers and screamed and shrank from me, because you saw me as a monster. No wonder you wished to forget. Who would want to see their own sister so?

But instead of saying the words, she gathered her papers into a neat pile and pressed them into the storage area of the writing slope. She kissed her sister's cheek, catching a brief hint of her scent and of her excitement at the thought of an evening out.

"Cassandra, if I said that we should absolutely not go to the Great House but I could not give you a reason why, would you abide by my wishes?"

Cassandra laughed. "When I remember the young Miss Jane who was such a determined flirt and whose only aim in life was to shock our neighbors, I'm surprised that you take such a high moral stance with Anna. Have you forgotten what it is to be young?"

"It's not about Anna," said Jane. "Not as much as it is about them, Edward's tenants. I do not think we should consort with them."

"Oh, don't be foolish," Cassandra said. "Doubtless they intend to invite us once, and then, their duty to our brother done, they will ignore us for as long as they stay here. I doubt whether they will stay more than a month or so, for we are so very quiet here."

"What do you remember of Mr. Fitzpatrick?" Jane asked.

Cassandra took her arm and led her out of the dining room and up the stairs. "He was a very pleasant gentleman as I remember. He helped us find temporary lodgings when—when—" Her voice faltered.

"When the French wanted to arrest you and Mama and Papa, having arrested me."

"Jane!" Cassandra pushed her into their bedchamber. "We should not talk of that time. We agreed not to, do you not remember? It was a very unhappy time for us, and you were unwell, and . . . I shall unlace your gown so you can put on your best one, and you should really wash your face. You have a smudge of ink here." She licked her fingertip and rubbed a spot on Jane's cheek.

Oh, poor Cassandra. She was so frightened of letting loose a great flood of awful memories and unanswered questions. Jane embraced her, and Cassandra gave a squeak of surprise. "What was that for?"

"Oh, I merely felt like expressing my affection for my dearest sister."

"You squeezed me half to death!" Cassandra said, releasing herself. "Come along, you silly sentimental creature, you must hurry."

After a little sisterly bickering—Cassandra had borrowed the pair of silk stockings that Jane herself had intended to wear, claiming that the other pair were finer, although Jane pointed out that they were held together by a cobweb of darns—the sisters descended the stairs. Mrs. Austen, majestic in her refurbished turban, stood with Anna, who was quite pale with nervousness.

"Will it be so very grand?" Anna asked.

"Of course not," Jane said. "This is the country."

She was wrong. The house was ablaze with lights, something that caused the thrifty Mrs. Austen to gasp and speculate aloud how much the household must spend a year on wax candles. Footmen, all of them young and handsome—why was Jane not surprised?—were everywhere, and she hoped she and Cassandra between them could come up with a respectable amount of pennies for vails. These footmen, however, looked as if anything below a shilling apiece was beneath their notice.

Dorcas moved forward to greet them as the Austens were shown into what had once been the Great Hall of the house several centuries before, where about a dozen people were gathered.

"Why, Jane, you sly thing! You quite outdo me in taste and elegance." Dorcas, whose luxurious, flowing gown was the height of fashion along with the silver and paste comb in her hair, linked her arm in Jane's.

"You flatter me," Jane said.

"Nonsense! Such elegance of figure and face—yes, you are one of us, it is clear to all now. Come, you must see William. I assure you he has been in such a state, anticipating your reunion."

"Indeed? And what sort of state would that be?" Jane cast a glance over her shoulder. She was relieved to see her mother, sister, and niece talking to Mr. Papillon, the curate, and his sister, but as she was led across the room, a wake of whispers followed, as her neighbors speculated upon Miss Jane Austen and her handsome friend. Had she been a good ten years younger and the comments related to her looks and gown, she would have been mightily flattered. Now, she was alarmed to be associated with Dorcas.

"I think my mother may need me," she managed feebly.

"Good heavens, no, she is deep in the subject of herbaceous borders with her neighbors." Dorcas led her back into the entrance hall and past the Jacobean staircase. A footman sprang forward to open a door into a small book-lined room.

Jane took a deep breath.

"My dear Jane." William stepped forward and took her hands, and thirteen years of pain and longing dropped away.

He looked the same; of course he would, and he would do so

for centuries more, tall and dark haired, handsome. He regarded her gravely.

"You need not tell me I am changed," she said. "Consider that I am older and wiser."

"You are still the most handsome woman of my acquaintance," William said.

Jane considered shrieking and slapping him with her fan—the Misses Steeles, recent literary inventions whom she was enjoying immensely, would almost certainly have done so. But instead she basked in his warmth and welcome.

"I was most sorry to hear of Mr. Austen's death," William said.

"I miss him still." She withdrew her hands. "What do you want, William? You are behaving almost as—as any normal gentleman might, yet I know you for what you are."

"So you should. I am your Creator."

"A pity you did not say so with such ardor thirteen years ago."

"It was a—a difficult time." He spread his hands in supplication. "Can you forgive me for my callousness and neglect?"

Jane walked away from him and took a turn of the room, noting the ancient mullioned windows and tapestries, faded with age, that adorned the walls. The planks beneath her feet were wide and glowed with the patina of centuries.

She turned back to him. "Sir, you created and abandoned me, breaking the rules of your own kind—and pray do not bleat of difficult times, for you sound like my sister and mother at their most peevish. No one will speak of what is past. Yet it is done and we live with the consequences, I with my decision to become mortal again, and you—"

"You? Mortal?" He moved to her side, fast and graceful. "I think not, Jane."

She glared at him. "Oh, very well. At the moment I am neither fish nor fowl."

He reached out to her again, but she evaded his hand. "Over a decade, William, I have wandered, unable to settle because of family circumstances. Now and again I would take out my manuscripts and look at them, yet I could not bear to return to what had given me so much joy. I was afraid that I had lost everything, that my small gift as a writer had faded. And now, now when we are settled and my mother and sister have as much happiness as women in their situation can expect, I have started to work once more, and it is the greatest delight of my life. Shall it be taken from me again, William?" She stamped her foot like a younger Anna in a rage. "It is so damned unfair!"

"I will atone," he said. "I swear it."

She snorted. "Oh, certainly. You sound like someone in an Italian opera. Or in a book—a bad one. Some gothic horror with an ancient house and mysterious creatures dwelling therein."

He smiled. "Life imitates art, my dear Jane."

"It depends entirely upon your definition of life, sir."

"Still as witty and as passionate as ever, Jane. Jane, let me be your Bearleader. Let me guide you through this maze. I abandoned you the first time. I will not do so a second time."

She had forgotten his power over her, the seductive thrill of his voice and person, but he had failed her before.

"Enough of your high-flown eloquence, William. Now tell me what you want from me."

He walked past her to the window and leaned his forehead on the glass. "In a matter of hours it will be dark, and every night I hope . . . Jane, you are the last of my fledglings. Do not leave me."

A long silence. The timbers of the ancient house made small sounds as it settled with the fading warmth of the day, and a shower of sparks arose as a log shifted in the fireplace.

"Luke?" Jane said, her voice tight and the sadness that she had worked so hard to conquer rising in her. "What has happened to

Luke?" Her former lover was old, for one of the Damned, almost as old as William, his Creator. He might well be gone to dust and to the fires of hell.

"He lives still," William said. "But he is—he left to join another household. There is a rift between us."

"I am sorry to hear it," Jane said.

"And as for George, well, he is the Prince of Wales and his memory is short. He is ungrateful and intemperate. He has thrown us over entirely, Jane, as a child throws away the toys he has tired of."

"So I have heard." She smiled, but she was anxious not to talk of Luke. "And so that is why you try so hard to be country gentry."

He gave a rueful laugh and turned from the window. "And how do we do?"

"Quite badly, I fear. You really must do something about the horses, you know. People like them in the country, and dogs, too."

He grimaced. "We have some dogs for appearances' sake. They hate us. Quite often I'm tempted to bite them back. "

"Most unfortunate," Jane said, relieved that they no longer spoke of Luke. "But why? Why do you go against your nature so?"

"We are out of fashion," William said. "It has happened before and it will happen again. We have found it wisest to lie low, to practice discretion in our ways. It is how we survive. We shall wait a century or so and see how taste and fashions change, and when the time is right, we shall take our rightful place in society once more. Consider, for example, that once we could not go out in the daytime; we have changed over the centuries."

"I must say I was astonished to meet one of the Damned fully dressed—although very badly—at ten of the morning, when Dorcas came to call," Jane said.

"She told me of it. Join us, Jane. It is time."

She shook her head. "No, William. I cannot. I shall pray, for myself and for you, but I will not hurt my family."

He strolled to the fireplace and kicked the logs into a blaze. "At the least, be good neighbors to us, Jane, for I must care for my family, too, this household. And I shall help you, for I see a metamorphosis has begun in you. So it is with those who take the waters as Cure; often it is not complete. Have you been *en sanglant* yet?"

"No, but my teeth ache. Of course, at my advanced age that is to be expected, but this is different. Of late I have been able to feel things and hear others' thoughts. I hate it, William. I should rather do anything than become one of the Damned again."

"And—this is indelicate, forgive me—you feel no urge to dine?"

"I should quite like some dinner, William, but I know that is not what you mean. No. Not yet, but I fear I shall hunger."

"You must come to me when it happens. Promise me." He held out his hand to her. "I shall help."

She took his hand and allowed herself to be lulled into the web of warmth and safety and, yes, love that he spun around her. But it was not enough, and it was not what she wanted.

"You know I shall never leave Cassandra again," she said. "I value my soul, sir, and I value my small gift for writing. I shall fight with prayer and all human means to preserve myself. But if my metamorphosis continues, I wish to know what I may expect."

He bowed his head in acknowledgment. "I admit we chart unknown waters. I cannot tell you how long it will take the metamorphosis to take place or what human qualities you will lose."

"If I were able to write still . . ." She looked away, horrified. Was her soul of so little concern that she should place her writing above everything?

He shook his head. "I wish I could set your mind at ease."

For a moment she almost pitied him, her once-powerful Creator admitting that even despite his centuries of existence, his knowledge was limited.

"Do we dine?" she said. "I mean—that is, maybe it is time we should go into dinner. I trust you do not have designs upon your neighbors' persons."

"Ah. Once . . ." William smiled. "But no, those days are past. We are entirely respectable now. But it is time for me to play host, and we shall join the others."

He offered his arm to escort her.

"Then how do you . . . I trust I am not indelicate, but I hardly think you have developed a taste for good English beef. I could not help but notice your footmen."

He cleared his throat. "Indeed."

"How very convenient that there are so many and all so handsome," Jane commented as they entered the Great Hall again.

"And a few adventurous ladies find reasons to call. They are most welcome."

"Indeed! Now I shall wonder who among my acquaintance succumbs to the charms of your company. But you do not need to tell me, William; I shall find them out. I have an eye for an adulteress."

Jane enjoyed dinner, as much for the food and wine as for watching the Damned, William, and his alleged sister-in-law Dorcas and her brother Tom (the blood tie that bound them was not a human one and they might even be lovers or bound as Consorts according to the customs of the Damned). Their deception and appearance were innocent; they ate little and encouraged their guests to talk of country matters, crops and the weather, gossip of neighbors and their activities.

Anna, she was pleased to see, looked exceedingly pretty and, although shy, responded readily when those seated close to her engaged her in conversation.

After dinner, Dorcas led her female guests upstairs to the parlor, where one of the handsome footmen assisted in pouring and handing out tea.

"How very polite we—you—have become," Jane said to her in a low voice, thinking of the activities in which the Damned indulged when she had last been among them.

Dorcas sighed. "I know. It is so very tedious. But tell me, Miss Jane"—in a slightly louder voice—"how long does your charming niece stay with you?"

"A month or so," Jane replied. *Lay one finger, or one tooth upon her, you or any of your kind, and I shall rip out your throat.*

"I am most saddened you trust us so little," Dorcas replied quietly. "But do you not see? It is your true nature as one of the Damned that makes you so very protective of your family."

"You are mistaken, ma'am. My family has always been my first loyalty."

A flicker of canine appeared at Dorcas's lip. "William is of your family. By extension, so am I and Tom. We shall stand by you, whatever you feel, although your ingratitude pains me."

Jane bowed her head. She declined an invitation to perform at the pianoforte, a handsome instrument she envied, but encouraged Anna to do so, and was gratified at the warm applause that met the young woman's playing.

"Charming, quite charming," Tom announced, as he and William entered the drawing room. "You play exceedingly well, Miss Anna. Do you sing, too?"

Anna gazed at Tom with obvious admiration, making no effort to hide her attraction, and a small triumphant smile played over Tom's beautiful lips.

Jane clapped a hand to her mouth as pain surged through her

canines. Horrified, she fought to regain control. William gave her a concerned look.

"Why, what is the matter, Jane?" Mrs. Austen asked.

"Toothache," Jane muttered from behind her hand. "Do not concern yourself, ma'am." Sure enough, her canines were aching and sensitive and sharp to her tongue. She was not quite *en sanglant,* but it was the nearest she had come so far.

"We really must take you to the dentist if things do not improve," Mrs. Austen said. "What do you think, Martha?"

"Dear Jane, allow me to look," Martha said, and touched Jane's hand with her own. They both wore lace mittens, and the effect of bare skin touching her own was too much. Martha's anxiety flooded her mind, overwhelmed her.

Jane leaped to her feet. "I beg of you—"

"Jane, you must drink this." William was at her side, a small glass of wine in his hand.

A drop of something dark coiled and spread in the wine, dissipating like smoke and releasing a rich scent. She reached for the glass and its precious liquid, a single drop of William's blood dissolved in wine, the first time he had ever allowed her this great privilege. A great sense of well-being and safety spread through her as she drank her Creator's gift.

"So. Do you feel better?" William took the glass from her and placed it on a tray held by a footman who lingered nearby. Jane suspected, from the gleam in his eye, that the footman might take the glass away and scoop out any last drops for himself.

"Much better, thank you." Her teeth were once more under control, and her anxiety and rage had ebbed away, leaving peace and happiness in their wake.

"Let us repair to the Great Gallery, ladies!" Dorcas moved forward to take William's arm. "I believe I can hear our musicians tuning their instruments."

Cassandra joined Jane as the ladies, gathering shawls and fans, prepared to follow their hosts. "Fie on you, flirting so!" She giggled.

"But he is so very handsome," Anna whispered.

"Nonsense. We are old friends, William and I, and he most kindly gave me some wine. You have such an imagination, sister. Maybe you should write a book."

Cassandra stuck her tongue out at Jane in a most unladylike way while Anna looked on in amazement.

"Oh, behave yourselves," Martha said. "May I help you with your shawl, Mrs. Austen?"

"Thank you, my dear. I fear my daughters are neglectful of me, so determined are they to behave like children, although I must say as young girls you two were much better behaved." But Mrs. Austen smiled as she spoke. "I was not aware you knew Mr. Fitzpatrick so intimately, Jane. I can scarcely remember you speaking to him when we met him in Bath. But there was another gentleman, was there not? I fancied you harbored a *tendresse* for—"

"Ma'am, how can I set an example to my niece if you insist on revealing my scandalous past?" Jane took her mother's arm. "Anna, if you are to learn anything of this, it is not to overindulge in a host's excellent wine at dinner. I fear Martha may be busy making draughts for our aching heads tomorrow."

"Indeed, yes, and they will taste exceedingly unpleasant!" Martha smiled. "Will you dance, Jane?"

"Of course not. I have had enough dissipation for the evening. I intend to sit by the fire and make tomorrow's medicine worthwhile with some more wine. But I hope Anna will dance every dance." As she spoke she guided her family toward the fireplace in the long room running the length of the house, where once ladies in outlandish ruffs and farthingales had taken their exercise. A group of musicians, whom Jane recognized as the village waits who played at Christmas and on other festive occasions, struck up a lively tune.

William approached the Austens and bowed. "Jane, you'll dance with me, I hope. And Mr. Fuller would very much like to be introduced to Miss Anna for the first dance."

Jane, aware that but a few minutes ago Tom Fuller's interest in her niece enraged her, smiled as the introductions were made and rested her hand in William's. Other couples joined them, but before the dance could begin, a footman made his way to William's side.

"Sir, I beg your pardon, but the others, you know, sir, *they* are here, and . . ."

"Pray excuse me, ma'am." William bowed to Jane and drew the servant aside. The man seemed to be in some state of consternation.

"Very well," William said to him after a short exchange. "Show them in."

But already a group of newcomers had arrived in the Gallery, half a dozen members of the Damned.

Jane gasped as pain shot through her teeth once more.

William came back to her side. "I regret I must leave you to talk with my new guests. I shall claim another dance this evening, Jane. Is everything well with you?" He added in a lower voice.

"Well enough." She took her place on the couch next to Cassandra.

Cassandra squeezed her hand. "Never mind, I am sure you will dance again. Who are those people? The red-haired lady and the gentleman with her look very familiar."

"Oh, yes," Jane said. "Most familiar indeed."

Chapter 4

William's stance, as he moved toward his new guests, was one Jane recognized: one of the Damned ready to attack. What could this mean, that William, grieving for his fledgling, should show such aggression toward him? A brief conversation followed that Jane could not make out above the noise of the music, the thud of feet on the wooden floor, and the laughter and conversations of the dancers. At one point, Luke stepped back, hands spread, in a gesture of appeasement.

Luke Venning, for a short time her Consort, was the man she had abandoned for mortality and Cassandra. She had not seen him since their last painful exchange, although even now she would see a gentleman who would remind her of Luke and her heart would give a painful lurch. Just as some features of the Damned remained with her—her lean build and her long stride—so a part of her heart remained Luke's.

He was deep in conversation with William, but his companion, a beautiful redheaded woman, met Jane's gaze across the room. Her expression registered surprise and then contempt.

With a slow smile she tucked one hand into the crook of Luke's arm. So Margaret was once again Luke's Consort.

William and Luke seemed to come to some sort of an agreement; a brief handshake followed.

The dance came to an end with a jubilant final chord, and Anna came to Jane's side. "Aunt Jane, Mr. Fuller asked if he could dance again with me; and I said he must ask you."

"Very proper," Jane said to Anna and Tom. "I believe your reputation will not suffer."

She certainly didn't want Anna to have any contact with the Damned who accompanied Luke—they looked almost a different breed, arrogant and dangerous. She watched Anna and Tom return to the center of the room and spoke quietly to Cassandra. "My dear, pray do not encourage any of the gentlemen who have just arrived to partner Anna, even if Mrs. Kettering introduces them."

"But they are very handsome," Cassandra said.

"Trust me. I shall explain later."

"Very well." Cassandra fanned herself. "I wonder where Mr. Fitzpatrick and Mr. Venning have gone?"

"They have left?"

"Yes, they went through the doorway we came through— Jane, where are you going?"

Bearleader and Creator together. She could not help herself. For a moment the room swam, the sound of the musicians discordant, and then she gathered her senses and strode toward the doorway that led out of the Great Gallery. A footman opened it and she passed through, guided by fierce longing.

A man stood outside the door of the Withdrawing Room where earlier the ladies had gathered for tea. Not a servant, but one of the Damned, and she suspected he was but newly created from his tentative glance at her.

"I beg your pardon, ma'am. You cannot go in there."

She bared her teeth. Even though she was not *en sanglant,* it was still a threatening gesture.

He stepped back. "I—they'll be angry. With you as well as me."

"Let me pass."

As he hesitated, she pushed him aside. Whether it was the return of her strength or a natural reticence to oppose a lady's wishes that made the man hesitate, she did not care. She flung the door open.

William and Luke stood close together in the small extension at the far end of the room, a cozy space with windows on three sides, created for a particular sort of intimacy on view to anyone else in the room. Earlier a harp had stood in the space. The instrument had been moved to one side, and the fire had burned almost out, leaving the room in darkness except for the pools of light created by candles. In the golden light Luke appeared as handsome as ever, his high cheekbones cast into relief.

"And what of her?" William was saying as Jane entered.

Luke shrugged. "She is so altered that I would not have known her again."

"She—" William looked up to meet Jane's gaze.

"I do not need the powers of the Damned to know you speak of me," Jane said.

Luke said nothing but made a stiff bow.

"Jane—"

But she did not answer William's entreaty, turning and blundering from the room, half blinded with tears, pushing past the doorkeeper.

"Jane," William said from behind her.

She swiped at her eyes, not wanting him to see she wept.

"I fear you injured him greatly," William said.

"How very foolish of me. Of course he has all of eternity to nurse his broken heart. Why, near thirteen years must feel like mere seconds to him, yet he proves his inconstancy by becoming Margaret's lover once again."

"They are not lovers," William said with a touch of impatience. "They are in the same household."

"Why? Why should he leave you to go where she is?"

"I regret I cannot tell you at present."

"Did you know he would come tonight?"

"I thought it more than likely, yes."

She turned away, angry with him, and pretended a great interest in the tapestry hanging on the wall next to them. He should have warned her.

"You are right," he said.

"Pray do not read my mind. It is ungentlemanly."

He bowed and offered his arm. "Do you wish to return to your charming niece?"

She curtsied in reply, and he escorted her back to the room where the dancing continued. Having provided her with a glass of wine, William left her with Cassandra, Mrs. Austen, and Martha.

"Dear Anna is quite the success!" Mrs. Austen commented. "I hope she will not tire herself with dancing for too long."

"Oh, we Austens are made of sterner stuff than that," Jane replied. "Cassandra and I would dance for hours, do you not remember, ma'am?"

"She is such a pretty girl," Martha said. "And Mr. Fuller seems very taken with her. I wonder if he will ask for a third dance?"

For at that moment the final chord sounded, and the dancers bowed and curtsied. Tom led Anna back toward the Austens, she smiling and pink in the face.

"I daresay you do not remember me, Mrs. Austen." The lady who emerged from the shadows beyond the fireplace was handsome and beautifully dressed.

"Why—can it be—Miss Venning!" Mrs. Austen shook her hand. "Why, my dear, your hand is so cold. You must sit with us by the fire and warm yourself. These old houses can be so drafty. Jane, it is Miss Venning—you and she were almost inseparable that winter in Bath . . ." Mrs. Austen's voice trailed into silence, but then she resumed with great good cheer. "And Miss Venning, you remember Cassandra, of course, and this is our friend Miss Martha Lloyd."

Clarissa Venning gave Jane a cool nod. Whether she and Luke were actually siblings was highly unlikely; Jane had long suspected that the term was used to account for them sharing the same house, just as Dorcas Kettering claimed to be William's sister-in-law.

Jane returned her nod with equal coolness.

"You left me as well as Luke," Clarissa said to her quietly. "It was badly done, Jane. And now you return. Will you break Luke's heart anew? Deprive William of his fledgling once again? Why, Tom!"—with a sudden coquettishness—"Your young partner is charming, but you promised to dance with me, remember. Mrs. Austen, allow me to present Mr. Duval Richards."

Of course Clarissa would be accompanied by a young man of outstanding beauty, but even for one of the Damned he was extraordinary, with dark liquid eyes beneath a handsome head of wavy hair. An air of romance and danger hung around him, as though, Jane thought with a curl of her lip, he were an engraving of a hero in a gothic romance; he was certainly someone who should not be allowed to dance with an innocent young girl.

Clarissa's gaze pinned Jane like a specimen on a collection board. Jane could not speak or utter any sort of warning to her family, who fluttered and smiled upon Duval, and gave him permission to dance with Anna. Anna stared at him, apparently entranced, with the pride of a woman who has been singled out by the most handsome man in the room.

"Why, Jane, you frown so!" Cassandra patted her hand. "What a handsome young man. I could not quite discern with which family he is connected, but Miss Venning knows him, so he must be genteel. You know, she puts us dowdy country spinsters to shame, for she hardly looks a day older than when we met her first."

"No. He's not genteel," Jane croaked, but her voice was barely a whisper. Furious at her weakness, and at Clarissa, who was almost certainly the cause of it, she drained her glass and looked around for a footman to refill it. But William, his hand held out, had returned.

"Come, Jane, you promised me a dance and I have come to claim it."

Her mother and sister exchanged a glance at Jane being addressed with such familiarity.

Her voice returned. "I beg your pardon, sir. I shall not dance. It is unbecoming to a woman of my age and station."

Don't be a ninny. William replied aloud, "I must insist, ma'am."

"Oh, very well." She stood and strode past him to where the dancers formed sets. "And I'm not a ninny," she said over her shoulder.

She had never danced with William before and was surprised at how well matched they were, at the effortless touch of their hands and telling glances. Onlookers, her family included, might well think they were at the very least flirting, if not planning a liaison.

An elderly gentleman tugged them out of the dance, to compliment them on the elegance of their dancing, breathing claret fumes over them, so that when they could escape him they had lost their places entirely. Some inelegant scrambling back into the set righted matters.

As she and William progressed through the dance, they met Anna and the fascinatingly beautiful member of the Damned. Jane did her best to communicate mind to mind how strongly she disapproved of the way his hands lingered over Anna's and that his ardent attentions to her niece smacked of impropriety. He gave a smirk in her direction and directed his smoldering gaze at Anna's pretty white neck.

"That young man is most improper," she said to William.

"He is not young, Jane."

"Precisely. Do I have reason to fear for my niece?"

"I should think not, in my house, and among friends and neighbors."

"It is not your house. It is my brother Edward's." She watched in annoyance as Duval's hand lingered on Anna's waist. "And are you sure he is a friend? I saw how you greeted his party, whom it was obvious you did not expect, or esteem them highly enough to invite them to dine—to dinner, that is."

"Pay attention, my dear Jane, or else we shall receive no more compliments on the elegance of our dancing." William pushed her back into place.

"Any savage can dance," Jane said. "Whereas it takes a being of great subtlety to change the subject so adroitly. But I shall make you talk of it whether you wish to or not."

He was not someone who smiled easily or often, and she had noticed before how she reacted with a mix of pain and pleasure; that the fleeting moment as he smiled upon her was a tiny speck even in mortal time, the swift passage of a bird flying through darkness back into the light.

"You grow philosophical," he commented.

"I cannot help it. I have gazed upon the torments of hell and escaped—or so I thought." She changed the subject. "Do you see how my sister and mother and Martha have their heads together? Doubtless they speculate upon your intentions. They are already most excited that you address me by my Christian name."

"I wonder that you never married," William said.

"It is no wonder at all. I am too sharp of tongue and have no money." She laughed. "I shall have to put up with veiled hints and knowing smiles at home for days about how I danced and flirted with that handsome Mr. Fitzpatrick. Doubtless they discuss how at my age the candlelight is flattering and I have always been at my best when dancing."

She glanced over her shoulder at Anna and Duval, who continued to flirt openly with each other, and for a moment envied Anna her youthful energy and boldness—or, it might not be boldness, but imprudence.

"Tell me more of Duval," she said. "If he is to pay my niece such attention, I must be sure he means only a flirtation and nothing more serious."

"He is my guest and will abide by my standards of propriety."

His answer hardly satisfied her, but after all they were in public, with plenty of neighbors present, and William had told her the Damned sought to be inconspicuous. She took another glance at her family. Mrs. Austen was deep in conversation with Dorcas Kettering, and Mr. Papillon and his sister, Elizabeth, had joined Cassandra and Martha, doubtless in a discussion of needy villagers.

"Is Fitzpatrick truly your surname? William Fitzwilliam: what a dreadful name. I am not surprised you chose to change it."

"I have long since ceased to use my real name," he replied, "but it is not Fitzwilliam, or Fitzpatrick, or even William. We become used to changing our names."

"And you will not tell me what your real name is."

He shook his head with a faint smile, and she knew she must be satisfied with that answer.

The dance came to an end, with bows and curtsies and laughter, and women fanning themselves. The musicians laid their instruments down and left the room with a footman, doubtless to quench their thirst with beer. William bowed, telling Jane he must act as host and see that his guests were supplied with refreshments, and she pushed her disordered curls to rights beneath her cap, thinking more wine would be most welcome. Anna must have had the same idea, for she was nowhere in sight.

Jane threaded her way through the crowd to where the Austen ladies sat, but Anna was not there, and a faint uneasiness stirred in her mind.

She accepted a glass of wine and strolled around the room. One of the musicians had not gone with the others but sat replacing a string on his violin. Jane asked him if he had seen a pretty, very young lady and a handsome gentleman leave the room through the nearby door.

"Why, yes, ma'am, I surely did." He tucked the instrument beneath his chin and plucked the new string, grimacing. "I wouldn't let any girl I know go anywhere with the likes of him."

Jane stepped through the doorway and closed the door behind her. There were no footmen present; and the gentlemanly guard who had unsuccessfully prevented her from interrupting William and Luke's conversation was gone also. She stood listening to the sounds of a house creaking and settling as the night air chilled. A candelabra with guttering candles gave off only a dim light. The door to the parlor was ajar, a little grayish-blue moonlight spilling onto the floor, for by now the fire and candles had burned down. All was quiet.

"Anna?" she called.

There was no answer. She moved forward into the shadows, her step becoming soft and quiet, a huntress following her prey, and turned into the soft welcoming darkness of the hall.

She froze. A quiet sound, a breath, a sigh, came from beyond a closed doorway to her left. The room held no light; only the grayish glimmer of moonlight showed beneath the door.

She closed her hand around the handle and turned it, calf muscles tensing in preparation for the leap forward she might need. No, *would* need, for the scent of blood, mixed with Anna's scent of apple blossom, sharp and fresh and young, was strong in the air.

She flung the door open to see Duval on the bed with Anna motionless in his arms, his mouth dark with blood. He raised his head and snarled.

"Let her go, damn you!"

He pushed Anna aside and met Jane's attack. She went for his throat, but he gripped her wrists and they slid from the bed to the floor, Jane attempting to knee him in the groin. Long ago she'd been taught to fight in an ungentlemanly style, and her training served her well, but she was at a disadvantage against the strength of one fully Damned; moreover, one interrupted while dining, which was much like interrupting a dog at a bone. She broke a hand free and attempted to claw his eyes, but he cursed and thrust her away.

She landed in a tangle of skirts and petticoats, made worse by the heavy satin bedcover, which had been dragged from the bed by their struggle, depositing Anna, still in a swoon, onto the floor. Duval leaped to his feet, reaching inside his waistcoat; he must have a weapon there. A weapon? The Damned needed no such thing—

His arm flashed down and Jane rolled to her side and bit his ankle, ripping his silk stockings. She heard a howl of pain as her teeth slid over bone and skin.

A dull coldness radiated from her collarbone. She was hurt in a way she couldn't quite define, injured, weakened. No, more than injured: she was fading in a chill grayness like fog where sight and sound slid away.

Pray for me, Cassandra, I beg of you. Pray for me.

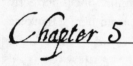 

Chapter 5

"Jane! Wake and speak to me!"

She was too tired to respond to that beloved voice, and the vigorous shaking to which she was subjected merely annoyed her. The frozen grayness into which she had sunk was not welcoming, but any response would take too much effort.

"Damn you! Wake!"

"Pray moderate your language, sir," she managed. "And have I not already been damned once?"

"That's better. Come, drink."

The rim of a glass nudged at her mouth, and she opened for wine flavored with the blood that once had been dearest in the world to her, a flood of desire and strength spinning through her body.

She opened her eyes before she said something foolish of love or of her injured feelings and gazed into Luke's face. To her mortification she lay in his arms, both of them sprawled on the floor among the bloodstained folds of the satin coverlet. As her strength returned she pushed herself away.

He held his wrist out to her and a bolt of excitement ran

through her, but he merely wished her to button his cuff again. She did so.

"Anna! Where is she?"

"William has escorted her back to your family. She is perfectly well. Duval had very little chance to dine from her." His voice was cool.

"And what of him?"

"Oh, he's perfectly well, although somewhat irritated at your most rude interruption, and he has a torn stocking."

"Forgive me if I seem unsympathetic to his plight. He must look elsewhere for his dinner." She disentangled herself from him and straightened her gown and cap.

"What do you expect? A pretty young girl shows her partiality and willingness to accompany one of us alone. As you should know, our nature is such that we must take advantage of such situations." He stood and offered his hand.

"Duval is no gentleman. What did he do to me?"

"Ask your Creator," he said. "My blood has revived you, and you will experience no lasting effect. I shall tell you no more."

She pressed her hand to her collarbone, feeling a cold patch, and moved to the mirror that hung on the wall. Her reflection showed still, although somewhat fuzzy around the edges, and, as she expected, of Luke there was no sign at all. A mark like a bruise showed on her skin.

"I thank you for your intervention, Luke. I believe I should have been destroyed had you not come along."

"I particularly admired the way you bit his ankle, like an enraged terrier," Luke said. "I am sure I did not teach you that. If you are feeling well enough, may I accompany you back to the Gallery?"

If he was determined to be so proper, then so was she. Doubtless he felt he was justified, for had she not left him? Yet he had immediately returned to the arms of his former Consort, whereas she had mourned her loss, unsettled for years, refusing the few offers she had received.

"Margaret is not my Consort," he said with some impatience.

"Oh, do stop reading my thoughts, Luke. It is so very tiresome."

"I beg your pardon."

His face was set and expressionless as he opened the bedchamber door.

"Why, Luke," she said with unseemly delight, "surely you are not jealous that William takes such an interest in me now."

"I assure you it is none of my business. I am delighted your Creator should guide you as is proper."

"You *are* jealous!" She shook his arm. "Oh, come, Luke, enough of this foolishness. Tell me how you do."

"I do well enough." He stopped and looked at her, met her gaze for the first time. "I am surprised to see you, although doubtless your presence in the neighborhood is one of the reasons William leased this house. A Creator always wants his fledglings nearby."

He took her arm and they strolled through the dark corridor toward the sound of music and merrymaking. "Had you been more Damned than human, you would have been in serious danger tonight. I shall say no more."

She trod warily, feeling stiffness in her limbs and bruises from the unaccustomed exertion of a fight, and the bruise at her collarbone aching—she supposed it was a bruise; what else could it be? But she was cheered by the evidence that she was not yet fully Damned and aware that she would have to put up with a great deal of teasing from her family the next day. Any visible stiffness in her movements could be attributed to too much dancing.

Before they entered the Great Gallery, Luke took her hand and raised it to his lips. "You and I spent a great deal of time bidding each other farewell, and I must do so again. Duval will be chastised, do not fear."

"I wish you would be more open with me, Luke. Something is wrong among our—your—kind. Will you not tell me of it?"

"Be careful, Jane." He held her hand still.

"Be careful? What sort of advice is that? I assure you I shall have to be very careful. If the signs are correct, I have years of deception and lying to my family to look forward to. I do not want to be Damned again, Luke. And I never hoped or expected to see you again, so I shall gladly say farewell."

She walked through the doorway ahead of him and looked for the Austen family. Yes, there they were, and the sight of them— particularly of Anna, who looked only as tired as any young lady after a night of vigorous dancing—made her smile with relief, so blessedly normal did they appear. The party was breaking up, it seemed, for people were gathering fans and shawls, and William and Dorcas were shaking hands and bidding their guests good night.

"But of course we shall see you tomorrow, Mr. Fitzwilliam!" Jane cried. She really could not resist the opportunity.

"We shall, ma'am?"

"Indeed, yes, for tomorrow is Sunday and we shall see you at church."

It was one of the few times she had seen William at a loss for words. Indeed, she felt a little apprehensive herself; the church was old and not in good repair, and a thunderbolt could do it irreparable damage.

"An excellent sermon, Mr. Papillon," William said gravely as the congregation left the church the next morning.

"Thank you, sir. I trust you did not find the church too damp. I find that I am particularly susceptible and I recommend that my parishioners dress warmly. But not too warmly, for . . ." Mr. Papillon glanced at his sister who gazed at William with the helpless, dazed look that mortals tended to assume when looking upon the Damned.

"What a charming bonnet, Elizabeth," Jane said, and pinched the woman's wrist.

"Oh. Oh, indeed, do you think so, Miss Jane?—I was saying to my brother—well, of course now I have seen Miss Anna's it is—but, oh there is Miss Benn, poor thing, I must . . ."

Jane smiled as Elizabeth Papillon's torrent of words washed over her and hoped that William would not be so indiscreet as to invite Miss Elizabeth to dine.

Do you think she'd stop talking? Dorcas Kettering took Jane's arm. "You must come and take tea with me, Miss Jane." *I have a particularly delicious footman in mind for you if you want something a little more potent.* "And do bring your sister and mother and Miss Lloyd."

"Thank you, Mrs. Kettering," Jane answered vaguely. She planned to return home and write; it probably wasn't quite proper on the Sabbath, but she might not have much time. During the sermon she had found herself staring at her neighbors, wondering how they would taste, and picking up the seductive counterpoint of a number of pulses within an enclosed space—not to mention her neighbors' thoughts and fantasies, some of which were most surprising.

But not nearly as surprising as the Damned behaving in church with the utmost propriety, bellowing responses and taking communion along with everyone else, although they had fumbled a little with their prayer books as though they had not opened such a volume in some time.

She did not hunger, not yet, but she found an inordinate interest in the slivers of neck visible above gentlemen's neckcloths and their male scent, which had quite enlivened Mr. Papillon's earnest but dull sermon. Mr. Papillon, now, he would taste of honey, for he enjoyed his beehives, and. . .

"Come along, Jane." Cassandra giggled and tugged her sister's arm. "You are looking at poor Mr. Papillon as though you wanted to eat him. I fear you may yet scandalize the village; the sooner you are married to him, the better. I shall get Edward to write to him and tell him he must make you an offer immediately."

"Oh, indeed, it is better to marry than to burn," Jane murmured. Was she experiencing merely human lust and not the hunger of the Damned?

"Jane!" Cassandra led her through the churchyard. "You need dinner, that is your problem, for see how distracted and ridiculous you are. Where is Anna? Oh, here you are, my dear. I am sorry you did not see that handsome Mr. Richards at church, but I found out that he and his party are staying at the inn in Alton and they must have gone to church there."

"We should not receive him," Jane said, emerging from her tangled thoughts—the charms of gentlemen all tied up with her writing; she really must scribble some notes down when they were back at home—and promptly trod into a puddle.

"Oh! Why not?" Anna said.

Jane shook muddy water from her foot. "Because we promised your papa you would lead a virtuous country existence. We already let him down last night."

Anna's lower lip protruded a little. "It was a perfectly ordinary evening with our neighbors. What was the harm in it?"

Jane took her niece's arm and drew her a little ahead of the others. "My dear, I must ask you something rather delicate. I hope Mr. Richards did not behave inappropriately last night."

Anna giggled. "Indeed, no. He flirted a little while we danced and then we took a turn around the room."

"No more?"

Anna shook her head, and Jane saw the dazed, blank look her sister and mother so often assumed when contact with one of the Damned was mentioned. So Anna remembered nothing of accompanying Duval to the bedchamber or his attack, for so she presumed it must be.

"Good. And you do not feel fatigued from dancing so much?"

"Oh, not at all. In fact, I feel extraordinarily well."

William had revived her. As soon as the thought crossed her mind, Jane knew it to be true. He had given Anna a glass of wine with a drop of his blood while Jane lay in a swoon from whatever it was Duval Richards had done to her; what else would explain the child's vivacity and extraordinary good looks today?

"We shall not visit the Great House again," she said. "I trust you will contain your disappointment, Anna. Mr. Fitzpatrick has done his duty to his landlord's poor relatives, and that is an end to the matter."

"Sister!" Cassandra, who had caught up with them, frowned at her. "There is no need for such harshness."

"I can't understand why Uncle Edward does not let you live in the Great House," Anna said.

"Oh, it would be ridiculous, we three ladies there," Cassandra said. "We are not bred to such luxury. It would not suit us at all. No, we are quite snug in our cottage. It is very good of your uncle Edward to provide for us."

Jane, although feeling that Cassandra protested a little too much, was compelled to agree with her. "We would have so much more work with the servants and the responsibilities of the house we'd scarcely have time to ourselves."

And time to herself was what she cherished most these days,

now the words flowed easily from her mind onto paper, and she laughed aloud with pleasure at what she wrote. Or so she'd thought. Now, the prospect of time, stretching dizzily before her, and she alone and bereft of the company of Cassandra, appeared only as a curse.

Chapter 6

"Is not Martha home yet?"

Jane, dazed from several hours of writing, looked up from her manuscript and smiled at her sister. She laid down her pen and stretched. "I thought she was helping our mother."

"No. She was going to visit Miss Benn, but Anna and I called on our way home and she had not been there."

Jane tapped her papers straight. "I daresay she changed her mind."

"Now I shall have to help get dinner ready, else it will be late."

"Anna can help you."

"It is not like Martha." Grumbling, Cassandra left the dining room, and Jane stood to look out the window. Outside, a cart lumbered by, a boy sitting on the tail, swinging his legs and trailing a stick in the dirt of the road. It was the Monday after the Austens' eventful weekend, and everything was back to normal again; everything except herself, that is.

She picked up a cup of tea, long since grown cold, and sipped. She was pleased with the day's work and knew that now she should probably assist Cassandra and Anna in the kitchen, but a few minutes' leisure appealed to her. She wiped her pen clean, packed her papers into her writing desk, and adjusted the chemisette at her neckline. A little fresh air might be pleasant, and she could see how her mother's labors in the garden progressed.

Her fingertips brushed the strange grayish mark on her breast. She had examined it in the mirror in the bedchamber that morning and seen not a bruise as she had first thought, but something similar to a stain on her skin, regular in color, and still cold to the touch. She considered consulting a physician, but possibly modern medicine might have no explanation; besides, she might be obliged to explain how she had received the injury. Almost certainly she would be declared insane.

Her writing things tidied away, she left the house through the back door and spotted her mother with a watering can, tending to the cuttings she had planted the other day. Jane bent to scoop up a pile of weeds. "The garden looks very fine, ma'am."

"It does, and it gives me great pleasure, which I admit is more important," Mrs. Austen replied. "We may have some early lettuce and cabbage soon, the boy tells me."

"I'm looking for Martha," Jane said. "Have you seen her, ma'am?"

"I daresay she is out and has lost track of time," Mrs. Austen said, clearly finding the subject of little interest. "I shall have to give this slip of lavender a firm talking-to. It is really not trying hard enough!"

"Quite so, ma'am," Jane said. "I shall continue my search."

She walked out through the yard, dodging past the kitchen windows again, afraid that she might be summoned to help with dinner preparations, and this one time might turn into many times and cut into her precious writing time. She returned to the dining room, put thoughts of Martha and household matters from her mind, and became absorbed once more in her work.

When she looked up next, it was to see Cassandra urging her to help her set the table for dinner.

"But where is Martha?" Jane asked.

"Possibly she dines with Miss Benn. I wish she had told us, though."

The four ladies dined alone, but by the time they had finished and had drunk tea in the parlor, Jane was concerned. Her mother and sister were busy with their sewing and Anna read aloud; normally Jane would have enjoyed her niece's musical voice and sensitive reading of Cowper, but now it was almost dark and she announced she would walk to Miss Benn's and bring Martha home.

Outside the house she looked up and down, hoping to see the familiar figure of Martha, bonnet slightly askew and her red cloak billowing as she strode down the road.

Jane pressed herself against the wall of the house as a carriage passed with a thunder of hooves and splash of mud and continued smartly on the Winchester Road toward Alton. Now she could see someone hurrying toward her, but as the figure drew near she recognized it as the youngest boy of the Andrews family, Edward's tenants at New Park Farm, accompanied by a dog. He had a look of great agitation and, when he saw her, increased his pace.

"Miss Jane!" he cried. " 'Tis Miss Lloyd. You must come at once, if you please, that is, ma'am."

She searched for and remembered his name. Samuel, that was it. She crossed the road to meet him. "Why, Samuel, what's wrong?"

"We found her in a swoon in the woods, ma'am. Peter, my dog here, was much agitated and led us to her, and my father and one of the men brought her into our house on a hurdle, ma'am, and we cannot rouse her."

She hurried along the muddy road, the boy's head bobbing at her elbow as he ran to keep up with her long stride, the dog staying close to him and occasionally showing his teeth at her. "How long since did you find her?" she asked.

"Half an hour, I think, for I had to run to the house and tell my father. My mother fears the lady may be hurt and did not want to move her again, for fear of hurting her further. So they sent me to tell you."

They passed a scatter of cottages, where this was any ordinary evening, a few men working in their gardens in the last of the daylight, smoke rising from chimneys and the scent of dinner lingering still on the air. Why on earth had Martha gone into Chawton Park Woods alone? Maybe she fancied the exercise, for it was a favorite spot for walks and, in warmer weather, picnics.

"How is your reading coming along, Samuel?" Jane asked, remembering that Cassandra frequently called at the farm to teach him and his brothers and sisters their letters.

"Pretty well, ma'am." His step slowed and he clutched his side. "Beg your pardon, Miss Jane, I have a stitch from running."

"No, I am sorry for rushing you so. I shall go ahead—"

"Beg your pardon, Miss Jane, but father said I should not let you walk on your own. He made a point of it, Miss Jane." The boy's chest heaved with exertion.

What on earth had happened to Martha? Jane's sense of unease grew. Had Martha been attacked in some way, assaulted?

"That's most thoughtful of you and your father," she said. "When you are ready to walk again, we shall proceed, and I promise I shall not rush you too much. But tell me, are there gypsies abroad?"

"No, ma'am, he says worse than gypsies."

Jane, seeing her young companion's fearful glance at the woods at the side of the road, did not pursue the topic further.

Only a few more minutes, and they had arrived at New Park Farm, and Jane splashed her way across the muck of the cobbled farmyard. Mr. Andrews, who sat outside smoking a pipe, rose to his feet as she approached.

"Mrs. Andrews wanted me out of the house, Miss Jane. This is a sorry business."

"Has she regained her senses?" Jane asked.

"Not yet."

Jane nodded and tapped at the farmhouse door. The door opened a crack and Mrs. Andrews peered out. "Oh, thank heavens, 'tis you, Miss Jane. She won't rouse at all. I have burned feathers under her nose."

Sure enough, as Jane stepped inside the house, the pungent scent of feathers mixed with the scents of the dinner cooked at the open hearth.

"You'll take some tea, Miss Jane?"

Jane didn't answer her. The hurdle that had borne Martha lay on the floor, and Martha was stretched upon it, inert and pale, diminished, a smear of blood on her bosom.

"Martha, my dear." Jane knelt and took Martha's cold limp hand in her own. "Can you hear me?" To Mrs. Andrews she said, "Where is she hurt?"

"I can't rightly tell, Miss Jane. I can see no mark, but maybe she took a hit to the head."

Jane eased off Martha's cap. Her bonnet was gone, maybe fallen off. She ran her hand over Martha's scalp and felt nothing. No telltale bump, or heat, and certainly, with the part of her mind that was of the Damned, no thought or memory. Nothing.

"I have bricks beneath her feet and at her sides to warm her," Mrs. Andrews said.

"Thank you for all you have done." Jane chafed her friend's hand and shook her gently. "Martha! Martha, wake up!"

But Martha didn't move.

Behind her Jane heard the clink of china as Mrs. Andrews made tea.

"I've always thought her a healthy sort of lady," Mrs. Andrews said. "Not slender, but now . . . there's hardly anything of her. I never saw a woman so changed."

Hardly anything of her, indeed. Flattened and inert and pale with only a thread of a pulse and only a flutter of movement at her throat to show she breathed. An odd, wild sort of scent hung about her; not an unpleasant scent, at least not to Jane; there was something familiar about it.

"We'll send for some of the men to take her home," Mrs. Andrews continued.

She was scarcely aware of Mrs. Andrews pulling forward a chair and placing a cup of tea upon it.

"Of course. I cannot thank you enough for looking after her."

Mrs. Andrews turned back to her spinning wheel.

Jane took a sip from the cup of tea. It was poor stuff, probably used and dried at least once, and she reminded herself to give the Andrewses some of their own tea by way of thanks. She poured a very little into the saucer, praying that what she would do might help Martha and not kill her, although, with her powers so diminished, it might achieve nothing. She willed herself to become *en sanglant,* shaming herself by thinking of Luke—that is, Luke in a state of undress no gentlewoman should contemplate—and her teeth ached and smarted. She could not become entirely *en sanglant,* but her canines were sharp enough to do what was necessary. A quick nip into her own wrist, and a drop of her blood and then more until the tea was dark and opaque. She had no idea of the strength of her blood, but it could not be very powerful.

She stanched the wound, afraid Mrs. Andrews would turn and see what she was about, and lifted Martha's head, tilting the saucer so that a little of the liquid ran into her mouth. Some dribbled down her chin and Jane scooped it back between Martha's lips, not wanting to waste any. "Wake up, dearest friend," she murmured.

Martha's eyes fluttered beneath her eyelids as though she dreamed, and a slow smile spread over her face.

Then her eyes opened wide. Jane clasped her hand. "My dear, how do you feel? I—"

The smile on Martha's face faded. She looked at Jane and screamed.

The whirr and thud of the spinning wheel ceased. Mrs. Andrews said, "Why, Miss Lloyd, you're awake, thank the Lord—"

"Get her away from me!" Martha screamed. "She's one of them!"

What could Martha see in her? She was not *en sanglant*. Had her appearance changed in some subtle, horrifying way?

Mrs. Andrews meanwhile bent over Martha, murmuring soothing words. She looked up at Jane. "She is not herself, Miss Jane. Whatever shall we do?"

Martha was curled upon herself, sobbing.

Jane touched her friend's arm. "Martha, dearest, you must listen to me. Look at me."

As Martha raised her head and met her gaze, Jane summoned the strength of the Damned to soothe her. "You are mistaken. You know me as your dearest friend, one who will never harm you."

Martha's face relaxed and she nodded. "Oh, dear me! Why, Jane, what has happened?"

Jane helped her to her feet and into a chair. "You swooned in the woods. Young Samuel found you, and Mr. Andrews brought you here."

"I'm glad to see you are feeling better, Miss Lloyd," Mrs. Andrews said. "I'll make some more tea—"

"Pray do not trouble yourself, Mrs. Andrews. Miss Lloyd may finish mine." Jane tipped tea from the saucer back into the cup and handed it to Martha. Her friend might as well receive as much benefit as she could from the drops of Jane's blood.

Indeed, as Martha drank, the color returned to her face and the brightness was restored to her handsome eyes. In no time at all, she said, "I feel so much better and refreshed. I think I am ready to walk home, for I do not wish to impose upon your hospitality further, Mrs. Andrews."

"If you think so, Miss Lloyd. We could take you in our cart, although it's not fit for a lady. I'll let Samuel and Mr. Andrews know you're recovered. I know they'll be much relieved." Mrs. Andrews glanced at Martha in astonishment, much, as Jane thought, as Lazarus's companions must have done. Not only had Martha come back from the dead, or as good as, but she appeared to be bursting with energy.

"Well, well, Miss Lloyd, this is a welcome surprise," Mr. Andrews said as he and his son entered the kitchen. "We feared the worst."

"It's a good thing Samuel found you," Jane said. "You might have lain there for hours."

"You say I was in the woods?" Martha looked at them all with astonishment. "Why should I be in the woods?"

"You do not remember?" Jane asked.

For a moment Martha looked troubled before assuring everyone with a gay laugh that she was exceedingly well and looking forward to her own dinner. She and Jane left the Andrewses' house and set off for their own home.

"Why are you so angry, Jane?"

"I'm not angry with you. I was frightened for your sake. I was afraid you would die."

"It is exceedingly mysterious," Martha said. "I do not even remember how or why I arrived there. I had called in at some of the cottages here, meaning to return home after, and listened to the children say their lessons. I certainly did not intend to walk in the opposite direction. Jane, you do not think I am ill, do you? I have not felt better in my life, but to have such a thing happen . . . and this blood upon my bosom—how do you think it got there?"

"Maybe you had a nosebleed," Jane said.

On their return, the Austens fussed over Martha, giving her the most comfortable seat nearest the fire and discussing whether a doctor should be called.

Jane meanwhile raged inwardly while maintaining an outward appearance of tranquillity. She played the pianoforte for the ladies, encouraged Anna to sing, and joined in a game of spillikins, a game at which she normally excelled, but which she now found tedious in the extreme. She was greatly relieved when her mother suggested they all have an early night, and Jane went upstairs with the others.

"What do you think we should do?" Cassandra asked her as soon as they were in their bedchamber. "Do you think she should see a doctor? It is a dreadful thing to have happened."

"It is my fault," Jane said.

"What!" Cassandra, in the act of unpinning her hair, looked at her with astonishment. "No, of course it is not. How could it possibly be your fault?"

"I should have protected her," Jane said and floundered to a stop, not knowing how else to proceed. "Cassandra, I must confide in you. I believe I am becoming . . . unwell again."

"Unwell?"

"You remember when I had to take the Cure in Bath a dozen years ago. The symptoms are returning."

For a moment Cassandra looked at her with sheer terror. "No! You look so very well. It cannot be. We shall ask Martha to make you up a draught and all will be well."

"I fear that my good looks are part of the symptoms. I *know,* Cassandra. Trust me."

"We cannot go to Bath. Not after Papa . . ." Cassandra swallowed. "I shall pray for you, Jane. I shall pray you are wrong. But surely you do not think one of those vile creatures attacked Martha?"

"I think it more than likely."

"Nonsense! This is an English village, not the sinister Italian landscape of a gothic novel. I am certain she had some sort of fit, which is worrying enough, but I do not believe she was the victim of any wrongdoing."

Jane took one look at her sister, frightened and close to tears, and moved behind Cassandra to unfasten her gown and stays. "Nevertheless, I do not think she should walk alone. What if she were to become ill again?"

"I think that an excellent idea," Cassandra said. "What's the matter?"

Jane could not speak of her disappointment at Cassandra's reaction to her confession. "I do not think I shall sleep. I think it best if I go downstairs to write."

"Very well." Cassandra pulled her mass of hair over her shoulder to braid it for the night. "You may wake me to help you undress."

"Thank you, but I should not dare do so. You are such a surly creature when awoken. I can rest well enough in my gown." She kissed Cassandra, half expecting her sister to shrink away from her and relieved that she did not; but was not that worse, that her sister did not believe her?

Jane went downstairs and sat in the parlor, listening to the creak of floorboards above as the household prepared for the night. A pad of footfalls the length of the house and the murmur of voices indicated that Cassandra, who liked to chat before sleep, had gone to visit Martha. Finally all was quiet, Cassandra back in her own bedchamber, and Jane took her cloak and left the house, closing the door quietly behind her. The night air smelled cool and sweet, and she fancied she could smell some early blossom on the air from the orchard. Keeping to the shadows—she was not sure she could melt into the darkness yet, a skill learned when she had been assuredly Damned—she made her way through the village and turned into the driveway of the Great House.

Since it was early yet, she was not surprised to see lights at the windows although no sound came from the house. Apparently the Damned did not entertain tonight, preferring to dine quietly at home. To her annoyance she was assailed by sudden, deep hunger. For how long would she be able to conceal her condition? How long before she became a monster, all human feelings and decency discarded?

At the front door of the house she raised the heavy knocker and brought it crashing down upon the ancient oak. The door swung open almost immediately to reveal William, in his shirtsleeves, his throat bare.

"I was expecting you, Jane."

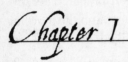

"So this is your idea of quiet country living—preying upon innocent women."

He stood aside and gestured to her. "Pray enter."

"Who was responsible for this outrage?" She stepped inside the house, anger flooding her with the full strength of the Damned.

He looked at her, considering. "You should dine."

"No! First, you should tell me who it was who attacked Martha this evening."

"And then what?"

"I shall kill him—or her."

"In that case you should definitely dine, although, Jane, I should not recommend your course of action. There are severe penalties among us for those who destroy their own kind."

She walked ahead of him into the small room lined with books where they had first met two nights before. A woman sat, or rather, sprawled in a chair, smiled and held out her hand to William as they entered.

"Ah. She hungers, too?" The woman giggled and rolled her

head back, exposing her neck to them. Jane recognized the euphoric tipsiness of a mortal pleasured and dined upon.

"I beg your pardon, sir. I did not realize you dined." Her words surprised her; she must be further developed as one of the Damned than she realized, to make an appropriate apology while she seethed with mortal anger.

William took the woman's hand and kissed her wrist. "A thousand apologies, *cara,* I must abandon you. You may visit Mr. Fuller, if you wish, or Mrs. Kettering." He pushed her from the room and closed the door.

"Now, Jane, we must talk. Sit."

She knew formalities must be observed. In the presence of her Creator, even though she believed he might be implicated in a heinous crime, she calmed and accepted a glass of wine. As she related her story, she hoped with all her heart that it was not he who was responsible.

"You are quite right," he said, settling in the chair opposite hers, a glass of wine in his hand. "It is indeed a heinous crime, and you must believe that neither I, nor any of this household, is guilty. But . . ." He leaned forward and prodded at a smoldering log in the fireplace. "But as for responsibility, I accept that fully."

The log fell into the glowing heart of the fire, sending sparks flying up the chimney. "I don't understand," Jane said. "Who attacked Martha?"

"I am not sure precisely who it was, although I have my suspicions. Let me explain something to you, Jane. The Prince of Wales and the *ton* abhor our company in these changed times. This household is one of many where we attempt to live quietly, waiting for a return to favor, or possibly a time when we may travel abroad to a more hospitable country. It is how we have survived, for centuries. But others are angry at our fall from favor. They seek revenge on England's displeasure by gaining sustenance, not through seduction but by force. This is a dreadful thing for us, Jane, we who have cleaved together for so long to be divided, households destroyed, and allegiances broken.

"Some who have been cast out by their fellows now hunt alone, with no society, no loyalties to any others, little better than beasts, and I believe it may have been one of them. Or, more dangerous yet, Duval's household embraces this most abhorrent behavior and welcomes those solitary creatures into their midst. We call them *les Sales,* the dirty, defiled ones."

"And Luke has joined Duval?"

"He is with them. I sent him and Clarissa as ambassadors, to persuade Duval to abandon *les Sales* and their unclean ways, and to destroy his weapons. I fear Luke may have cast his lot with them."

"Weapons? What weapons?"

"A weapon like the one that made the mark upon your breast. Had you been at the height of your powers as one of us, that blow would have destroyed you. As it was, you fell into a deep swoon, and it took Luke's blood to revive you."

"And you believe that one of *les Sales* attacked Martha? On Duval's orders?"

"Very likely, but as to it being upon Duval's orders, I think not. He allows them to roam as they will and gives them shelter. But soon I fear he will command them."

"What can Duval hope to gain?"

"Who knows?" William shrugged. "He and those with whom he is in sympathy are seduced by power. It divides us, Jane, at a time when we cannot afford a schism in our ranks. It is my responsibility to seek a solution, for I am the oldest and highest in rank in this county."

"But why should Luke revive me if he is one . . . one of them?"

"I believe you have a better understanding of Luke's mind than I do." He looked at her inquiringly.

"I don't believe I do. You are his Creator! Do you not know him best?"

"Not while he is among Duval and *les Sales,* and that is my burden. After what happened in this house when you were here, I have forbidden Duval ever to set foot here again. But I can no longer see Luke's mind."

She understood that, the isolation of the Damned who could not sense the presence of the ones they loved. "So fledgling has turned against Creator."

"So it would seem. But as you know, things have never been easy between us. We are too alike in temperament and age; I expect he told you of this."

"Tell me more of the weapons," Jane said, not wanting to talk of Luke. She touched the place near her collarbone as she spoke.

He stood to fetch the decanter and pour them more wine. "You may remember that after we found Margaret had betrayed you to the French, I gave you the choice of judgment: to banish or to destroy her. There was a weapon, a small sicklelike implement of graystone. You chose banishment. It is weapons like that knife that Duval and those who hold his views use. And yes, I still possess that knife, but I bring myself to that level of degradation should I, or any of my household, use it in warfare."

Jane nodded, remembering the cold burn of the graystone against her fingertips and her reluctance to send another of the Damned to hell. One of the Damned, alone, was as good as destroyed, might even become one of *les Sales.* Had she really made such a wise choice? Or even a humane choice? Yet Margaret had formed, or joined, another household.

"She was luckier than most," William said in answer to her

unspoken question. "Well, Jane. Is it not time you made a decision?"

"What do you mean?"

"To throw in your lot with us and hunt *les Sales.*"

"And my family?"

"You mean your mortal family. Join us, and they will be safer than if you do not."

She rose to her feet. "You are hardly persuasive, William."

He rose too. "I am honest. My family is my first priority. But consider, Jane. This is not a situation unique to Hampshire. All over England the Damned are divided, households and old alliances broken, fledglings turned against Creators, and more and more of us take to the ways of *les Sales.* It is your duty to help, as it was when the French invaded. "

"Your indifference to my family hardly convinces me to join you, William. I regret I must decline your offer."

"You may think differently when more fall foul of *les Sales.* Martha was lucky that you knew what to do."

"I must excuse myself. I suggest, sir, you and your kind protect this village in which you have chosen to live, and upon which you have brought trouble. It is the neighborly thing to do. Since I must hope and pray a metamorphosis never takes place I can be of little assistance."

He bent to throw a log onto the fire. They both watched as it settled in the embers, throwing off sparks, blue-gray smoke rising upward.

"If you do not dine soon," William said, "you will not have much strength as one of us, and it may well affect your strength and health as a mortal. You put your precious family in danger."

Tonight she had experienced the first stirrings of hunger. Time might be running out for her. He knew it as well as she.

She placed her wineglass on the mantelpiece before she was

tempted to throw it in his face. "Even though you barely let me into your mind, I note you have no compunction whatsoever for roaming freely through mine. I trust you enjoy yourself there."

William bowed. "I shall send for my steward."

"You will excuse me. I do not wish to dine."

"I was merely offering you an escort home."

"I am much obliged." She turned away from him, mortified by her mistake and insulted that he did not offer to escort her himself. Doubtless he wished to return to the harlot upon whom he dined, whoever she might be.

"Jane?"

He merely held out her cloak, which she had tossed upon a chair on entering the room. She grabbed it and threw it around her shoulders, hearing, from the tinkle of breaking glass, that she had managed to dislodge her wineglass from the mantelpiece. She hoped William had not noticed the broken glass, but he was in conversation with someone outside the door.

"This is Raphael, my steward. He will see you safely home," William said.

Jane nodded at the steward—she had a vague impression of a strong profile, black hair streaked with silver—and walked ahead of him out of the room and toward the front door. The steward stepped beside her to open the door and an intoxicating scent arose from him—healthy male sweat and his blood, oh heavens, she could smell his blood, and hear the sound of his pulse.

"Steady there, ma'am!" He grasped her elbow.

She must have lost her footing. His touch melted his thoughts to her . . . *one of them? A handsome lady despite her anger . . .*

Snarling, she shook his arm away and marched ahead of him down the drive. Now she was apart from William, and unnerved by her violent reaction to the man who followed her, she wondered if she had made the right decision. She had no part in the quarrel between the Damned and *les Sales;* she had seen the contemptuous attitude of many of the Damned toward mortals, regarding them as convenient sources of pleasure, service, and sustenance. From thence, it could only be one small, wicked step to regard mortals as prey.

But still it made no sense. For was not one of the delights of the Damned to give pleasure far beyond any mortal sensual experience? Did the pleasures of the hunt outweigh the luxury of a seduction? Memories of strength and power, the fierce joy of pursuit and capture, came back to her. However much she might justify her actions as a soldier might justify his killing during a war, she could not deny the pleasure of ripping into an enemy's throat, the exultation of his blood and fear . . .

"Ma'am, if you please." She heard the crunch of gravel behind her.

"Yes?"

"Ma'am, my instructions are to stay close." There was something, a hint of a foreign accent in his voice.

"Very well." She stood and listened. She could hear Raphael's breath; beyond him, in the meadow at the side of the driveway, a scamper of small furred beings, the brush of an owl's wing in the dark, the hectic rush of air as a bat turned and skittered . . . sounds no mortal could or should hear, and yet she still deluded herself that she was not one of the Damned! Further into the darkness, cattle stirred, made uneasy by her presence—or was it by the presence of another like herself? A breath of wind sent a faint scent to her nostrils, the scent that had clung about Martha earlier that day, rank and musky yet with the familiarity of the Damned about it. The scent of an animal.

Some hunt alone, with no society, no loyalties to any others, little better than beasts . . .

"Take my arm," she whispered. "Come closer to me."

After a moment's hesitation, he did so. She now stood between him and *le Sale,* for that was what it must be.

She pulled the hood of her cloak up over her head. "Whisper quietly to me as though . . ."

His hand moved to his hip and she saw against the silk lining of his coat the gleam of finely polished wood and steel with a delicate tracery of ivory. "As though we're courting . . ."

With a smooth, easy movement he withdrew the pistol and cocked it.

She slowed their pace and listened, ignoring the distraction of his person so close to hers, hip to hip, his arm around her waist beneath her cloak.

He gave a soft murmur of laughter. "Ah, a good servant enjoys his work, ma'am."

She who had once hunted at night was now prey. The creature moved clumsily, doubtless weak from hunger, lonely and fearful, almost as though it didn't care that she could hear.

She gave a low growl, and beside her Raphael's breath hitched; if he had had any doubt of her nature, now it was clear what she was, or what she was becoming.

The creature was on her with a sudden burst of speed and a desperate clumsiness, but even so it was stronger than she. Its prey was not Jane, but Raphael—she found herself knocked to the ground as it leaped on Raphael, *en sanglant* agleam in the moonlight, a woman with wild hair and eyes, a once-fine gown in shreds and tatters, her movements weak and frantic as though she had not dined in some time. The pistol exploded with a streak of fire and left the scent of powder in the air. Whether the ball found its target she didn't know—certainly the woman did not slow down.

Jane grasped the woman's matted hair. "Leave him!"

From her appearance it looked as though the woman was

more animal than human, and Jane was surprised when she spoke. "He is mine!"

"He does not consent. Go to the house. They have willing humans there."

But even as starved as she was, the woman had strength beyond Jane's, and one blow of her arm sent Jane reeling back, stars bursting before her eyes. She found herself flung several feet away. As she struggled to her feet there was another loud explosion and flash of fire; Raphael had managed to grasp the second of the pair of pistols, and this time his shot was true.

The woman fell back with a cry, dark blood staining the ruined bodice of her gown. She fell and began a painful crawl away from them. The wound, which would have proved fatal to a human, merely weakened her enough to cause her to abandon her attempt to dine.

Jane ran to her. "I beg of you, do not go!"

"I am dishonored; I am *sale*. Leave me." The woman snarled and melted into the darkness.

"Let her go," Raphael said. He got to his feet, brushing his coat off, and bent to retrieve the pistol that had fallen. "What do you think would happen to her if she came to the house?"

"I don't know."

"William would show her little clemency or mercy, ma'am." He examined the pistol and tucked it inside his coat again. "She would receive justice. This way she survives a little longer. Shall we continue?"

Jane nodded and brushed dirt from her cloak.

The moon was a small sickle in the sky, but there was light enough from the stars for her keen sight to observe the wound on Raphael's knuckle, a bright trail of blood that made its way with tantalizing slowness down his finger (powerful, elegant hands; how had she not noticed before?). And the scent, God forgive her, mixed with that of gunpowder and scorched fabric and flesh, which brought hurtling back memories of other nights and other hunts.

"You bleed," she said.

"Aye, ma'am, so I do." He was not one to be overcome by her powers (whatever they might be; she wasn't sure of her capabilities. Had not *la Sale* thrown her as easily as a man might throw a sack of grain onto a cart?). This man would yield only if he wished; all the seductive powers of the Damned could not help her.

He raised his hand to his mouth and licked the knuckle clean, a deliberate and tantalizing gesture.

She let out a small sigh of disappointment. But the blood welled anew.

"You wish . . . ?" He offered his hand. It might have been an invitation to walk on, and she stood, frozen, watching the scarlet trail, imagining how that would feel and taste on her tongue, the pleasure of his male taste and smell, the touch of hands whose refinements were marred with a little roughness.

And if she drank his blood she was Damned and there would be no turning back; there would be no more doubt or uncertainty.

If she would not yield as one of the Damned, she could yield as a woman. She stepped up to him and kissed him on the lips, receiving the shock of an aftertaste of his blood, delicious with the flavors of almonds, of honey, and, yes, a little of bitter herbs she could not identify.

He made a soft sound of surprise and gathered her close. She clutched the lapels of his coat as though she drowned and he were her only rescue, but she wanted to sink into sweet, deep oblivion. He winced as her sharp teeth scraped the softness inside his lips, but she would not allow herself to draw blood. This, for the moment, was enough.

"So." He put her from him, and she wondered if she too wore a look of dazed wonder, her lips swollen from kissing. "My instructions are to see you safely home."

"You will." She looked upon him with pleasure, a tall, well-made man, although not a young man—the silver in his hair attested to that—muscular and graceful with a body made to dance or fight or, yes, make love. Definitely a body for making love.

"Come," he said, and led her through the starlight, onto the road and past the darkened cottages and finally by the pond where a duck gave a comical sleepy quack.

They did not speak, she wanting to savor the moment, for almost certainly she would want his blood, or another's, and sooner than she cared to think about. She could have entered his mind, but delicacy forbade it. For all she knew, he might regard her as an easy conquest; he might be one of those who craved to provide the sustenance of the Damned as others craved gaming or strong drink or opium. For this night, she wanted to keep her illusions beautifully intact.

He kissed her hand at her front door—or, rather, he kissed her wrist at exactly the point he would have chosen had he been Damned and wished to dine—and she thought she might swoon with pleasure. He bade her good night with grave formality, and while she could not bear to let him go, she could not wait to rush inside and light a candle from the banked-up fire.

She had a lot to write about.

"Go away." Jane's pen scratched over the paper before her.

"We have callers," Cassandra said.

"I'm barely fit to be seen."

"And whose fault is that? If you had not stayed up all night, you would not be such a bear with a sore head this morning."

Jane leaned back in her chair and shook the sheet of paper dry. "I am a busy bear with a sore head, sister, and I am not in the mood to exchange polite idiocies over tea."

"Not even with handsome gentlemen?"

"We don't know any, and I doubt these mythical handsome gentlemen have come to see me. Or you, for that matter."

"Of course not." One of the annoying things about Cassandra was her refusal to be provoked. "They—or rather he—has come to see Anna."

"But Anna is not here in Chawton to see gentlemen—wait, who do you mean?" She stood, alarmed, and straightened her papers, absently wiping her pen on her handkerchief.

"Duval—Jane, you look a fright, come back."

Jane, her appearance forgotten, ran into the parlor where Anna, Mrs. Austen, and Martha sat. Duval stood and bowed as she entered.

She longed to attack him, but the mayhem of spilled blood, the possibility of his being armed, and, not least, the cruelty of revealing her true nature to her family stilled her.

"I trust you are well, Miss Jane," he murmured. He cast an amused glance at her. She was fairly sure she had a smudge of ink on her cheek, and her gown bore the brunt of the fight last night. Altogether she was fairly sure that she looked exactly what she was: a woman of a certain age, bedraggled and slightly grubby. He, on the other hand, was impeccably handsome and elegant, and to Jane's dismay Anna was gazing at him with besotted admiration.

"It is most kind of you to call, sir, but I regret we must bid you farewell."

"Jane!" her mother exclaimed.

"Have you not forgotten, ma'am, that the chimney sweep is due to visit today? We must cover the furniture."

"No, Jane, you are mistaken," Martha said. "Sir, my friend is all at sixes and sevens when she is writing; you must forgive her."

"You write, Miss Jane?"

"Yes, sir. I write novels."

"Oh. Novels." He looked at her with some pity.

"They are very good," Anna said. "And a publisher was very interested in one of them once, am I not right, Aunt?"

Jane sighed in exasperation. "It has been very kind of you to visit, Mr. Richards, but it is not proper for we ladies to receive you."

He bowed and picked up his hat. "It was delightful to see you, ladies."

After he had left, Cassandra turned on her sister. "What on earth is the matter with you, Jane? All this nonsense about a chimney sweep! Why were you so rude to him?"

"He is most unsuitable company for Anna . . ." Jane stopped as she saw Anna's look of avid interest.

"Why, Aunt Jane?" Anna asked.

"Delicacy forbids me from saying more. He is more dangerous than you can imagine. We should not receive him again. If necessary I shall write to your father and he—" She stopped as the front doorbell rang again. "This place is a madhouse this morning, and I am busy. You must entertain yourselves and the next herd of visitors without my presence."

As she stepped into the vestibule she heard the murmur of voices and darted forward to greet the new guests.

"My dear Jane!" Dorcas Kettering grasped her hands. "How delightful to see you. I am afraid we had to bring Raphael with us, but as William's steward he is most respectable, almost a gentleman. What do you think of my gown today? I borrowed it from one of our servants." She wore a striped cotton gown that revealed a lot of ankle.

"Oh. Much better, although I think the original owner must have been considerably shorter than you. The paste earrings, however—"

"Diamonds, my dear."

"Not at all suitable, I fear. They are quite lovely, but not in the daytime."

William, clearly annoyed by talk of feminine frippery, interrupted. "Duval was here. We saw him leave. Is everyone safe?"

"Yes. Perfectly safe. Raphael, how very pleasant to see you again." She wondered if William knew what had transpired between her and Raphael last night and concluded he probably did. "I made Duval leave."

"You *made* him leave? How?" William asked.

"I told him the chimney sweep was expected at any moment and I was quite rude. I embarrassed my family."

He frowned. "Duval and his kind need stronger measures than bad manners, as you know."

He stood back to allow her and Dorcas to enter the parlor, where Cassandra looked at Jane with a satirical air and Anna looked sulky.

"I thought you had to write, Aunt Jane."

"Oh, I can spare a few minutes yet." She introduced Raphael to them and prepared to enjoy the sight of her family gravely exchanging pleasantries about the weather with the Damned.

Raphael sat next to her, making her acutely aware of her bedraggled appearance.

"I have been awake all night," she muttered to him.

"I too."

"I was working," she added, in case he harbored any illusions that her wakefulness was caused by thoughts of him. "Writing."

"So was I. Hunting." He shifted so his coat swung aside to reveal a pistol.

Finding herself gazing at his muscular thighs clad in tight-fitting buckskins, she cleared her throat. "Would you care for some more tea?" As she poured, she muttered, "Hunting *les Sales*?"

He nodded.

"Do you kill them?"

"What are you two talking about so very seriously?" Mrs. Austen found it necessary to intervene.

"We are talking of vermin, ma'am," Raphael replied.

"How charming," Mrs. Austen replied. "More tea, Mrs. Kettering? My son sends us this tea from London. It is a most superior blend, do you not agree?"

"What are you, Raphael?" Jane asked in a whisper. "You are not one of the Damned, yet you—"

"Oh, how very kind!" Cassandra cried. "Jane, Mrs. Kettering has offered to let us copy some of her music. My sister, Mrs. Kettering, has the clearest penmanship on a manuscript; it is as good as printed music."

"Most kind indeed," Jane said, trying not to look at William. *You hunger?*

I'm not sure. But she looked at Raphael and couldn't tell exactly what she hungered for.

He is my servant, but you could do worse than to take him as a lover. You will have need of him, or another, when you wish to dine.

You, sir, are offensive, and I assure you once again I shall fight a metamorphosis with all my strength.

"I think, Miss Jane, you and I must establish a musical club and have regular weekly meetings at your house, or ours," Dorcas cried.

Jane glanced around the parlor, trying to imagine it crammed not only with the gentry of Chawton but also with a cluster of the Damned, notorious for their indifference to music, wondering on whom they should first dine. "That is a very fine idea, but—"

"We are in agreement then! What do you think, William?"

"Excellent. Since it is Dorcas's idea, we should play host first. I invite you all to the Great House tomorrow afternoon, if that is convenient. Raphael will see to invitations to others in the village."

"Will Mr. Richards attend?" Anna asked.

"Regretfully, no, Miss Anna," William replied. "He is not at all suitable company for a gently bred young lady like yourself. He has a reputation as an unscrupulous rake who is heavily in debt and gambles—"

"Quite unsuitable, as I have told you," Jane said, dismayed by Anna's avid interest.

"But my brother, Mr. Fuller, will be there," Dorcas said. "He is very fond of music."

"I regret we cannot attend," Jane said, but she was interrupted by her sister, mother, and Martha, exclaiming that the family would be delighted to attend, while Anna beamed with pleasure.

Shortly after, their guests took their leave, with Jane unable to continue an unspoken conversation with William or a whispered one with Raphael.

"Why, we are becoming quite fashionable," Mrs. Austen commented. "And Mr. Raphael seemed quite gentlemanly for a steward, although when I was a girl it was a very respected profession for a younger son. I think, however, that Mr. Fitzpatrick is an old-fashioned sort of gentleman. I do wonder why he has not married. But who is this Mr. Raphael? He sounds foreign."

"I am sure Aunt Jane can tell us more of him. She talked only to him the whole time," Anna said.

"A slight exaggeration," Jane said. "May I remind us all that Anna has not been sent to stay with us to enjoy society but to reflect upon her errors. We should not visit the Great House tomorrow."

"Oh, certainly," Cassandra said. "We should stay home and read sermons aloud to one another. I do think, Jane, considering the good works our mother and I do in the village—"

"It was agreed, sister, when we moved here, that I should be at liberty to write, and I too do my share of Christian duty—"

"Girls!" Mrs. Austen looked at her daughters with disapproval. "This does not become you at all, to quarrel like a pair of children."

"As I was saying, we lead exemplary lives and we deserve the occasional visit to our neighbors," Cassandra continued. "Besides, if we go tomorrow, Jane, you will be able to flirt with Mr. Raphael all you want."

"I do not flirt!" Jane said with some savagery. As she left the room, she heard a burst of laughter in her wake.

She, once the most frivolous and silly flirt in Hampshire, according to some, was now turning into the sour, pious sister of the family. It certainly explained the origins of Mary among the Bennet sisters, a character who'd surprised her by emerging fully formed out of nowhere. At any moment she'd start quoting homilies from sermons and setting her cap for Mr. Papillon in earnest.

"I'd rather be Damned," she said and was glad there was no one to hear.

Chapter 8

Exhaustion finally overtook her that day and she lay on the sofa for a while before dinner. She could barely eat, however, and the others expressed concern. Her concern was of a different sort; almost certainly her lack of appetite was another sign of her deterioration, her restlessness the beginning of the compulsion to dine. Beneath the clatter of cutlery on china and conversation she heard the others' heartbeats and loathed herself for her inability to control the symptoms of the Damned.

Inevitably the conversation turned from her health to Martha's, and they all agreed what a remarkable recovery she had made the day before. Anna volunteered to deliver the Andrews family some tea the next day as a gift for their hospitality, and conversation turned to the morrow's activities and the anticipated pleasures of the music club at the Great House.

"Martha and Cassandra and I shall accompany you when you visit the Andrews family," Jane said at breakfast the next morning.

"Oh, you don't have to," Anna said.

"I think it would be courteous," Jane said and caught a flash of disappointment on Anna's face. While passing Anna a slice of toast, she brushed her hand against the young woman's wrist, but caught only vague meanderings on what she should wear and whether she really should eat this second slice, or forgo the jam, for she did not want to get fat.

"Austens don't get fat. We're lucky," Jane said, before she could stop herself.

Everyone stared at her.

"How did you know what I thought?" Anna said, blushing.

Jane wondered about that blush. What had she missed? "Why, you said so yourself. You asked for another slice of toast and said that you didn't want to get fat but the jam was so very good. Well, of course it is good, for it is one of Martha's recipes."

"I don't think I did say that," Anna said.

"Your grandmother used to read our minds all the time," Jane said, improvising as best she could. "Do you not remember, ma'am, when you would have your back turned to us yet you would know exactly what mischief we undertook?"

"Indeed yes," Mrs. Austen said. "Your papa, Anna, was so often a badly behaved child, forever getting into trouble."

"Really?" Anna sighed. "I miss Papa. I wonder if he's still angry with me."

"I am sure he has forgiven you, particularly if you act with good sense in the future." Jane watched Anna. Certainly the girl was up to something, and she hoped she had not been so foolish as to agree to meet Duval secretly. But how could she have arranged such an assignment? She made up her mind that she would guard Anna very closely even if she could not convince her family of the very real danger that lurked at nightfall in the peaceful fields and woods of the village.

The devil of it was that Anna was safer with Duval than one

of the Damned would be if he had only seduction on his mind; she was in no more danger than any other woman with one of the Damned. But the proprieties must be observed: Jane must accompany Anna whenever she went out. If Jane herself was in danger, William would come to rescue his fledgling, ideally with Raphael and his pistols.

It would play havoc with her plans to write this morning, and while she rather liked the idea of Raphael coming to the rescue, she was still extraordinarily offended by William's encouragement for her to take Raphael as her lover. She was a respectable spinster who had to set an example in the village and uphold the good name of the Austen family, and moreover she was far too old for such foolish dalliance. She had kissed the man within minutes of meeting him. She wanted to do it again. And more.

"What are you thinking about, Aunt Jane? Can anyone tell what my aunt is thinking about?"

Sometimes the child was too sharp for her own good. "I was thinking about how I, too, enjoy Martha's jam," Jane replied. "It is so very sweet and dark and delicious and . . . well!" She jumped to her feet, sending her knife clattering to the floor. "Look at the time! Let us put our bonnets on and visit the Andrewses."

Mrs. Austen, muttering of an assignation with a boy who was to spread manure, left for the garden, and the four ladies set off on their visit. Almost to Jane's disappointment, no sinister figures lurked behind trees; and even though she revisited the scene of her attack for the first time, Martha had no recollection at all of what had happened to her.

"Do you remember the picnic we had in the woods the last time I visited?" Anna said as they returned. "That was such a happy time, but I was young then."

"Indeed, you are now all of fifteen, quite in your dotage," Jane replied teasingly with a smile and stopped dead as a figure materialized from the darkness of the trees ahead of them.

"Why, is not that one of the ladies who attended the dancing at the Great House?" Cassandra said.

"Wait here!" Jane snapped to her companions.

"What's the matter?" Martha asked, but Jane ignored her. She walked forward, her tread becoming light and wary.

Margaret stood still, waiting for Jane to reach her.

Jane wished she could become *en sanglant,* but nothing happened. Margaret smiled. "You're not so advanced as I had been led to believe."

"Do you carry a weapon?" Jane said, annoyed that Margaret saw her deficiencies so clearly.

"Would I tell you if I did?"

"What do you want?" Jane asked.

"Why, Miss Jane, I am merely taking the air in these most pleasant woods. This is very pretty countryside."

Jane laughed. "Mrs. Cole—I presume you still use your husband's name?—I have to thank you."

"Thank me?"

"Oh yes. You have proved very useful to me. I remembered a certain conversation we had regarding my intentions toward Mr. Venning, and a character in one of my books spoke your words exactly. I raised her a little higher, however; she was a lady of quality, and not a known adulteress. I trust you have not come to ask me the same question again."

Margaret smiled, very slightly *en sanglant:* enough to indicate that she felt the sting of Jane's words. "Yes, I am still Mrs. Cole; I begin to believe Mr. Cole is immortal too. I wish to give you some advice, Jane. Do not become Raphael's *amorata* and do not trust William. I know he is your Creator, but remember he rejected you as such once before."

"Oh, for heaven's sake! I trust you do not set your cap—or your teeth, rather, I should say—for Raphael or William. May I give you some advice, also—or rather, advice for one of your companions? If Duval comes near Anna again, I shall kill him."

"She is not handsome enough to tempt *him,* I assure you, other than as an easy conquest; no more. Besides, I doubt whether destruction of one of us is within your grasp, although Duval complained that you bit his ankle like an annoying puppy."

"He seemed to be perfectly recovered when he came to call upon us yesterday. Pray convey him our thanks for his civility, but he—none of you—is welcome in our house."

"Jane." Margaret touched her wrist, and bolts of power and sensation tore through her; to her surprise there was some genuine friendliness there, some regret, all mixed with distrust. "Once we fought side by side. Do not forget that. I have paid dearly for the wrongs I did you."

"Jane, will you not introduce us?" Cassandra tugged at her arm.

Jane made introductions and watched, appalled, as Margaret turned her easy charm on the women.

"Oh, but we have met your brother, Mr. Richards," Cassandra said. "He called upon us yesterday."

"Yes, he was here to supervise the unpacking, but now we are quite snug."

"Why, you have moved into our village? He did not tell us; how like a man. But how very delightful," Martha cried. "Which house have you taken, Mrs. Cole?"

"We are very close neighbors indeed to you. We have taken Prowtings."

This was far worse than Jane had anticipated. Only a stile and a meadow, a walk of a few minutes, separated the handsome house from the Austens' cottage. "Where are Mr. Prowting and his daughter? I had not heard they left."

"Mr. Prowting's business demanded that he go to London," Margaret replied, "and of course Miss Prowting accompanied him. Such a pleasant gentleman! He was so pleased to have us as tenants at such short notice. Duval's great friend Luke Venning and his sister, Miss Clarissa Venning, whom I believe you know, will move into the house with us today or tomorrow. They stay at the inn in Alton at present."

Somehow Jane doubted that Mr. Prowting would be pleased to hear that he had rented his house to the Damned.

"We shall interrupt your walk no further," Jane said hastily before Martha or Cassandra could invite more of the Damned to take tea, discuss the drains or chimneys at Prowtings, or fulfill other social niceties. She grabbed her sister's arm. "Come, Cassandra, we must return home."

Cassandra gave her a curious glance, but polite farewells were said, and the Austen ladies set off toward home.

"What a handsome lady," Anna said. "I never saw anyone with such beautiful red hair before."

"I regret to tell you that her presence at Prowtings makes it impossible for us to have any contact at all with her, Duval Richards, or the Vennings," Jane said. She was about to play her trump card, and, even better, it was absolutely true. She lowered her voice. "Forgive me for the indelicacy, but I must tell you that we cannot receive anyone from that household—Mrs. Cole is an adulteress."

"Oh dear," Cassandra said. She stopped walking. "I have a stone in my shoe. Pray wait while I undo the laces."

"I said, Cassandra," Jane said, "Mrs. Cole is an adulteress. Did you not hear me? It is well known that she left her husband and now enjoys illicit relationships with others."

"Truly?" Anna cried, her eyes wide with excitement.

"Anna, it is wicked!" Jane said. "Martha, Cassandra, pray acknowledge the truth of the matter. We cannot let a delicately bred young lady like Anna associate with such people. Our brother would be most displeased."

Cassandra, standing on one foot, shook her shoe to dislodge the stone. "Oh, come, Jane, did not Our Lord forgive the woman taken in adultery?"

"The difference being that the woman in question repented. Margaret—Mrs. Cole—is entirely unrepentant."

"But we should set an example of Christian charity to our neighbors," Cassandra said. "To err is human, my dear Jane. Besides, how do you know about this?"

"Mr. Fitzpatrick told me of it. He was most displeased when Mrs. Cole and her party arrived at the party in his house, but he could not ask them to leave without causing his guests embarrassment."

"But he and Mr. Venning seemed to be the best of friends," Martha said. "And in a village this size, and with so few families of quality, it is almost certain that our paths shall cross. We must be civil."

"We should not receive their calls," Jane said, annoyed at the outflowing of Christian charity that Martha and her sister displayed, and she was appalled at the dreamy wonder on Anna's face.

"But that is so romantic," Anna said. "To sacrifice all—one's reputation and honor—all for love. It shows great courage. Is it not like Admiral Nelson and Lady Hamilton?—I know you admired him greatly, Aunt Jane."

"You are mistaken," Jane said. "He was England's hero and

much can be forgiven him. This is merely tawdry and a stain upon our pleasant village. I deeply regret such people are our neighbors."

Cassandra's shoelace now tied, the party continued forward.

"Jane, help me look for mushrooms," Martha said.

Jane saw they were close to the cluster of cottages where the path turned onto the road known as the Shrave and considered that Cassandra and Anna, deep in conversation about naval heroes, would be safe enough. She followed her friend into the stillness of the woods, where the grass was still wet with dew and the trees bright with early greenery. A few birds twittered overhead.

"Oh, you know I am no good at this. I shall poison us all."

"No, you won't. I am extremely knowledgeable." Martha prodded at some half-rotted leafy matter with her toe and turned it over. "Jane, what troubles you?"

"You are very perceptive," Jane said, wishing she could confide in her friend. "There is something that weighs heavily upon my mind, but I regret I cannot tell you what it is."

"Is it to do with Mr. Fitzpatrick? Mrs. Austen said your family met him in Bath, but I did not know you were acquainted with him. It is some years since you and he last met, but I can tell there is—or was—something between you."

"It is like a novel," Jane said. "It would actually make a very good novel, if anyone wished to read about a woman who ages and displays none of the usual characteristics of a heroine."

"The usual characteristics? What are those?

"Oh, the long golden hair, the wealth of accomplishments, the extraordinary beauty, the unassailable virtue; and the tendency to explore secret passages in sinister buildings at dead of night during thunderstorms while wearing a nightgown. You know of what I speak." Jane smiled.

"Oh yes, indeed. They are so tiresome, those girls. Promise me you will never write such a paragon of excellence, or possibly a paragon of stupidity; I do not think I could bear it."

Jane idly poked a fungus growing on a tree. "I could not bear it, either, and I would be stuck with the wretched girl for three volumes. Martha, what of this one?"

"Certain bellyache, although it would not kill you. But what of Mr. Fitzpatrick?"

"No bellyache, I am glad to say. Or a big belly when I was young and foolish. But yes, there was an understanding of sorts between us."

"Oh, Jane!" Martha cried. "Don't you realize?"

"Realize what?"

Martha looked around her with great caution. "He is one— one of *them*. One of—one of the Damned." Her face pinkened a little at the word. "Yes, I can tell. Some people can, you know, but this is something I only recently acquired. Only, in fact, since my—my mishap of a couple of days ago. And I believe our visitors this morning and Mrs. Cole are, too."

"Dear me. Is there anyone else?" Jane waited.

"Oh, you do not believe me!"

"I do. Why should you make up such a thing? It is shocking, I admit, for Mr. Fitzpatrick seems such a gentlemanly man, but it explains certain eccentricities."

"Yes, it is quite surprising. Of course I know things were different in Bath in '97 when . . . but possibly you were forced to consort with those wicked beings when things were in such turmoil."

"Those wicked beings saved us from the French, Martha, whatever other depravities they commit." She stopped, realizing that she damaged her own case. "But Martha, my dear, I do not at all like the idea of Mr. Richards, if he is one of them, making love to Anna. We have yet another most excellent reason to prevent Mr. Richards and others of his household from visiting us, and we must tell Cassandra and my mother immediately."

"But what of Mr. Fitzpatrick and his relatives?"

"What of them?"

"He is your brother's tenant, and I feel that it is our duty to the Knight family to be good neighbors," Martha said, her cheeks flushing a delicate pink again. "I think, if it does not sound absurd, that he is a better one of their kind."

"Ah. If by that you mean you wish to attend the music party this afternoon—"

"Oh, yes! I mean, of course we should. It would be impolite to not go after saying we shall." In some agitation, Martha plucked a pallid mushroom, examined it, sniffed its root, and threw it away.

"Calm yourself, my dear. We do not want you to poison us for dinner. I think it may be correct for us to attend the Great House today. After all, we escaped one evening there unscathed." *Mostly,* she added silently. "And, as you say, Mr. Fitzpatrick is quite gentlemanly."

"Oh, I am so glad to hear you say that!" Martha beamed. "Come, let us catch up with the others."

"But the mushrooms?" Jane said.

"The mushrooms," Martha said with a giggle, "may go to the—well, I mean we shall not find any, and . . . Jane, have you heard that when one of the Damned feeds upon someone that it is intensely pleasurable? For the one who is being fed upon, that is."

"It is indecent. No virtuous woman would contemplate such a thing."

"That's not what I have heard," Martha said with great cheer.

"I fear you are asking the wrong person," Jane said.

She followed Martha out of the woods and back onto the path, relieved that her friend, with her newfound perception, did not recognize Jane as one of the Damned. And Margaret, who had little reason to lie, had scoffed at what powers of the Damned Jane possessed. Maybe she could remain mortal after all.

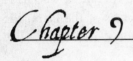 

Chapter 9

"We shall be late!" Jane said, tapping her foot as they waited in the vestibule of the cottage that afternoon. "What on earth is Martha up to?"

"She is arranging her hair, I believe," Cassandra said. "Do you have your music, Jane?"

"At her age? That is ridiculous. Now, Anna, I can understand you fussing with your appearance, but Martha looks perfectly respectable and that is adequate."

"Charity, dear Jane," Mrs. Austen murmured. "We shall see how you fare in ten years, whether you are as careless of your own appearance then as you are now."

"She looks perfectly well without . . . without new blue ribbons on her hat. Martha, at last; we have been waiting a good ten minutes for you."

Martha made a careful descent down the stairs, a newly trimmed hat in her hand.

"Oh, how pretty, Aunt Martha," Anna said, with the easy generosity of a much younger woman aware of her own good looks.

"Thank you, my dear." Martha took a quick look in the mirror as she tied the blue ribbons beneath her chin. "Jane, you look excessively annoyed."

"You will make us late," Jane said, relieved that she yet had a reflection to express annoyance.

"Oh, is that all? Is it not fashionable to arrive slightly late?"

"Maybe, but all the refreshments will have been eaten. You know our neighbors are like pigs at a trough."

"Now, Jane, curb that tongue of yours." Mrs. Austen seized her umbrella. "I hope it does not rain, although the garden and crops are in sore need."

The ladies left their house, and Jane nudged Martha. "I expected you to speak at nuncheon."

"Oh. Yes, indeed. It is rather awkward."

"Would you like me to tell them?"

"No. I shall speak now." Martha cleared her throat. "Ma'am, Cassandra, Anna, I have something important to say."

A large cart, reeking of manure and with one sorry-looking pig in the back, lumbered past, forcing the ladies into single file. The driver touched his hat as he passed.

"Now you can tell us," Jane said as they turned onto the quieter fork of the road that led to the Great House.

"Very well." Martha cleared her throat. "I regret to tell you that Duval Richards, who has moved into Prowtings, is one of the Damned."

Mrs. Austen and Cassandra burst into peals of laughter.

"I assure you, it is true. Moreover, one of the ladies in the house is a notorious adulteress." Martha glanced at Jane for help.

"Poor thing," Mrs. Austen said. "If that is indeed true, we must pity her. Mr. Richards has moved into Prowtings, you say? I did hear a rumor that Mr. Prowting was summoned to London suddenly, but how very fortunate that he could let his house so quickly."

"Ma'am, Christian charity is all very well, but she too is one of the Damned," Jane said.

"Oh come," Mrs. Austen replied, "you have joked about this long enough, Jane. How ridiculous! I am surprised you should encourage Martha in such silly beliefs."

"But Martha, how do you know?" Cassandra asked.

"Oh." Martha looked embarrassed. She twisted her hands. "It is—well, ever since my bad turn in the woods, I have been able to tell. We—Jane and I—believe one of the Damned was responsible for my . . . accident."

"But if that were so, how did you survive?" Mrs. Austen asked.

"I don't know," Martha said.

Jane, who did know, said nothing. What could she say, after all? That it was a generous dose of her blood, the blood of someone who was reverting to a state of Damnation, that had brought Martha back to life?

"My dear child," Mrs. Austen said to Martha, "I think you are unwell from your fit, or whatever it was you suffered. If you did not look so exceptionally well—is not her complexion quite splendid, girls?—I should summon a physician. But you do look so very . . . blooming."

"Why, thank you, ma'am," Martha said.

They turned into the driveway of the house, and Jane, clutching her sheaf of music in one hand, found herself anticipating a few hours of music with great pleasure. If she should encounter Raphael at the house—he might possibly attend, for his status landed him at the brink of gentility—that was all well and good; and here was William, come to greet them at the front door, looking for all the world like a respected and landed gentleman. He showed them into the Great Hall, where a handsome instrument and several music stands stood.

Chawton's vicar, Mr. Papillon, was already there with his sister, Elizabeth; Jane could hear her talking to Dorcas and Tom, or rather at them, a flow of words with little sense and apparently little thought behind them. Elizabeth must prove an obstacle to any marital inclinations Mr. Papillon might have, but any bride moving into that household would need a great deal of patience and fortitude to deal with the vicar alone.

Dorcas saw Jane and her family and came to greet them.

"Do let me know if you would prefer a footman," she murmured to Jane. "Welcome all. Pray have some refreshments. Will you take a slice of apple tart?"

"An apple tart!" Mr. Papillon said. "A very little slice, my dear ladies, will do you no harm. It might even be wholesome, for these are apples from the Knights' orchard and I always say they are the most healthful apples in all of Hampshire. You will find out, Mrs. Kettering, how very superior the fruits of the estate are. Mr. Knight has always made sure that a gift is given to the rectory when the first asparagus comes in; why, I think that should be quite soon."

"Next month," Mrs. Austen said with an air of authority. "Now, we have been eating early greens from our garden these past few days, some lettuce and rocket, and—"

"Oh, that reminds me—did I not say, dear brother, that I must ask Miss Lloyd for her recipe—you remember last Easter when we—for I wore a new cap and . . ."

Jane smiled and blocked out the waterfall of words.

"I have a pug," Dorcas announced as though confessing to an embarrassing ailment. "You should like to see it, would you not?" She called one of the footmen over. "Where has the pug gone?"

"Hiding, ma'am, I daresay, as usual," the man replied.

Jane peered over the back of the sofa on which she sat. "I thought I could smell—Dorcas, perhaps you should summon a servant with a mop—your pug is here."

The small, miserable furry bundle saw Jane, whined, and ran out into the room. It hesitated for a moment and then dashed to Anna, a safe haven among the Damned.

Anna scooped the dog into her lap. "Oh, what a sweet creature! What is his name, Mrs. Kettering?"

"His name." Again Dorcas consulted the footman. "Oh, yes. His name is Jacques. Keep him, my dear Miss Anna. He doesn't seem to like any of us very much."

Anna giggled as the pug licked her chin and wriggled with joy. "Oh, may I, Grandmother? I should so love to have a pug. But will he not miss you, Mrs. Kettering?"

"I am sure he will be much happier with you, Miss Anna." As she spoke, a lurcher slunk from under a table and made a dash for the door.

"I think the dogs may feel a draft," Mr. Papillon pronounced. "I am most susceptible to the cold, but I have found a flannel waistcoat just the thing. In June it may be safe to remove it."

"I wish you happy, my dear," Martha whispered to Jane. "How will you contain yourself until the waistcoat is removed?" They both tried to stifle giggles while Mrs. Austen shot them a stern look.

Elizabeth, despite her nervous chatter, was an accomplished musician, and she and Jane took their places at the pianoforte for a duet. How strange it was to see the Damned, for whose sensitive ears music was generally a mass of discordant sound, nodding and smiling as she played. Tom Fuller even offered to turn the pages for them, although it was obvious to Jane that he had some trouble in following the music. She had to elbow him several times to prompt him.

But at the end of the first movement, Jane stopped. "I think the instrument is out of tune."

"Impossible, my dear Miss Jane!" Tom said. "Why, we had it tuned yesterday, and this is one of Mr. Broadwood's best instruments. It should hold its tune better than that."

Everyone else hastened to assure Jane that the instrument was perfectly fine, but her observation distressed her. A sensitivity to pitch and tone could mean only that her Damnation advanced. But she smiled and, striking a few notes, claimed she had been mistaken, and she and Elizabeth continued to the end of the piece.

Jane asked Dorcas if she would care to perform, wondering exactly how far the Damned would go in their impersonation of the gentry. She declined, and the company was in agreement when Dorcas asked if Anna would sing next.

Jane was relieved when Tom left to join the others, for the accompaniment to the Scottish song Anna wished to sing was quite simple and she could easily turn the pages herself. Tom, she imagined, wished to admire Anna without distractions. She did not entirely approve, but she trusted William would make sure his companions behaved respectably.

Spirited applause broke out at the end of Anna's performance, and the little pug jumped from Mrs. Austen's lap and trotted over to her, the stump of its tail wagging as best it could. Blushing, Anna agreed to sing again and started another song, Jacques seated at her feet.

"I have delighted them long enough," Anna said to Jane when the second song was finished. "We should let Elizabeth play. I think Mr. Fitzpatrick finds her conversation overwhelming."

Sure enough, both Dorcas and William sat in astonishment as the Papillons bombarded them with meaningless chatter. Elizabeth talked (as far as Jane could tell) of embroidery thread and tea and the church roof; Mr. Papillon entertained them with an explanation of how the butter in Hampshire, particularly that of the Knights' estate, was superior and most healthful because of . . . well, who could tell, for he certainly did not reach any conclusion.

"Elizabeth, you must play for us," Jane cried, feeling like a boulder swept away in the conversational stream. "I should so like to hear the new piece you were telling me about. What better place to play it than among friends!" Then, because she could not help herself, she said to Mr. Papillon, "Mrs. Kettering has a particular interest in the Sermon on the Mount. I know she would love to hear your opinions."

"Of course, my dear madam!" And he launched into a long-winded theological discourse.

William gave a sigh of relief as Jane sat next to him. "I am not sure how we shall spend a decade, let alone a century, in the company of such dull people."

"There are superior people with interesting conversation to be found; my brothers, for instance, although I shall not introduce you."

"Why?"

"Because they would think what my mother and sister are thinking when they see us having a private conversation. I do not want to raise their hopes, and neither can I reveal what our true relation is. By the by, Martha is now able to identify the Damned, but she does not recognize me as such."

"Indeed. She will, when the time comes, and that will be soon, Jane."

She did not reply, afraid that he was right. But had not he himself expressed ignorance of how her metamorphosis would advance? He wished to have her return as his fledgling, after all, and would seize on anything he thought might be significant.

"But where is Martha?" Jane, while relieved to introduce a change of topic, was concerned that Martha was missing from the room. And so was Tom.

She rose, and William did, too. On the other side of the room, Cassandra and her mother whispered together. "Where is she?"

"I believe they left for the dining room."

The dining room, indeed! "And you did not stop them?"

"To do so would have been discourteous and ungentlemanly. I assure you she was willing."

"She is a gentlewoman!" Jane hissed at him and turned on her heel. "Pray do not follow me. It will give rise to all sorts of speculation."

As inconspicuously as she could, she left the room, hoping that Cassandra would not follow, and cursing the etiquette of the Damned. Now she remembered Martha's speculations about the sensual pleasures the Damned could provide. It seemed as though Martha's brush with one of *les Sales* and mortality had revealed hidden aspects of her friend's character, the least of which was her ability to identify the Damned.

She flung open the dining room door.

Martha was sprawled upon Tom's lap, a wide grin upon her face as he dined at her neck, one of his hands thrust into her bosom.

"Sir! Unhand Miss Lloyd this instant!" She looked him in the eye, a direct challenge by the standards of the Damned; or, she remembered somewhat belatedly, a request to join in.

Tom lifted his head, blood around his mouth, and smiled. "Such a sweet lady, Jane. Pray join me."

To her mortification, Jane's teeth tingled and ached. Lifting a hand to her mouth, she said, "This is most improper! Martha, what were you thinking?"

"Oh, Jane," Martha said. "I never realized . . ." Her head lolled to the side and Tom resumed dining.

"It's indecent!" Jane said, outraged and aroused. "Sir, she is old enough to be your mother!"

"No, she isn't."

True enough. "Tom, if you please, have you not dined your fill?"

"No," they both said.

Jane stood, tapping her foot and trying to maintain her expression of disapproval.

Tom raised his head again and a trickle of blood ran like a small scarlet stream into Martha's bosom. "Jane, you are spoiling my appetite with your sourness."

"I am delighted to hear it."

He snarled, and his voice became cold. "Your behavior is most improper. William will not be pleased to hear of your discourtesy."

"Damn William and damn you. Let her go!"

Tom snarled again and breathed on Martha's neck to close the wound, licking it clean. Jane remembered doing that herself, and the small gesture brought desire and memories rushing back.

"Are you satisfied, madam?" he said to Jane.

"No. Do it again," Martha said, her eyes closed.

"Martha!" Jane stared helplessly as Tom hoisted her friend onto the table, where she sprawled, skirts awry, bosom half bared.

Tom put his own clothing to rights, finally reaching for his coat that hung neatly on the back of a chair. That enraged Jane more than anything, that his dining upon Martha was so calculated a seduction that he had taken care not to crease his clothes.

"Martha!" Jane said again and shook her friend's arm. She pulled Martha's skirts down, noting that Martha had borrowed (without asking) a pair of her own precious silk stockings and sported garters of red silk and gold wire; heaven only knew where those originated.

"Tom, look at her! She is almost insensible. You must revive her immediately."

"I beg your pardon. I do not take orders from you."

"If you please," Jane said, forcing herself into civility. She fetched a bottle of wine and a glass that stood on the sideboard. "She is your guest, after all."

With a look of distaste upon his face, Tom bit into his own wrist and let a drop of blood fall into the wine. "This sort of activity is suited to the kitchen, not above stairs."

"Times have changed, sir. This lady is your neighbor and now your equal." During her time with the Damned, it had been a fledgling's duty to provide the blood that revived the source of the previous night's entertainment; she remembered a group of men and women—whores, servants, laborers—smiling and wobbly and sated, seated at the kitchen table and watching drops of her blood dissolving into breakfast small beer.

She slid an arm beneath Martha's head. "Martha, my dear, please drink this."

Martha giggled and presented her neck to Jane.

"Martha!" Jane said and slapped her.

"Oh!" Martha blinked. "What is the matter, dear Jane?"

"Please drink this."

Martha drank, smacking her lips. "How delicious. May I have some more?"

"Certainly not." Jane took the glass from her hand. "I believe Mr. Fuller has something to say to you."

Tom approached, straightening his neckcloth, and bent over Martha's hand. "Dearest creature. You have done me great honor."

"Oh, you sweet boy." Martha ruffled his hair. "On the contrary, you have honored me. When may we next—"

"You should apologize, Tom!" Jane said, entirely out of patience with them both. "And this is never to happen again!"

"I don't believe that's your decision, Jane," Martha said, bright-eyed and energetic once more. But she smiled at Tom and slipped off the table, straightening her skirts.

The dining room door opened and William entered. "Tom, the ladies have requested that you play your flute for them. Miss Anna will accompany you."

"He plays the flute?" One of the Damned, playing a musical instrument—Jane was dumbfounded.

"Yes, I picked it up a few months ago," Tom said. "I believe I'm quite accomplished. I have been practicing an Irish air. Will you not come and listen, Martha?"

"Miss Lloyd to you, sir," Jane said.

"I shall enter separately so as not to cause gossip," Martha said. She gave a sigh as William and Tom left. "They are both so handsome, are they not, Jane?"

"Oh, Martha, that you should fall into the hands of that vile seducer," Jane said, close to tears. "I am so sorry I could not prevent it."

"Indeed." Martha looked at her with very little warmth. "You interrupted us!"

"Thank God I did."

"I wish you had not. No, let me speak, dearest Jane. I am forty-three and I have never known passion in my life, nor am I likely to. Why should I not take this opportunity to experience that of which the poets sing? Oh, Jane, it was a revelation; he made me feel beautiful, desired. Young." She smiled. "And he was so happy to oblige, although he was a little shy at first."

"You asked him?" Jane did not know which astonished her

more: Martha's proposition or one of the Damned assuming shyness.

"Of course. I had to; I don't believe he would have spoken. Well, I feel most refreshed and invigorated. Let us go and hear dear Tom perform on his flute."

"I daresay you've worn his own flute quite out," Jane said, trailing after Martha as she left the room. "And next time, if you please, wear your own stockings."

"There is no need for vulgarity," Martha responded with crushing dignity.

Chapter 10

"Oh, I do so love Mr. Darcy," Anna said dreamily as they sat around the fire at home later that evening.

"Indeed. How interesting. All he has done so far is refuse to dance with our heroine." Jane laid the papers on her lap, her reading aloud concluded, and well pleased at Anna's observation.

"Oh, yes. You know he is handsome and will be an ardent lover. How do you do that, Aunt Jane?"

"Anna!" Jane said, annoyed to see Martha nodding in agreement. "All I have done is arranged the words and made sure the characters are not in two places at once. I should never have agreed to read after dinner if I had known I was to be such a corrupting influence."

"I do so want to know what happens next," Anna said, stroking her pug's head.

"I trust Mrs. Bennet is not based upon me," Mrs. Austen said with a smile.

"Oh, no, ma'am, for you obviously lack that single-minded ferocity to get your daughters married."

Mrs. Austen and Cassandra exchanged a glance.

Martha stood and stretched languorously as far as her stays would allow. "Ladies, I think I shall retire to bed. I find I am quite fatigued. I wish you all good night."

"Indeed, it has been an exciting day," Jane said. "Pray wash my stockings before you return them to me."

"And good night to you, too, Jane. Come, Anna, you sit there yawning." Martha and Anna took candlesticks from the mantelpiece and made their way upstairs.

Jane stood to leave for the dining room and her writing, but her mother spoke. "My dear, your sister and I are very concerned. We must speak with you."

So they knew. Cassandra must have confided in their mother. Overcome with shame and relief, but full of gratitude too that they accepted her condition with such equanimity, she stammered, "Indeed, I cannot help it. I am shamed, for I did not expect this, and particularly at such a time in my life. I fear for my soul and that I must leave you—"

"My dear girl," her mother said, "I hardly think your soul is in danger. Your heart, almost certainly, and that is why we wish to ask if you are engaged to Mr. Fitzpatrick."

"Engaged! To William!" Oh, no. How could she have been so mistaken?

"Yes, we notice you use each other's Christian names."

"It is quite romantic, that you should meet again after a dozen years," Cassandra said. "He is still very handsome. I remarked to our mother that he has hardly changed since we met him in Bath. You would not think him more than twenty-eight or so. But we did not realize how well you knew each other then, although I suppose you must have seen him when you stayed at Miss Venning's house. Did you part on bad terms? I wish you had confided in us then."

"He shows you marked partiality," Mrs. Austen continued.

"We cannot help but notice it, so you may be assured our neighbors do, too. It is so difficult without a man in the family, for if your father were alive, he could take Mr. Fitzpatrick aside and have the matter settled in a moment. Maybe when James or Edward visits next, we—"

"Ma'am, Cassandra, I assure you, you are mistaken. Mr. Fitzpatrick and I will never marry, and there is no need to consult my brothers." Of that she was quite certain; among the Damned, any sort of carnal activity between Creator and fledgling was considered incest and therefore forbidden.

"And so you are not in love with him?" her mother asked.

"No, ma'am. He is a good man, and I am proud he is Edward's tenant and one of our neighbors."

"Except that they are such a dull lot, and Mr. Fitzpatrick is not dull," Cassandra said. "He is quiet, but he seems possessed of good sense and manners."

"I am much relieved that your heart is untouched," Mrs. Austen said, "although I should like to see both Cassandra and you settled. There is yet time, for you are both handsome and clever, if no longer young."

"I trust you did not think he pursued me for my money," Jane said, and all three of them laughed, easy again. "But, ma'am, Cassandra, since we are to speak plain, what would you say if I were to tell you that dangers lurk in our friendly fields and woods, and that we must exercise the greatest caution?"

Cassandra looked at Mrs. Austen, and they both burst into raucous laughter.

"I should advise you, Jane, to read Fordyce's sermons and not Mrs. Radcliffe's horrid novels," Cassandra said, shaking her head. "Come, you sound like an ignorant village girl, not a rational being. Why, only the other day, Betty Cooper was saying something equally ridiculous."

"I remember you saying Betty had suffered a fit that sounds remarkably similar to poor Martha's," Jane said. Poor Martha indeed! She had certainly had the best time that afternoon of any of the guests.

"I think Betty was drunk," Mrs. Austen said. "I regret the family has a tendency to overindulge in strong drink."

"So much for Christian charity, then." Jane rose to take her candle from the mantelpiece. "I'll bid you good night, ma'am, Cassandra. I am going to write."

In the dining room she gave a longing glance at her writing slope but did not open it, too unsettled by the events of the day, particularly the last conversation with her sister and mother. She placed the candlestick on the windowsill and thought longingly of when she had slipped out at night to dress in men's clothes to hunt the French, the welcoming friendliness of the darkness and the excitement of the chase. She cracked open the shutters at the window and peered out at the night, the deep velvet shadows, the trees sculpted against a starry sky.

The moon moved from beyond the buildings opposite, spilling a little blue-gray light into the room. Around her the house creaked and settled, something small scampered with a scratch of claws beneath the floorboards (its pulse a rapid thrum, but she would pay no attention), and a distant burst of song came from the direction of the alehouse.

Jane.

The summons came as strong as though William whispered in her ear.

Come to the back door.

What are you doing here? she replied, but there was no answer.

She should ignore the summons, but she could not. She found herself drawn to her Creator, walking through the quiet house to the back door, which she unbolted and eased open.

William, Tom, and another figure a little behind them stood there.

"We've come to see if you remember how to fight," William said.

"Naturally. In the middle of the night. I know how to fight; I learned in Bath, as well you know, but I see no need of it now." She noticed the third member of the group was Raphael, and her heartbeat kicked into a slightly higher pace. She hoped William and Tom paid it no attention. And even as she spoke, the idea of going out into the darkness, of experiencing once more the freedom afforded by men's clothing, increased her excitement.

"I doubt you have put in much practice recently. These are for you." William pushed a bundle of clothing at her. "I hope you haven't got fat."

"I have not! But—" She snatched the clothes, a full suit of men's garments and linen, from him. The pair of boots atop threatened to tumble to the floor, and she grabbed them beneath her chin. So: now she had accepted the clothes even though her natural modesty insisted she should go no further with this madness.

Additionally, there was a problem, that, to her embarrassment, she must overcome. "Is Dorcas with you?"

"No. Hurry up," William said.

"It's my stays."

"What of them?"

"I need help unlacing them. I could wake my sister but then she would wonder why I did not go to bed—"

"Turn around, if you please," William said.

Fingers tugged at the ties of her gown, but she became overcome with embarrassment. She gave a muffled shriek. "Not you, Raphael!" That Raphael should touch her when her thoughts had turned to him for most of the day was intolerable.

"Good God," William grumbled. "And to think you were the fearless girl who hunted the French and dined with us—allow me, Raphael."

"I, sir, am a respectable spinster in a village where everyone knows one another and what they do not know about us they invent—" Her gown, loosened, slid, and she clutched it to her body.

"Well, come, Miss Jane Austen, how would they know who unlaces your stays? Unless you boast of it to your neighbors." William's fingers plucked at the strings of her stays and they fell away, a breath of cool night air caressing her through the cotton of her shift.

She retreated into the house and stripped off her clothes, which she hung on a peg by the door, underneath one of the cloaks that hung there. She'd have to be sure to return before the house was stirring, or she would have to counter some very awkward questions. She paused before opening the door, accustoming herself to the unfamiliar touch of cotton encasing her legs, the stiffness of leather boots against her calves, the heavy swing of coattails against the backs of her knees; above all, the shock of moving without the rustle and drag of skirts.

But there was another detail, because although William had thought to include an extra neckcloth to bind her breasts, he had forgotten another item necessary for her to assume a truly masculine appearance. She pushed the sleeves of the coat up a little, releasing a faint scent of horse and tobacco.

"William!"

"What now?"

"I need an extra stocking."

"What for? You do not have three legs."

"Not as such, sir. I need to look like a man."

To her mortification all three men laughed.

"This isn't a social call, Jane," William said. "If you must fill out your breeches, use one of your own stockings."

"Oh, very well. But I also need a pin."

A sigh. "We gentlemen do not carry pins. Go without."

No, she hadn't become fat, still strong and slender from her regimen of frequent long, energetic walks. She opened the door and took a step forward, assuming an arrogant masculine swagger, aware of Raphael's look of admiration and William's approval.

"I trust I will do, sirs," she said.

"Well enough," William said. "Into the shadows with you, then."

She found herself standing alone in the yard. *Think of the darkness,* she reminded herself. *Think of something dark.*

Raphael's eyes.

Absolutely not!

The black of poorly dyed mourning clothes and the darkness of their lodgings in Bath after her father's death.

Even worse.

William appeared and touched her arm. "I see the time is not right. We must wait until the metamorphosis is more advanced. Raphael, walk with Jane, if you please."

"Where are we going?" But their direction through the gardens was familiar, and across the fields the lights of Prowtings glimmered. "Not to Prowtings!"

"Not to Prowtings, exactly. That is, we do not pay a call. We go merely to see what is going on there," Raphael told her. He was friendly enough, but not as familiar as she would have liked, although this was no time for amorous dalliance; he withheld himself from her.

She could not help laughing with delight as she clambered over the stile on the hedgeline that separated the properties. "Oh, what a great thing it is not to be hampered by skirts!"

Ignoring Raphael's outheld hand, she jumped to the ground. William and Tom were somewhere close, having taken to the shadows, whereas she and Raphael walked in the full light of the moon, the night bright enough for shadows to be cast.

"We stand out like sore thumbs."

"I regret we're the bait."

"The bait! You mean we are the worm on the hook?"

"Precisely so. We are safe enough. Have you ever fired a pistol?"

"No, but I have some skill—or I did have, once—in fighting hand to hand. Luke taught me. You know Luke, I suppose."

"I do." He paused. "I would tell you of myself, but now is not the time."

She smiled in agreement but was alerted by a movement ahead.

Raphael's hand moved casually to a pistol inside his coat. "Keep walking," he said softly. "They have set guards."

"Why?"

"Because they expect us."

"This is madness," Jane said.

"On the contrary, they are not mad. Would they were. They are ruthless and single-minded and dangerous."

"So are all the Damned."

"Indeed. But they wish to give us a demonstration of their power, so they let us approach."

They were close to the low stone wall that separated the meadow from the garden of the house, an ancient piece of masonry with ferns and small flowers and moss sharing the space between the stones that Jane had often admired on her way to visit the house. She was barely surprised when Luke stepped out of the wall's shadow in his shirtsleeves, a glass of wine in his hand, as though he took his ease in his own drawing room.

"Your servant, gentlemen. And Miss Jane." He gave her a careless bow. "A fine night, is it not?"

"Where are the others?" William asked as he and Tom emerged from the shadows.

"Up to their usual mischief, or so you would call it. Do you wish to see the night's sport?" He glanced at Jane. "Do you hunger?"

"No."

"You will. Remember when we hunted? Here we do so once again."

William moved forward and took Luke's arm, engaging him in quiet, forceful conversation, but Luke laughed and broke free. "No, you should see—your two eunuchs should see also."

"Eunuchs? He means us? There, I was right. I know I should have used an extra stocking. But why—"

"Come, we must follow," Raphael said. Already William and Tom followed Luke, falling easily into the fast lope of the Damned, gracefully skimming over fallen logs and ducking to avoid low branches as they left the meadow for woodland. Jane, used to vigorous walking, found herself picking up their rhythm and, while lagging behind, was pleased with her strength. It was not the strength of the Damned; not quite, and pray God it would not be. Raphael, she suspected, could keep up with them, but his efforts were more mortal than vampire. He grabbed his hat as a branch swooped it from his head and cursed as he slipped on leaf mold.

"We must be close to the London road," Jane commented, out of breath.

"We are." He stopped, a pistol in his hand. "Look to your right."

She saw the trees end raggedly at the road, the ruts showing clear in the moonlight, and someone moved ahead of them. Not William or Tom—she thought they and Luke were a little farther off. This creature was one of *les Sales,* lean to the point of emaciation and desperately hungry, scenting her.

"Come, my pretty," he crooned.

"Try. You won't forget." Jane felt a familiar jolt of pain in her canines, a rush of power in her limbs. Her gaze on *le Sale,* she bent to grasp a fallen branch. Behind her Raphael cocked the pistol.

But *le Sale* was distracted, and a few seconds later Jane heard the cause of his interest, the sounds of an approaching carriage, the thud of hooves and creak of wheels. The carriage lights appeared first, and the horses snorted, uneasy at the presence of the Damned—there were more of them, Jane knew, hidden among the trees, waiting. *Le Sale* erupted from the trees and flung himself at the closest horse, which came to a rearing stop. The horse next to it plunged in the traces, and the carriage came to a jolting stop.

The driver fumbled among the capes of his coat, possibly looking for a weapon, and then gave a shout of terror and aimed his whip at the team. "Get off, you devil!"

"He dines on the horse," Raphael said.

Sure enough, *le Sale* had leaped onto the horse, which screamed half mad with terror. A jet of blood sprayed onto the road.

The window of the carriage was pushed down from the inside, and a gentleman poked his head out. "What the devil—"

The Damned, maybe a half dozen of them, swarmed over the carriage, bearing its occupant down inside, the door half wrenched off its hinges. Meanwhile the screaming, plunging horse had fallen, crushing *le Sale* beneath its hooves. The air was thick with terror and the scent of blood.

"Shoot them!" Jane said, horrified. She tried to pull the pistol from Raphael's grasp.

"Have a care! It's cocked. We'll not shoot unless they attack us."

William touched her shoulder. "Remember they are armed with worse than pistols. We have seen enough. Come, Jane, Raphael. We must leave."

He led the way back through the woods at a slower pace.

Jane's teeth chattered, her legs felt weak, and she stumbled on the path. Raphael put an arm around her shoulders. "Be brave, Jane."

"We should have saved him—them. Why did we do nothing?"

"William wanted you to see how dangerous they are, how they use *les Sales* as their cannon fodder. *Les Sales* will destroy themselves willingly, for they have lost their honor and their family."

"Why cannot they join another household? Why must they wander like beasts?"

"They are dishonored," Raphael said. "No respectable household would wish to have them join, and they would refuse."

"How many are there?"

"A dozen or so, we think, but it is their masters, Duval and the others, we must fear. He has made it clear that he will tolerate them. So he assembles an army of sorts, ready for the day when civil war breaks out among the Damned."

"You think it cannot be avoided? So that is why William wishes his fledglings to return."

"Indeed."

She realized now where they were, close to the Great House, and leaving the woods for an open meadow. A little light came from the shuttered cottages that lined the road ahead.

"And you, Raphael. You too are what Luke calls a eunuch, neither Damned nor mortal? Are you one whose metamorphosis is halted? What is William to you?"

To Jane's annoyance, William, ahead of them, turned at the mention of his name, thus effectively breaking the flow of conversation. For someone who was so keen to have her take Raphael as her lover, William's behavior was certainly contradictory.

"Raphael, if you will, fetch some lanterns and bring them to the barn." He waited for Jane to catch up with him. "I hope you realize now the severity of our situation. I see you are shocked by what you witnessed."

Tom handed her a flask and the brandy fumes made her eyes sting, but a good gulp of the spirits made her feel a little stronger. "Indeed I am. How long before more in the village are attacked? What of my family?"

"You should persuade your family to leave the cottage to visit one of your brothers, and you should move to the Great House. They will be safer elsewhere and you may continue your metamorphosis. I am concerned you have progressed no further." He led her to the outbuildings that clustered at the side of the house.

"But . . . I pray I shall remain mortal. Every night, William. I do not wish to progress."

"So be it. If it is any consolation, Jane, *les Sales* rarely hunt in the day, despite your friend's unfortunate experience. You should, however, be concerned with Duval's interest in your niece."

"What do you think he intends? You think seduction or draining her is not bad enough?"

"He may intend to create her. She is not of high rank, but you, even in your half-formed state, have power, and it is likely he believes she may have the same potential." He pushed open the door of one of the larger buildings. "He needs more to rally to his cause."

"As do you, William." She couldn't help the ironic laugh that welled within her. "How the mighty are fallen, that the Damned stoop to create from among the gentry."

His expression, however, was serious. "Be assured, Jane, I shall do all in my power to have you return as one of us, however hard you pray. Did you enjoy wearing men's clothes and running through the darkness tonight?—nay, you do not need to answer, for I see you did. Do you not remember what it was to be even stronger and swifter, invincible? Do you remember the pulse of blood on your tongue? No?"

"Where do you want these lanterns?" Raphael, carrying a pair of lanterns, approached them.

William gave him a brief nod of thanks and gestured to a nearby bench. He continued, "At the least, you must be armed. I shall provide you with pistols and a knife. I remember you had some skill in fighting."

Jane nodded and yawned. The effect of the brandy, after its initial bracing shock, was to now make her feel discontented and sleepy. She longed for her bed. "Could we not resume this tomorrow?"

"I regret not. Mr. Papillon has invited me to view his collection of curiosities and to dine."

Jane laughed. "You will certainly need to reserve your strength, then. I trust he will not display his sister in his cabinet of curiosities. Tongues will wag, you know."

"I see you still possess the unfortunate tendency to speak to your Creator with disrespect. Let us continue." William gave a curt nod to Raphael. "Pray show her how to use the pistol."

A glint of amusement in Raphael's eyes nearly sent Jane into a fit of inappropriate laughter, but she managed to keep her countenance.

Raphael removed his coat. "It's best to learn in your shirtsleeves, Miss Jane. You have a greater range of movement."

Aware that she had been watching him slide the garment from his shoulders and admiring his form as he stood before her in shirtsleeves and waistcoat, she nodded and removed her own coat. She wore no waistcoat; her skin prickled with a chill that was only partly the effect of the cool air.

"So." Raphael handed her one of his pistols. "A beautiful instrument of death, Jane."

She weighed it in her hand, sliding her fingertips over the polished wood and the delicate tooling. Inlaid ivory and silver scrollwork depicted flowers, as though it were a piece of embroidery. "It is very fine work," she said.

He came to her side, his shoulder touching hers. "So, here. This is at half cock. And now full cock, ready to fire. It is empty, so it is safe to show you. Try it."

She placed her thumb on the silver lever and imitated his movements, hearing the quiet clicks as she manipulated it.

"Good. Now raise it. You practice first as though for sport, not for real life." His hands on her shoulders turned her so she stood directly in front of him, her back against him, sharing the heat of his skin. His hand grasped her wrist. "Sight. Look along the barrel. Keep your arm straight. When you fire, you hold your breath. Aim at that knothole in the timber there. You see it?"

She nodded. The barrel wavered at the end of her outstretched arm, and she laughed.

"Try again. Hold your breath. Fire."

"May I try with it loaded now?" She lowered the pistol and turned her head to Raphael's.

They stood for a moment, their lips almost touching, his chest close to her shoulders, their skin separated by only a few layers of cotton. "So," he said and stepped away. "Yes. Yes, I think so."

He fumbled in his waistcoat pocket. "Here. This is your powder. Hand me the pistol, Miss Jane, and I shall show you."

He held a small twist of paper and bit the top off quickly, so Jane could not tell if he was *en sanglant* or not. "Some of the powder down the barrel. You keep a little for the firing pan. This is the ball. It goes after the powder, and you ram it firm with the rod." He drew a slender steel rod from the underside of the pistol, so cunningly nestled in a groove, Jane had not seen it there. "You learn to do this fast."

He handed the pistol back to Jane. "Place it on half cock, if you please. The rest of the powder goes into the firing pan. And now it is ready to fire when you place it on full cock."

He stepped away and Jane raised the pistol, aiming at the knot in the wood she had sighted before. She held her breath and pulled the trigger and was taken aback by the loud explosion and the scent of burned powder. Through a haze of smoke, the walls of the barn turned into a row of houses built of Bath stone and the shouts of battle echoed in her ears.

The illusion lasted but a moment, and as she came to her senses she caught William's disapproving stare.

Her canines were bared in a snarl, not *en sanglant* (not yet) but sharp and sensitive.

"I beg your pardon," she muttered, and raised her other hand to her mouth.

"Not bad," Tom said. "You missed the timber but not by much."

"Good." Raphael, leaning against the wall of the barn, arms crossed, smiled at her with friendly encouragement. "Try again. This time you load. Here." He held out another packet of powder and a ball.

She ran through the routine again and again, until the beaten earth floor around her feet was littered with scraps of paper, and a pall of gray smoke hung around the barn. The pistol gained a familiarity in her hand as she learned to appreciate its heft and balance and grew accustomed to the kick of firing, the sharp explosion that rang in her ears. She could load without thought, her movements swift and economical.

"Well enough," William said. "Try a moving target."

"I beg your pardon?" She lowered the pistol.

"Tom, if you will?" At William's suggestion, Tom moved into the center of the barn, his coat removed to save the garment from damage.

"Not my head, if you please," Tom said. "Or my bollocks, however much you resent my intimacy with Martha."

"I quite understand," Jane said. "In short, I should avoid an injury to the part that governs you."

Tom grinned with great good nature and took a turn around the barn, hands linked beneath his coattails.

Jane raised and sighted down the barrel. Tom darted out of range, moving with the unearthly rapidity of the Damned. She swung the pistol, her finger tightening, and her shot went wide.

"Try again." Raphael handed her a loaded pistol.

This time Tom ran slowly, zigzagging across the barn, but making sudden, unexpected feints. "Look lively, Jane. I'm barely moving."

"Keep your arm straight," Raphael said. "Don't let him taunt you."

She concentrated, her arm weaving, finger stilled, then took a breath, held it, and fired.

"Ow!" Tom staggered, clutching his arm, and the dim space filled with the intoxicating scent of blood. He dropped to one knee, a dark stain spreading over his shirtsleeve.

"Serves you right," Jane said. She lowered her arm and took a deep breath.

There was no denying the desire she felt for the spilled blood, the gorgeous richness of a fellow vampire's blood, and the invitation in Tom's gaze.

Victor's spoils. She remembered fighting with Luke, lapping the blood from his skin, a rare and luxurious flavor . . .

She took a step toward him. The blood had soaked the sleeve and spread onto his hand. He clenched his fist and scarlet drops fell onto the floor, the tiny splashes magnified by her sensitivity.

"Come," Tom said.

She knew what he expected, that she should lick his wound clean and breathe it closed.

"Does the ball remain in your flesh?" Her voice was hoarse.

Another step.

"No, it passed through the muscle. Two wounds for you, Jane."

He unbuttoned his cuff and rolled up the sleeve, the light from the lanterns gilding the hairs on his arm and turning the streaks of scarlet to glistening trails.

Her breath caught.

He smiled. "Drink, Jane. Come back to us."

Come back, my dear fledgling.

And then she knew. She turned to William, and the rejection of the blood of the Damned felt like a rip in her own heart, leaving her raw and hungering. "So this is what this is all really about, is it not?"

William bowed his head in acknowledgment. "I told you I would do all I could to persuade you to throw your lot in with ours."

"You have played me for a fool!"

"I seek to hasten what is inevitable, Jane."

She turned to the bench where the second of the pair of pistols lay. It was loaded, she knew, and she moved faster than she would have thought possible.

She raised the pistol and pointed it at Tom's head. "You shall lose an ally and a companion, William. Is this really what you want?"

No one moved. Tom, who had watched the scene with amusement, now became still and serious, staring into the barrel of the pistol.

"Tell me, why I should not dispatch him. I have been deceived, by you, William, my Creator."

"I admit it." His voice was rich and quiet and resigned. "I think only of what is best for you. All I do, it is for love."

She shifted, as though arranging her feet for a dance; turned her right foot from the heel, adjusting her stance, and swinging her arm with the gleaming pistol to aim at William. Her shot could banish him to hell: immortal, yes, but indestructible, certainly not.

"All for love. I think not, sir. You might have some concern for my soul, as I do. I have every justification for pulling the trigger. One small movement of my finger, that is all."

"It is your choice," William said.

She knew it was the part of her that was Damned that stilled her finger, and equally, it was her instinct as a Christian and as a woman to spare him. But the anger and despair burned within her.

"You deceived me once when you created me and abandoned me. That was an unnatural act, was it not? You should have loved me then, William; you should have been a true Creator to me. So I shall end this sad charade now."

She took the breath that would precede the tightening of her finger upon the trigger, but a warmth enveloped her, stole around her with the scent of spices and herbs. Raphael's arm wrapped around her shoulders. His other hand grasped hers and lowered the pistol, took it from her hand. She heard the quick metallic sound as he uncocked it, still holding her in his embrace.

"Well, that was exciting," Tom commented. He licked his wound himself and breathed it closed. "I wonder what would have happened if we'd chosen Raphael for your target practice?"

He viewed his ruined shirt with distaste. "I need to dine. I'll bid you good morning."

He opened the door of the barn, and a little grayish light, that of a very early morning, seeped inside.

William walked out of the barn, not looking at Jane. Tom gave her a rueful glance and followed him, leaving Jane still wrapped in Raphael's embrace.

Chapter 11

Jane turned and laid her face against Raphael's shoulder, too weary and sick at heart to feel arousal at his embrace. A little hunger lingered, fighting with exhaustion.

"I could sleep like a horse, standing up," she murmured.

"Do you wish to come to the house?"

"No. And am I to think you are yet another temptation cast before me by William?"

He stepped away from her, his face severe and rigid. "You insult me. I hope I am my own man, still."

"I beg your pardon." She reached for her discarded coat and shrugged it onto her shoulders.

"But I fear our continued association may well have dire results and propel us both toward Damnation. It is better, madam, that we associate no more."

"Oh, for heaven's sake. I am wearing men's clothes and you address me as 'madam.' And I believe that the decision regarding our continued association is mine also. So I have judged right, Raphael. You are one such as me. But what is your association with William?"

He paused, one arm halfway into his coat. "William is my brother. Yes, brother by blood and by birth, and my Creator, the one I hate and love most in the world."

"So you also are his fledgling."

"I was." He pulled his coat onto his shoulders and reached to adjust her lapel, smoothing it. "Some twenty years ago I took the Cure. There was a lady who would not countenance marriage—or any other sort of liaison—to one of the Damned."

"You are married?"

"No, no." He shook his head with an ironic smile, and in that gesture she could see William. "The Cure was lengthy and difficult, for I had been Damned so long, and I retired to a monastery to recover. She would not wait. I cannot blame her. I had leisure to contemplate my soul and repent of the evil I had done as the Damned." He opened the barn door.

Jane stepped outside into the chill gray of early morning. A tentative flute and whistle indicated the start of the dawn chorus. "You took vows?" She tried to suppress an inappropriate laugh. "I beg your pardon, it is like something from a gothic novel."

"Life in the monastery gave me the opportunity to undertake scientific studies to find a true cure for the Damned. Even then I knew taking the waters was a difficult and imperfect process that might not work permanently."

"And did you succeed?"

"I did, after correspondence with some of the leading men of science throughout Europe. It is why I came to England, to confer with a Mr. Davy in Cornwall and Mr. Herschel, the Astronomer Royal. I believe I have the solution. If it is successful, it will not only provide a permanent cure but make the person who takes it safe from the lures of the Damned so they may never be created again. And William asked to see me, so, here I am."

"Why?"

"He is my Creator," Raphael said. "And my brother. Is not that reason enough? He wants his fledglings, even if, like me, they seek to destroy what he is, or, like you, reject him. It is what he is."

Their boots crunched on the gravel of the house as they walked back toward the village. A sleepy child, yawning, accompanied by a calf on a rope, passed them, gazing at them with curiosity.

"Will you take your cure yourself?" Jane said.

He shook his head. "I hope I shall not need to. It may kill if taken as a preventative. I do not know, for I have but one small flask of the solution and I fear it is an imperfect solution at present." He sighed. "I fear, however, that I may need it soon. You have noticed, my dear Jane, that association with the Damned, in our state of imperfect metamorphosis, speeds the process. Our association with each other, also, for our vampire tendencies are stronger than our human souls."

"You mean we damage each other," Jane said. "Well, my mother will be disappointed but relieved that I do not contemplate an affair of the heart with a Roman Catholic. I believe that making the choice between a papist and one of the Damned as a son-in-law might prove a weighty moral dilemma for her."

"You jest about it. I admire you for that."

"What else can I do?" She walked ahead of him as a cart clattered by on the road, for they had now left the driveway of the Great House. "Surely at my time of life to think of love is absurd."

"My dear, I am older than you even in human terms."

She nodded. "I shall go the rest of the way alone. I thank you for coming with me."

She turned away quickly, ignoring his outstretched hand. A handshake between two friends, what harm could there be in that? Merely the danger of bursting into tears of disappointment and anger, and she did not want him to see her weep. She entered the yard of the cottage, where chickens stretched and fluffed themselves but scattered at her approach, and let herself in through the back door of the house. From the kitchen came the sound of banging pots and the servants' voices; the household was awake.

She grabbed her own clothes from the peg where she had hung them last night and crept into the shuttered, dim dining room to change into her shift, and then barefoot, and hoping Cassandra would not awake to ask awkward questions about the boots and men's clothes she carried, ascended the stairs and entered their bedchamber.

Cassandra lay asleep, as usual buried beneath the bedclothes.

Jane thrust the men's clothes beneath her bed. She would have to send them back to the Great House, for she would not go herself. William's presence, as her Creator, was too strong, and she did not want to see Raphael again.

She substituted her nightgown and cap for the shift and crawled beneath the chill sheets.

She should have tumbled Raphael in a haystack when she had the opportunity, and to the devil with her reputation as a respectable spinster, daughter of the late Mr. Austen, rector of Steventon. Damn Raphael for his scruples. She thought of that one kiss and sighed, remembering the richness of his taste and smell.

She was damned one way or the other, at the very least to eternal spinsterhood.

She woke once to grayness and the spatter of rain on the window and turned to see Cassandra's bed was empty. So it was not early, but she fell back into sleep.

"Jane! Will you not wake?" Sometime later, Cassandra shook her awake. "We let you sleep for I thought you might be unwell. Do you not want to write? It's close to noon."

"I'm quite well, thank you." Jane sat and swung her legs over the side of the bed, wincing as she did so. She was still mortal enough to feel the effects of the previous night's energetic run through the woods and fields. "What is everyone up to? I see you've been outside; your skirts are sadly bedraggled."

"It is indeed a dirty sort of day. Martha is in the kitchen. I'm afraid our mother has taken to her bed."

"I'm most sorry to hear it." Mrs. Austen, for all her great energy and good humor, suffered from frequent bouts of melancholy where she would spend her days in bed, the curtains drawn, and refusing any efforts by others to rouse or cheer her.

"Anna is reading to her."

"Poor child. She'll probably leave with a flea in her ear." Jane looked at the rain trickling down the window and thought her mother had chosen a good day to stay abed.

When she was dressed, she retired to her usual spot in the dining room, annoyed at the extravagance of a candle, for the day was greatly overcast, and set to work. This is what she should do; she must resist the Damned and all they stood for, and she would certainly not brood over Raphael, a gentleman she barely knew. And a Catholic, she reminded herself. The house was quiet apart from the scratch of her pen and faint sounds from the kitchen.

Someone tapped at the door. "Jane?"

Jane laid down her pen. "What is it, Martha?"

A giggle and a shuffling sound. So both she and Cassandra were there. "A servant is here from the Great House with something for you."

"Very well. Leave it outside."

"But we want to see what it is! And which of the gentlemen sent it to you."

Jane stood and stretched, stiff from having sat in the same position for so long. She walked to the door and opened it. Cassandra and Martha stood there, and one of the handsome foot-men presented her with a parcel wrapped in paper. Inside was a large reticule, a beautiful silk and leather bag with tassels and embroidery.

Jane took the reticule, surely one of the finer items of fashion she had ever owned, and slipped her hand inside it. She pulled out a card. "It is from Mrs. Kettering. How very kind of her." She glared at her sister and friend. "And here is the music she promised she would lend Anna." She certainly wasn't going to tell them the reticule also contained pistols, shot, and powder.

"Oh, how very generous!" Cassandra cried. "And Anna can copy the music, since it is too wet to go outside."

Jane said to the footman, whose livery was dark with rain, "Perhaps you could wait in the kitchen and have some refreshment while I compose a note to Mrs. Kettering."

Before Cassandra or Martha could inquire too closely into the contents of the reticule, she took it upstairs and stowed the pistols and ammunition beneath her bed, wishing she had some way of returning the men's clothing to the Great House. She could return the reticule, but then how would she carry the weapons? She was determined not to succumb to the lures of the Damned, but even her pride would not allow her to turn down this opportunity to protect her family.

The letter (a polite and formal note of thanks) was written and returned to the footman, who sat with a pot of ale and a hunk of bread and cheese, his clothes steaming from the heat of the kitchen fire and not in any hurry to go back into the rain. Jane found Cassandra and Martha deep in conversation in the parlor.

" . . . but I think it is from Mr. Fitzpatrick, not Mr. Raphael—oh, Jane, there you are. Look at this music Mrs. Kettering has sent! Some of the very latest airs and compositions that are fashionable in London. How splendid!"

"Pray do not speculate on my admirers," Jane said. "At my age, it is ridiculous. I shall fetch Anna downstairs. She will enjoy this music, and I must bid our mother good day."

But when she entered her mother's bedchamber, Mrs. Austen was alone. Jane's heart sank as she approached the bed. "How do you do, ma'am? I am sorry you are unwell."

"Why did you not come before? Too busy writing, I suppose, to care for the duty you owe your parent."

"Indeed not, ma'am. I was somewhat indisposed myself this morning but have felt a great deal better since rising." She continued hastily, "I am sorry Anna is not here to keep you company."

"That wretched poetry rants on so. I sent her away." Mrs. Austen turned over.

"I hope you feel better soon," Jane said. "Is there anything I may fetch you? A glass of wine? Some tea?"

As her mother made no reply, Jane left, closing the door quietly behind her. She returned downstairs and opened the parlor door, intending only to tell Martha and Cassandra that she was returning to her writing slope.

"But where is Anna?" Jane asked. "Our mother sent her away. Surely she has not gone outside on a day like this!"

The other two women exchanged a glance. "Well," Cassandra said, "she is certainly not in the house."

"She'll get soaked," Jane said. "Foolish girl. You should have—"

But at that moment she heard the rattle of the back door. Jacques the pug, who had been asleep, snoring noisily, on a cushion, jumped up and ran into the vestibule to meet his mistress. Jane followed him and found Anna standing in a puddle and shaking out an umbrella. As she had predicted, her niece was indeed soaked to the skin, but her glowing eyes and complexion indicated that the walk in the rain had been something more.

"For heaven's sake!" Jane said, relieved that Anna was home.

"Where have you been? And not to tell anyone! This was badly done, Anna. And look at you, soaked to the skin. I am certain you will catch a cold."

"I'm very well, Aunt." Anna stood the umbrella in a corner and tugged at her bonnet strings.

Jane reached to help her. A faint scent of blood and the feral scent of the Damned hung around Anna. She untied the bonnet strings and gathered the wet folds of Anna's red cloak. "Did you meet Mr. Richards?"

"Yes, I did, Aunt."

"You do not deny it!" Jane gritted her teeth. "Do you not see, Anna, this is precisely the reason why your father is so angry with you—that you pursue the dictates of your heart with so much thoughtlessness. Have we not given you warning enough to avoid Mr. Richards? If this continues, we shall have no choice but to send you to Kent."

"Pray, how else should I pursue the dictates of my heart? With cold reason? Is that why you have never married, Aunt Jane?" Anna brushed past her into the parlor, where Jane heard Cassandra and Martha exclaim over her bedraggled appearance and urge her to sit close to the fire.

Jane dropped the sodden cloak onto the floor and followed. "Cassandra, Martha, I have reason to believe that if Anna has not yielded to Duval Richards yet, she is well on the way to becoming his mistress, and her behavior must cease immediately."

All three of them stared at her, and then Anna cried, great childish sobs that shook her slender frame, while Cassandra and Martha comforted her and shot vicious glances at Jane.

"What is the matter with you?" Cassandra whispered to Jane. "I though Martha was the one given to odd fancies and fantasies, but you have become both vulgar and fantastical in your statements. Look at the poor child! See how upset she is!"

"You condone her assignation with a known libertine?"

"We have only hearsay on the matter. For that matter, we know very little of Mr. Fitzpatrick and his friends. How are we to know who speaks the truth? Next time Mr. Richards calls—"

"We should not receive him—"

"Next time we shall receive him graciously and note his behavior. You, Jane, sent him from the house, and is it any wonder then that Anna met him secretly?"

"But—"

Cassandra turned away and, talking of hot possets and warm bricks, left for the kitchen.

"I'm going to write," Jane said to no response from either Martha or Anna and returned to the bleakness of the dining room and her writing slope.

Chapter 12

The next day dawned bright and clear, and to the relief of the household, Mrs. Austen rose from her bed.

Jane, after a most satisfying few hours at her writing desk, emerged refreshed and cheerful to find what the rest of the family were doing. Mrs. Austen, having decided that the garden would be too wet for her to do any work outside that day, sat in the parlor, busy at her needlework. Martha, it turned out, had gone to call on Mrs. Chapple.

"Who is Mrs. Chapple?" Jane asked.

"The housekeeper at the Great House. Doubtless Martha has gone to exchange recipes."

"Oh, that's right, Mrs. Kettering's housekeeper. Hmm," Jane said. Martha was a grown woman; her activities should be of no concern to Jane, to whom it was perfectly obvious that recipes were not what drew her to the Great House. "I shall go to meet her there. And what are you and Anna up to, this fine day?"

"We shall visit Miss Benn."

"You look in fine fettle today, miss," Jane said, pinching her niece's cheek. "It's early yet, so I hope you are up to no mischief."

"Hardly at all, Aunt," Anna said with a smile. "A few assignations, a handful of love letters—nothing out of the ordinary."

Jane couldn't help laughing, even though her niece's remark was a little too close to the truth for comfort. She decided to accompany them to Miss Benn's house, since it was on the way to the Great House.

Anna insisted on taking a handful of crumbs for the geese and ducks in the pond at the crossroads, a gesture Jane found endearing. She watched her niece laugh at the birds' antics and at the pug's excited barks. Anna was little more than a child, still.

"Oh, to be young again," Cassandra said. "Do you ever wish for that, Jane?"

"Sometimes. I hope I grow wise as I grow older. You do, I am sure." She linked her arm in Cassandra's. "The child will be all over mud again."

If she and Cassandra had not had a wealthy brother, this is how they would have lived: poor, dark lodgings crammed with too much furniture, the relics of happier and easier times. Miss Mary Benn rose from her chair to greet them with cries of delight, her needlework laid aside.

"Why, Miss Anna, you have grown into such a pretty young lady. And Miss Austen and Miss Jane, you must take tea. What a pleasure to see you all! And is this little dog yours, Miss Anna? What a fine fellow he is indeed."

"Our brother Edward sent us some tea and we have brought you some; it is very good. We thought we must share our bounty with our neighbors," Jane said. Tea was a luxury for Miss Benn, and the fabrication of a gift a way the Austens might help her without hurting her pride.

"Most generous indeed!" Miss Benn reached for the kettle that simmered at the hearth, and Anna hastened to help her.

Miss Benn's hands, clad in mittens that were for warmth as well as an attempt at fashion (for her lodgings were cold and damp), were swollen and twisted. A tray containing a teapot and cups of fine china, carefully preserved from Miss Benn's more prosperous days, stood nearby.

"So you have heard the news?" Miss Benn asked. "My maid Fanny has told me highwaymen attacked a carriage on the London Road the night before last. A most important gentleman, an intimate of the Prince of Wales, so they say, and a lady . . ." She colored slightly, which Jane took to mean that the gentleman's companion was probably not a lady and certainly not a wife or relative. "Is that not shocking? All dead, even the horses, they say. What sort of times are these? Although if he was a friend of the Prince I regret to say he could not be a very good sort of man."

"Highwaymen!" Cassandra echoed. "I thought the profession had almost died out. Well, that part of the road was always thought to be notoriously unsafe."

"Indeed, yes. I remember my father used to speak of it. But now the whole village is abuzz with the news, and you know how superstitious the common people are hereabouts."

Miss Benn broke off her reminiscences to instruct Anna to offer the pug a saucer of milk, at which he lapped noisily.

"Why, what do the common people say?" Jane asked.

"My dear, they believe that fiends are among us, or ghosts, or some such nonsense. Is not that true, Fanny?"

Miss Benn's maid, who had just come in with more coals for the fire, nodded. "Oh, 'tis true, ma'am. They say they'll suck your blood and drag you down to hell, so no one must go out at night. Why, even the menfolk going for ale and shove ha'penny at the inn won't walk alone after dark. It's not safe, ma'am. And they say"—she looked around as though a supernatural creature were ready to burst out of the cupboard—"they say them up at the Great House are to blame."

"Oh, nonsense," Miss Benn said. "These ladies have paid calls at the Great House, so Mr. Knight's tenants must be respectable. Miss Jane, you tell her she is foolish to say such things."

"Indeed, Fanny, you are mistaken," Jane said. "But . . ." Her voice trailed away.

Fanny looked at her, one hand on her hip, eyebrows raised.

"But you should not be out after dark," Jane said firmly. "You must stay here and make sure your mistress is comfortable and not encourage wild stories."

"Miss Jane is quite right," Miss Benn said. "Back to the kitchen with you, Fanny. But Miss Jane, what a very handsome reticule that is! Is that also a gift from Mr. Edward Knight?"

"No. Mrs. Kettering gave it to me," Jane said. "She is sister-in-law to Mr. Fitzpatrick, our brother's tenant at the Great House."

To her annoyance, Cassandra and Miss Benn exchanged an arch glance and Anna giggled. Jane was tempted to produce the pistol and show her skill, but not wishing to destroy any of Miss Benn's beloved possessions (the milk jug, though; that had a crack and Jane was sure they could replace it with one of their own), she merely smiled and, making the excuse that she had another call to make, left the cottage.

When she arrived at the Great House, she went to the servants' entrance at the side of the house. Almost certainly William knew she was there, but meeting her Creator after threatening to kill him would be exceedingly awkward. She was still too angry to apologize, yet as she neared the house anger was replaced by a familiar yearning and the stirrings of hunger. It was as Raphael had said: the very presence of the Damned heightened and intensified her body's urge to return to being one of them.

The door stood open, and she stepped inside a dim hall lined with flagstones. The murmur of voices and clink of utensils and the scent of cooking food indicated that she was near the kitchen. The housekeeper in a house of this size would almost certainly remain aloof, keeping to her own room or suite of rooms that included living and working quarters.

Jane passed the kitchen, catching a glimpse of people hard at work—unless the Damned entertained that night, very little of the food would be eaten. A woman pushed stuffing inside a large fish, and at the table another rolled out a creamy sheet of pastry.

"May I help you, miss?" One of the handsome footmen, carrying a basket of greens, stepped from a doorway a little ways ahead.

"If you please, I'm looking for Mrs. Chapple and Miss Lloyd who pays a call on her."

"Mrs. Chapple's here, miss. I'll show you. I don't know if any other ladies came to call, though."

He turned on his heel and led her farther down the passage. He was not in livery, for he was at work downstairs, but he wore a leather apron over breeches and shirt. Jane found herself admiring his broad shoulders and strong thighs and chided herself for her indecent thoughts. Yes, she could blame it on Damnation, but more and more, particularly in this house, Jane of the Damned and Miss Jane Austen blurred and blended.

"In here, miss," the footman said, pointing to a doorway. His smile indicated that he had guessed her thoughts. "Half a crown, miss," he said to her softly, "for anything you fancy. I'll be in the kitchen if you need me."

Jane's face burned. "Thank you," she said with as much dignity as she could manage. Here, in this house, she was most definitely one of the Damned.

She tapped at the door. In the room, Mrs. Chapple—Jane recognized her now—stood at a scrubbed table, tipping the contents of a jar onto the pan of a set of scales. Whole cloves, sharp and fragrant, rattled as they fell.

"Good afternoon, ma'am." The housekeeper picked a few cloves out and returned them to the jar and pushed home a cork. She tipped the spices into a small crock the size of her fist. "It's Miss Austen, is it not?"

"Good afternoon, ma'am. I came to find my friend Martha Lloyd."

"Miss Lloyd? Why, she left some time ago."

"Oh. I'm sorry to have missed her. She must have gone home."

The woman nodded. "If you'll excuse me, ma'am, I have business in the kitchen." She picked up the crock that held the cloves, considering. "I believe she went upstairs."

"Upstairs!" Jane echoed. So her suspicions were correct.

Mrs. Chapple gestured to her right. "Continue this way, ma'am, and you'll reach the staircase." She ushered Jane out of the room and lifted the chatelaine at her waist, which held a variety of keys, and locked the door. "Good day to you."

Jane murmured a farewell and continued along the passage and then up the stairs. At the first landing she paused. She could hear no one in the house. When she turned to her right, she found herself at the end of the long Gallery and took the doorway that led to the parlor. The door stood ajar. Jane could hear the sound of sobbing.

She rushed inside to find Martha huddled in an armchair in the small extension at the end of the room, where only a few nights earlier she had come across William and Luke together.

"Martha, my dear!" Jane ran to her. "Oh, what has happened to you?"

But she knew; Martha's clothing was in disarray, her bosom half exposed, and, to Jane's annoyance, one of her—Jane's—silk stockings collapsing around her ankle.

"You borrowed my stockings again!" Jane said, fury replacing fear.

"You don't have anyone to wear them for," Martha said. "Why are you here?"

"After what happened last time, I was afraid for you. But why are you crying?"

Martha wiped her face. "I—I want to go home." She stood, and then collapsed back into the chair, giggling. "Heavens, I must have drunk too much."

"Or he did." So she needed to be revived, and to Jane's annoyance Tom was nowhere in sight. "Why has he left you here alone?"

"Well." Martha's face took on a slight tinge of pink. "He and I—well, we sat and conversed here for a little, and then we went to another room—"

To his bedchamber, Jane supposed. "What did he do?"

"What do you think?"

"I am quite sure I know what you mean, but why do you cry?"

"Another lady came to call. She—she was rude to me. And Tom laughed. And then Tom undid her gown and she asked if I wished to join them. And I said no. So I came back here to sit down and I do feel so very weak and foolish. I thought he liked me, Jane."

"My dear." Jane patted her hand. "He does like you, I am sure, or as much as one of the Damned is able to feel for one of us. I fear he may like your blood better than any other of your charms."

"That is unkind!" Martha pushed herself up a little straighter in the chair and attempted to straighten her gown.

Jane knelt to help her, and the scent of blood and spent pleasure made her dizzy. "I believe you need to be revived. You will feel better then."

She found a bellpull by the fireplace and tugged on it, angered by Tom's behavior. After some time, a footman entered and Jane ordered him to bring some wine.

She paced the room, knowing that what she must do would be disturbing. She did not dare try to use her own blood, even though her canines had once again assumed that disconcerting sharpness and rubbed painfully against her lip. When the footman returned, she took a sip of the wine herself for courage and, telling Martha that she would return soon, left the room.

She stood outside, concentrating, listening, half annoyed and half grateful that her condition was not yet so advanced that she could scent one of the Damned in the act of dining. And then she heard a sound, a muffled laugh, an intimate whisper from one of the rooms, the same room where Duval had assaulted Anna.

She knocked and threw the door open at the same time, to find Tom and a young woman together, sprawled sated on the bed.

"Oh, for heaven's sake, put some clothes on!" Jane said, trying to look away. It had been some years since she had last encountered a gentleman in a state of undress.

"Who's this?" The girl's voice was slurred, and she ran a proprietary hand down Tom's chest. "How many old women pursue you, my dear?"

"Be quiet, miss!" Jane held out the glass to Tom. "If you please. Not only have you hurt Martha's feelings, but you have left her alone and in need of revival. It was most unmannerly, sir."

He frowned. "I offered her further hospitality, my dear Jane. Jane, may I introduce you to Miss . . . so sorry, my sweet, I have quite forgotten your name."

"I am Arabella!" the young woman snapped.

"Dear, dear, Tom, have you dined so zealously your memory is affected?" Jane waved the glass in his face. "A drop of blood, sir, and I shall bother you no more, and you may exercise your charms upon Miss Arabella's person again."

"You are an infernal nuisance, Jane." Sighing heavily, Tom sat up and raised his wrist to his mouth. Arabella stared at his canines digging into the pale skin and released a faint moan when his blood welled. She leaned forward, lips parted, but Tom pushed her away. "Later, my love."

A delicious scent rose from the one drop of blood that fell into the wineglass. Jane hoped she did not look as avid and helpless as Arabella, but the sight of Tom's blood made her almost groan with hunger.

"You refused my blood the last time," Tom said. "I am not offended. Come, Jane. Join us. Your friend can wait. Arabella will not mind, will you, my dear? You'll like her taste, Jane."

She took a step toward the bed, her canines sharp against her lip before she came to her senses and stopped. Arabella leaned to lick Tom's arm and sagged against him, her eyes rolling back in her head.

"Oh, pray stop behaving like a male slut!" Jane said. "And is she well? I think she has swooned."

"So they do if they try to take our blood unmixed," Tom said. He shoved Arabella away. "She bores me, Jane. Your friend, Martha, for all she talks of silliness and of what she has cooked for dinner the night before—lord, how she talks—Martha entertains me more."

He stretched luxuriously on the sheets, smiling.

"Indeed. Entertainment. You do not care for her."

"Of course not. Just as you do not care to see me in my unclothed glory."

Jane snorted with laughter. "Your modesty does you credit, sir."

"So will you see William?"

"Possibly." Of course she would. They both knew it. William's presence called to her, tantalized her. "I do thank you, sir, for your generosity in allowing my friend one drop of your blood at such grave inconvenience to yourself. No, no, I assure you I am capable of opening the door myself. You must rest, Tom, to reserve your strength for the next bout with the lovely Miss Arabella."

He grinned. "You know, Jane, I almost forgive you for threatening to blow my head to pieces and my soul to hell."

"It is no laughing matter, sir." She raised the glass of wine. "I thank you for your assistance."

It was but a few steps to the next room, and as she walked she argued with herself. Perhaps Martha would be recovered; perhaps Tom would grant her another drop; Jane longed to drink the wine herself, and more, to drink from Tom or Arabella or . . .

"Martha, my dear!" Her voice sounded hoarse. She handed the glass to Martha.

Martha's hand shook, spilling a drop onto Jane's wrist. "Drink!" Jane said.

She held Martha's hand to assist her in drinking, and the single drop rolled into her cuff, absorbed by the fabric.

"So sweet," Martha said, smiling. "Oh, so sweet."

"You may sleep now, Miss Lloyd."

Jane turned at the sound of William's voice, impressed despite herself. How useful to be able to bid people to sleep and have them actually do it. Her thoughts flew to certain garrulous members of her family.

Martha yawned. "You know, Jane, there's something different about you . . ." She fell asleep as easily as a child.

"Now you have no choice but to talk with me," William said with a faint smile.

Chapter 13

"I cannot be all things," Jane said. She, who had started the day off cheerful and content, now found emotions spilling over and her fists clenched in agitation. She could not sit still; she paced like a wild creature, like one of the Damned, her limbs restless. "*Les Sales* have been seen in the village, and people are in fear of them. I cannot protect my family—I cannot even persuade Martha or Anna not to play with fire in consorting with the Damned—and I must write, and—oh, this is hopeless, William. Last night I nearly destroyed Tom, and I wished to destroy you also—"

"Oh, I would not have let you do it," William said. He smiled faintly. "You forget I have more speed and strength, however passionate you become."

She swallowed. "Pray forgive me for my intemperance. But I cannot forgive you for using Raphael as your bait. Two birds with one stone, I presume? Two fledglings returned to your nest?"

"Jane, my dear." He stepped into her path and took her hands. His power burned into her, and as much as she could she closed her mind to him. "Let the metamorphosis take its course. Do not fight it. Last night you were so close, almost *en sanglant,* and I hoped you would cross the divide to us. And Raphael burns for you; has he not persuaded you of his desire? Of course you should take a lover; a woman such as yourself, denied of all passion and sensuality—it is absurd!"

"I am Miss Jane Austen, spinster, sir, a respectable resident of this village where my brother is the main landowner. I have certain standards to maintain, the good name of my family to protect. I am not what you think I am."

"You are. Come back to us, Jane." Had he been a lover, the ardor in his voice would have thrilled her, moved her.

"I will not. But there is one thing I shall do, sir, and that is something I can accomplish as a mortal, not as one of the Damned. I shall put an end to your hostilities with Duval and his house."

"Indeed? Why do you think you can do so?" He released her hands and gestured to a chair. From the sofa, Martha gave a faint snore.

"You sent Luke as ambassador. He has failed. He is too involved with your cause, whereas I am not yet one of the Damned and I am determined not to become one again. I think and feel like a human woman; I am impartial, yet I know a little of the ways of the Damned. So I can represent both my family and the village, as the sister of the owner of the Great House; and I can also, in a lesser extent, represent the Damned. You, my Creator, are here; and my former Consort is with them."

She had said it as easily as she had hoped.

"Interesting." William sat opposite her, elbows on knees, absorbed in what she had to say. "What will you ask for?"

"That attacks on any of us, particularly the innocent people in the village, should cease. That *les Sales* be treated with pity and decency and taken into households—yes, even without letters of introductions, as shocking as that may seem. You cannot take revenge against the Prince of Wales without hurting the innocent. Did that gentleman's coachman and postilion deserve to die?"

"And the weapons?" William asked.

"Those graystone knives?" She shivered, the mark on her breast burning anew. "Abandon them. Bury them, destroy them however you may. If there is a way to take power from them, let it be done."

William shook his head. "They must remain. They are part of who we are. We may use them but once in a hundred years, but the gray knives are ours. But more to the point, Jane, what do you offer the Damned in return?"

"Acceptance. There is no need to masquerade as what you are not. I can use my brother Edward's connections to introduce you to country society here in Hampshire. A little while ago you would have thought company such as this beneath you, but consider the country squires and merchants and shopkeepers your allies. You may have lost the support of dukes and princes, but I can assure you the Prince of Wales is not much liked or respected here. And these middling people are not so likely to forget the debt they owe the Damned when our—your kind—saved them from the French. And you will also win the trust of the village, and that is important if you are to live here. Did you know the common people hereabouts consider the tenants of the Great House responsible for *les Sales*? They will not hesitate to rise up against you if they are roused enough."

"Very well. And what does Miss Jane Austen receive as reward?"

"My freedom."

"Your freedom?" he echoed. "I assure you, you are in no way in bondage, unless it is to your respectability."

"Let me go, William. Let your fledgling go in the way she chooses, even if it is not the way of the Damned."

He sat, elbows on his knees, hands clasped, silent for a moment.

"You don't understand, Jane. It is as much you as me. Once you were one of us. In the most secret and essential elements of flesh and bone and blood, you are one of the Damned still. You will always yearn for us; you will always have those powers of perception if not the physical strength, the ability to understand and observe—"

"I believe, sir, that my excellent powers of perception and understanding have always been a part of me." Her voice rose. On the sofa, Martha stirred and subsided into sleep. "William, promise me you will not try to trick me or bribe me. Do not, I pray, throw handsome footmen in my path or ask Tom to undress in front of me. He is quite shameless, and he does it so often I fear it will become as commonplace that he removes his breeches as others remove a hat. And above all, do not use Raphael as your pawn. I ask only that if I bring about peace, you leave me alone."

"What you suggest goes against our natures," William said. "You will yearn for the rest of your mortal life for what you cannot have, and I . . . I must spend eternity knowing I have failed you again."

"I'm sure you will find comfort one way or the other." She leaned forward and removed a long fair hair that clung to his coat. "You dine early today, I see."

He smiled. "I had to invite Mr. Papillon and his sister to dinner, and lest I be tempted by the lady . . ."

"Oh, surely you jest. I doubt even you dining upon her would stop her tongue. But let us talk of tactics if I am to be your herald."

"Indeed, yes. Will you come later tonight so I may instruct you? I must write a letter of introduction."

"Why? I have met Duval."

"It is good manners."

Jane shrugged. She had never grasped the intricacies of etiquette among the Damned, but she should let William guide her in this matter at least.

"I am sorry I have saddened you," she said.

"It has saddened you, too. I hope you are successful, Jane, for despite our natural longing for sensation and the thrill of the new, I and many of our kind abhor this state of war. We shall be an example to other counties."

She stood. "I cannot hide the secrets of my heart from you."

He held her hand briefly, then raised it to his lips. It was not the kiss of a lover—that could never be—but the acknowledgment of an ally, an equal.

Behind them on the couch Martha stirred and sighed.

"I hope you are feeling better, Miss Lloyd," William said.

"Oh, indeed. Much better." Martha blinked. "I thank you for your hospitality, but now it is time Jane and I returned home."

Jane detached her hand from William's, aware of Martha's keen glance. But Martha looked away, her lips tightening.

Several times that evening Jane caught Martha's curious gaze and wondered if Martha had overheard any of her conversation with William. Jane might well seem different in that house to one who possessed the gift of recognizing the Damned, but was that really what Martha's sleepy comment meant? Or was Martha embarrassed by her experience with Tom and fearful Jane might say something about it to the family?

After dinner, Anna played the piano and the ladies sewed, Jane glad that the music inhibited conversation. When the ladies rose to take their candlesticks upstairs, Jane announced that she would retire downstairs to write. It was easy enough by the light of two candles, and while Cassandra said her prayers, for Jane to tuck the bundle of men's clothing beneath her arm and quietly leave the bedchamber.

She waited in the darkened dining room for the maids, Eliza and Jenny, to finish the household chores and go upstairs to their beds. When all was quiet, she slung the reticule and its weapons over one shoulder and left for the Great House. The streets were almost deserted, apart from a few latecomers returning home from the alehouse, and only a handful of cottages showed the fitful dim light of candles or rushlights. She almost hoped that one of *les Sales* might burst from the darkness into her path, but by the time the lights of the Great House came into view the only attacker had been a stray cow that lumbered away, crashing through the furze bushes at the side of the road.

The door opened as she approached, and Dorcas ran out to meet her. "Is that your best gown, Jane?"

"Well, it is the one I generally wear in the evenings; the long sleeves can be removed, and I—"

"But this will not do. No indeed."

"Why not?" Jane asked.

"You must be very well dressed. When did you last take a bath?"

Jane tried to remember. "A week or so ago, I believe. I wash my hair frequently, but we have to bathe in the washhouse, for we have no menservants to bring water upstairs, and it is a great nuisance."

"I thought so," Dorcas said, to Jane's embarrassment.

She resisted the temptation to snuff at her own armpits. "I am perfectly clean!"

"But you'd like a bath, wouldn't you? And you must borrow one of my gowns."

"Oh, very well," Jane said, somewhat interested in seeing more of Dorcas's gowns and immediately regretting that she would not be able to tell Cassandra about them. "But how am I to get there?"

"You'll take the carriage," Dorcas replied. "We can't have you arriving with a foot of mud on your skirts. Come with me, my dear."

She led Jane upstairs and into a bedchamber where several footmen stood around chatting, having emptied buckets of hot water into a large tub.

"How did you know I was to arrive?" Jane asked.

"Of course we knew," Dorcas said. "Or rather, William did. Turn, my dear, so I may unfasten your gown."

"Pray send the footmen out!" Jane said in horror.

"Are you quite sure?"

"I am quite sure," Jane replied. The scent of healthy young men and the slow thud of their heartbeats made it hard to keep her resolve. "You must understand, I go to Prowtings as a representative of the village. They will know if I have dined recently."

"They will know you hunger, also, but if it is your wish . . ." Dorcas shrugged and nodded to the footmen, who gathered up the buckets and left.

A maid at the far end of the room took gowns from a linen press and laid them on the bed, and while Jane enjoyed the steaming water, Dorcas and the servant discussed which gown she should wear.

"No, I do not think she has the complexion for that . . . oh, you dirty girl, why did you not clean the blood from this one? He was a very enthusiastic gentleman. I think with the right jewels this might do. Jane?"

Jane, who was scrubbing the back of her neck, alarmed that she had patches of grime detectable only by the Damned, looked up. "Yes?"

"What do you think of this one?" Dorcas held up a gown of shot silk, gold that turned to crimson as she turned it.

"Too ostentatious."

"This one, then?" A striped green satin.

"Better," Jane said. "But is not the neck cut a little low?"

"Not at all," Dorcas said.

"I should wear a lace scarf if you have one."

"Nonsense. You have a fine bosom. Don't you think so, Maria?"

"Indeed, yes, ma'am," the girl said. "We'll lace you as much as we need to."

"Very well," Jane said, resigned to having her bosom presented to the world, or at least to the Damned at Prowtings. She knew they would be more interested in looking at her neck, that portion of the anatomy having more appeal for the Damned than any other female attributes.

Her bath over—she was grateful that Dorcas did not make any comments on the cloudy quality of the water—she dressed with the help of the maid.

"I'm too old for this," Jane said, regarding her expanse of revealed bosom.

"You know what the cure for that is," Dorcas said. "I'll invite a footman back in, if you like."

"No!"

Dorcas shrugged, amused by Jane's vehemence. "You'll do well enough by candlelight. By town standards you're quite decent, and I've seen women twice your age display more bosom."

"Very true, miss," the maid said with bored insolence. "Sit down, if you please, and I'll dress your hair."

She had the attitude Jane had noticed in London servants of performing their work as an extraordinary favor to those they served.

When Jane sat in front of the mirror, her reflection was still there, to her relief; and despite the immodesty of the gown, she thought she looked well. Not only did the maid dress her hair, but she added a headdress of tall ostrich feathers.

"I feel like a fool," Jane grumbled. "I'll have to bend my knees every time I pass through a doorway, and if I can step into the carriage managing the train and the feathers both, it will be a miracle."

"You'll do well enough, miss, I daresay," the maid said with a distinct lack of interest and a toss of her head.

Jane stood and walked across the room, accustoming herself to the drape of the train (she had not worn a gown with a train in some years) and the constriction of her stays, laced far tighter than normal. She glanced in the tall mirror that stood in a corner of the room—Dorcas and the other occupants of the house would have little need for it—and was surprised at her own elegance.

"You need a fan." Dorcas pressed one into her gloved hand. "There. Now you must speak with William."

Jane followed Dorcas out of the room and into the parlor, where William and Tom, both in breeches and silk stockings, bowed to her. She saw the admiration in Tom's gaze and fluttered her fan at him.

"Yes, indeed, you look very fine," William said. "Pray take this seriously, Jane."

"I assure you I do. I have as much, or possibly even more at stake in this venture than you."

He bowed his head. "Indeed. I have always admired you for your courage, Jane, although so often it takes the form of impropriety toward your Creator. Yet I do not think you anticipate the danger to which you subject yourself tonight."

"Sir, I cannot dwell on possible horrors or misery. It is not in my nature."

"I have sent a formal letter of introduction this afternoon, announcing your arrival."

"Why?" She had thought that she would take the letter with her, thus affording her arrival an element of surprise.

"It is the way things are done."

"Very well."

"But I have decided to break protocol by arming you."

"Arming me?" She glanced down at her bosom. "There is scarcely enough fabric to contain my person, let alone a pistol."

"Not that sort of a weapon." He reached into his pocket for a small key, with which he unlocked an ivory-inlaid mahogany box on the mantelpiece.

Jane shook her head and took a step away, raising one hand to her breast where her injury burned cold again even though the mark had faded. "I think not, sir."

He opened the box. "Keep your gloves on; the blade will not harm you. It will be in a leather sheath, and you may slip it into your stays."

The stone knife glowed gray on its bed of dark velvet. Tom and Dorcas gazed at in silence and then at her.

"I cannot do it, sir," she said. "It is not the action of a person in good faith."

"And if they do not act with good faith?"

"It is a risk I must take."

He closed the box, placed it back on the mantelpiece, and locked it. The sense of unease that Jane shared with Tom and Dorcas ebbed. William said, "I may not be able to help if things go wrong."

"I know. I shall make sure they do not."

"I shall follow you—in your mind, that is—for you must go alone. I have asked Raphael, since he is of like condition, to accompany you in the carriage. I hope that is acceptable? He will carry pistols."

"Thank you." What William said made sense, in case any of *les Sales* roamed the countryside, but she had not wished to see Raphael again, or at least be alone with him.

But she draped her train over her arm and took William's arm and descended the staircase. Footmen sprang forward to open the front door of the house, and armed with only her own wit and nerves, she stepped forward to do battle.

Chapter 14

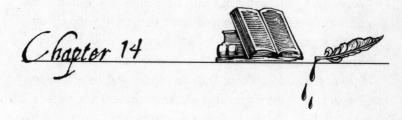

Raphael held open the carriage door, bowing, and Jane stepped inside, remembering only just in time to bend her head and save her ostrich feathers.

He stepped inside after her, closing the door, the carriage creaking and tilting with his weight.

"Pray say nothing of fine feathers," Jane said. "I assure you they are a nuisance."

He sat opposite her and laid a pistol on his knees. "If this were a normal evening, I should compliment you on your looks."

"You may do so if you wish. I cannot stop you." *Oh, for goodness' sake, Jane, stop flirting.* "But this is hardly a normal evening. Generally a gentleman does not accompany a lady in a carriage with his weapon exposed so." Worse and worse. "I beg your pardon, I am nervous and given to bawdy talk at such times. It has got me into trouble upon numerous occasions and earned me many a severe scolding from my sister. She says gentlemen do not marry a woman who talks so, yet she, who would not recognize a double entendre if it hit her on the head, remains unmarried still, so . . ." She came to a halt.

He leaned forward and laid his gloved hand upon hers. "Come, we shall be friends."

"Very well," she said. "But tell me, Raphael, I wonder that you have traveled all this way, at some danger to yourself on a continent at war, and after taking the Cure, to be with William, knowing what his presence and his influence could do."

"I do not wish to become Damned again, as I have told you, but I wish to be with my brother. After all these years, he is all I have left. But why did he abandon you after creating you?—that is, if you do not mind telling me. It seems unlike him. But I find I must learn my brother's ways all over again."

"He had good reasons to do so, for he was charged with the protection of the Prince of Wales."

"And little good that did him." His gaze, which had darted from her face to the darkness outside the carriage, returned to hers. "I am astonished."

"He wishes to make amends now." She shrugged. "I know I injure him by my refusal, but I feel I have no choice."

He looked outside again. "Every day I pray it will not happen, yet I fear my metamorphosis is inevitable."

"I, too, and this is why I have made a bargain with William."

"And yet he has arranged for us to be alone in a dark carriage."

"I know. And we are both in a celibate state, but I am sure we can resist temptation for this very short ride."

He held up a hand and shifted to the other side of the carriage, snuffing the air, then shook his head and returned to his former position. "I thought . . . it is a good thing I am charged with your protection, for it keeps me occupied."

"I shall ask you something, and you need not reply unless you wish to. You and I have both been celibate for some years—at least I presume you have been so, although I have been led to believe that life in a closed order is extraordinarily depraved—but if we met under different circumstances, without the curse of Damnation hanging over our heads, what then?"

He was silent for a while. "I would say you are one of the most witty and handsome women of my acquaintance, ma'am. I should be a fool not to pursue you."

"We are almost here, I believe. I can see the lights of the house. I barely have time to smack you with my fan and cry 'Fie upon you, sir,' or some such." She hesitated. "In truth, I believe I would put up little resistance. It is a great pity."

"It is, but I believe your affections are bound elsewhere."

Before she could respond, the carriage came to a halt. A footman emerged from the house to open the door of the carriage and lower the steps.

Jane ducked her head in time to preserve her headdress, gathered her train, and stepped down. She raised her head and walked toward the front door, held open by another footman, and into the house. It was an old-fashioned sort of place, ancient, expanded and improved by many generations, and she stepped into a flagstone hall that was similar to that at the Great House, but here dark oak panels reflected the light from a candelabra. The door shut quietly behind her as she heard the coachman click his tongue and the crunch of hooves and wheels on gravel from outside.

She was alone in the stillness of the house, a place she had previously considered friendly and welcoming, and that she had visited many times before. But now, standing in near darkness with the candles casting flickering light, the house breathed danger and hidden threats. The footman who admitted her to the house had disappeared, melted away into the shadows as easily as his masters.

It was a deliberate ploy to intimidate her, to keep her waiting in the dark, and almost certainly she was observed. She feigned a yawn and unfurled her fan. She admired as best she could in the dim light an elaborate painted mythical scene, the sticks and handle of gilded ivory, and wondered if it was of French origin, while willing herself to be calm and untroubled. What was worse even than being observed was the possibility that her thoughts and emotions were similarly open to view, and she was certainly going to give away as little as she could.

At last, footsteps, and she quenched as best she could the joy and desire that washed over her. He was close to her in the darkness, as he had been so many times before, and she reached out her hands before she could stop herself. A slight movement of cool air indicated his hesitation, and then her gloved hands were in his— no vivid thrill at the slide of bare skin, but eloquent and strong enough to intensify all she could hear and feel. The fan, hanging by its silk thread from her wrist, swung back against her skirts, and the feathers atop her head bobbed with her movements. Now she was aware of his form in the darkness and his beloved scent, but a jolt of pain in her canines and the sharpness against her lip reminded her once more of the danger of being with the Damned.

She loosened her hands from his and stepped back to make a curtsy. "I trust I find you well, Mr. Venning."

"Tolerably, ma'am. Come. The others are waiting for you."

"They send you to do their bidding?" she said as she walked beside him in the darkness, her hand laid on his arm.

"I am new to the household."

"Or they think you will dazzle me with your presence and charm me to a state where I will agree to anything."

"Oh, of course. That also." His answer matched hers in irony.

Once they had been well matched indeed, and her whole being, the mortal Jane and the vestiges of her existence as one of the Damned, yearned for him. Would it be the same if she had yielded to Raphael?

Beside her, Luke drew in a sharp breath.

He had been eavesdropping on her mind. "Jealous, sir?"

"I did not realize you contemplated taking him as a lover."

"I did not realize it was any of your business, sir." A door opened into a room crowded with wax candles (the thrifty spinster in her was appalled at the expense) where the other inhabitants of the house, Duval, Margaret, Clarissa, and a handful of others she remembered from the evening at the Great House, stood in a semicircle.

Duval walked forward and bowed.

She dropped into the deep curtsy she had practiced, holding the pose at some discomfort to her thigh muscles, and wondered, for an idiotic moment, if she and Duval were to remain frozen in a competition of manners, waiting to see who would yield first. But he straightened, and so did she.

"We are most honored by your attendance, Miss Austen."

She bowed her head.

"Let us be seated," Duval said and gestured to the large oval mahogany table that stood in the center of the room. A footman stepped forward to draw a chair out for Jane.

The table held three sets of candelabra and a footed china stand on which was heaped a pile of hothouse fruits—grapes, figs, nectarines, peaches, and pineapples—more for decoration than anything else, for if anyone were to pick a fruit, doubtless the whole edifice would collapse. The highly polished surface of the table held a reflection of the fruit arrangement and candles as though they stood on water.

Duval took a seat on the opposite side of the table, flanked by Margaret on one side and Clarissa and Luke on the other. Another footman approached with a tray holding a decanter and glasses, which he placed on the table at Duval's hand.

"Some wine, Miss Austen?"

"Thank you, sir." She was surprised that the wine was white, knowing the preference of the Damned was for red, and grateful that this way she would not become intoxicated if blood had been added.

Duval gave a small smile. Jane attempted to overhear his thoughts—for almost certainly he had intruded upon hers—but caught nothing. This would not do. "Before we begin, sir, may I request that none of you attempt to listen to my thoughts?"

"Of course. Is there anything else, Miss Austen?"

"Yes, sir. That we put aside all hurts and injuries between us and discuss this matter like rational beings. Doubtless you know, sir, that I was once the Consort of Luke and a friend to Clarissa; furthermore, that it was my decision to banish Margaret after she betrayed me to the French."

"That is all past," Duval said. "As for Margaret's banishment, I can only be grateful, for that is what brought her to my household." He took Margaret's hand as he spoke and raised it to his lips.

"May I suggest also, Miss Austen," Duval said, "that you do not let my association with Miss Anna influence you."

Jane took a sip of wine to cover her anger at Duval's arrogance. Anna's association with Duval could lead only to ruin or Damnation; there was no happier outcome, at least not for Anna.

My dear Jane, do not give him the upper hand so soon. He diverts you from the real reason for this meeting; he wishes emotions to sway your reason.

Luke! Well, she had asked Duval not to stray into her thoughts, and apparently he kept his word, for she did not think Luke would express himself so openly otherwise, but what of Margaret and Clarissa?

Do not concern yourself. Clarissa is your friend, still, but neither she nor Margaret hears us.

Jane smiled. "I assure you, Duval, Anna is a silly flirt who figures very little in the larger scheme of things, and I am sure you will tire of her before long. I have quite washed my hands of the girl. She is disobedient, and I long to return her to her father."

Duval poured a little more wine into Jane's glass. "So, Miss Austen, what is it that you wish of me?"

Slowly, Jane. Don't stab him right away. Feint a little. Flirt if you wish.

It was Luke who had taught her to fight. "Pray, address me as Jane. Once, I was one of you. I fought side by side with your present companions."

"You did, ma'am, and I honor you for it." Duval raised his glass.

"We few, we happy few, we band of brothers; / For he to-day that sheds his blood with me / Shall be my brother; be he ne'er so vile, / This day shall gentle his condition." Jane saw the look of recognition on their faces as she quoted the words. Had they attended a performance at Shakespeare's own theater?

"Ah, yes. We fought against the French at Agincourt, too," Luke said. "You were there, Duval, I believe."

"You enjoy the theater, Miss Austen?"

He's trying to divert you. Don't let him. He can see where this is going.

"Very much, sir. It is my great regret, however, that one of our band of brothers has behaved in a way unbefitting his rank."

Duval laughed. "We were princes when the Hapsburgs were grubbing in the dirt with their swine."

"I daresay, sir, but he is the one with the gilded palace now. And the debts to prove it. He wishes to forget those who saved his head and his throne, but others, like the people in this village, do not. They know what the Damned did. They remember and tell the tales around the hearth, father to son, mother to daughter. They shall not forget."

"He that shall live this day, and see old age, / Will yearly on the

*vigil feast his neighbors, / And say 'To-morrow is Saint Crispian.'
/ Then will he strip his sleeve and show his scars, / And say 'These
wounds I had on Crispian's day.'*" This time it was Luke who
quoted Shakespeare with such quiet intensity that Jane decided
he most likely had acted in Shakespeare's Wooden O.

"We talk then of loyalties," Clarissa said.

"Indeed. Yet you harbor a traitor here. There is reason to believe that William's ambassador has suffered a change of allegiance." She looked hard at Luke as she spoke.

Well said, Jane. Now watch him squirm on your hook.

"Do not you, too, represent the Great House?" Duval said.

"So I do, sir. My brother owns that house. My family—myself,
my sister, and my mother—are his representatives in the village
and on the estate. What the Damned do among themselves is
of little concern to me, but when my family and my home are
threatened, then it is indeed of grave consequence. So I ask you,
sir, because of the bonds between the Damned, that you cease
hostilities among yourselves. Princes come and go; they are of no
consequence."

"*Put not your trust in princes,*" Duval said.

"*Nor in the son of man, in whom there is no help.*" Luke finished the quotation.

"The Damned quoting the Old Testament—I am all astonishment," Jane said. "Yet I suppose you must while away the long
hours of eternity the best you can. As to you, sir"—she cast a look
of contempt at Luke, hoping she acted well enough to deceive
Duval (had she not excelled in Austen family theatricals?)—
"neither the Austen family nor the village expects your faith; we
expect civility and that the only bloodshed should be voluntary,
whether for pleasure or monetary gain."

The three of them were silent, and Jane knew they spoke
among themselves.

"We are somewhat in agreement," Duval said. "Yet what does this poor place have to offer such as us?"

Jane shrugged. "Our civility; acceptance among the gentry of the county—I should be most happy for my brother Mr. Edward Knight to supply letters of introduction to widen your circle of acquaintances. I must agree this is a poor place; we are very quiet people here. Yet good society lies within half a day's drive."

Another pause for silent discussion on the other side of the table.

Jane continued, as if unaware of their conversation, "I fear the worst may happen if the common people in this village live in fear. We may expect riots and worse."

"That would be unfortunate indeed," Duval said.

"Oh, I do not think you are in danger of losing your heads," Jane said. "Not yet."

Small signs—the clench of Duval's fist next to his wineglass, an exchange of glances between Luke and Cassandra, and Margaret's sharp intake of breath—showed that her comment had hit its mark. The Damned had good reason to fear the guillotine, after so many of their number had been destroyed in France, and it had seemed during the 1797 invasion that the same could happen here.

Dear, dear. That is a remark in extremely poor taste, even from one who rode the tumbril herself. Nicely done, ma'am.

Jane waited, enjoying Luke's scowl. She had no doubt he played devil's advocate among the four. How soon would it be before he declared his true allegiance? She had no doubt the bond between William and him would prevail, despite his flirtation with Duval and the rest. As for a bond between the two of them . . . but he was silent.

"I suppose you wish to speak of the disposition of *les Sales,*" Duval said. "We are ladies and gentlemen; we pose no threat."

"Of course not, sir! But they are your things." She wrinkled her nose in ladylike disgust.

"I have not turned them away as others have done. I have offered them hospitality."

"Indeed, sir. Yet I see none of them here."

"They're in the barn," Luke said. "Beg your pardon, Duval. Did I speak out of turn?"

"In the barn! As though they were animals! Do they need blankets or nourishing soup? Maybe my sister and I and other gentlewomen of the village can assist them."

"I assure you that will not be necessary," Duval said, but a gleam in his eye acknowledged Jane's teasing, and she liked him better for it.

"Why not formally invite them into your household, sir?"

"They are shamed," Duval said. "They have been cast out for disagreeing with their peers. Some wish only for an end, but most wish for punishment."

"But to be kept in a barn! Could you not take them on as servants for a specific period, as has been done in our former colonies, until their honor is restored?"

"A form of indentured servitude?" Duval said.

"Why not? You are all extraordinarily fond of claiming your descent from princes. What greater disgrace than to become a commoner? Unless that seems too cruel, I suppose." She gave a bright smile. "Since they are Damned, how worse could their existence be? Arrangements could be made, I am sure, for dining in the servants' hall."

Again the other side of the table fell silent. Jane stifled a yawn—a genuine one, for it was late—and thought longingly of her bed.

I think of you in your bed, too.

Oh, hold your tongue.

As for your tongue—
Sir! You forget yourself.

Surely the others at the table must be aware of her heated face and the acceleration of her pulse. She hoped they would think it merely the excitement of the negotiation.

"Miss Austen." Duval stood and offered his hand. "We are prepared to accept your terms. I shall write William a letter stating our intentions."

"I am most pleased to hear it, sir." She took his hand, grateful that she wore gloves, troubled but determined not to show it. She had only Duval's word; was not that enough? But why should he agree so easily?

"Will you take some more wine, or some fruit, Miss Austen?"

"No thank you, sir. I should return home."

Luke crossed the room to her side. "I'll keep Miss Austen company until her carriage arrives, if that's agreeable, Duval."

With the exchange of bows and courtesies, the others left, leaving Jane and Luke alone. Rather than look at him, she kept her gaze on the pyramid of fruit, imagining her family's cries of delight if they were to receive such bounty, the careful planning of preserves and pies and fools.

"Well?" he said.

"That seemed altogether too easy, but I am most grateful for your assistance."

"Grateful!" He plucked a peach from the artful arrangement, and fruit fell and rolled onto the dark surface of the table. "It is not gratitude I want from you, Jane Austen."

Chapter 15

"What do you want from me, Luke?" She hoped her carriage would arrive soon and looked toward the doorway, wondering who would stop her if she ran from him.

"You won't run. It's not in your nature. And the carriage will come only if I call for it."

She retrieved a nectarine that rolled toward the edge of the table and placed it back onto the stand. He was in her mind, where she had allowed him to roam, and she made a conscious effort to think of something that would be of no interest to him. Quilting, that was good; the painstaking piecing and arranging of scraps of fabric, her needle dipping in and out of the seam with small, neat stitches, the growth of the quilt day by day, week by week . . .

"Enough!"

"No, sir, I am the one who should call for a halt to this. Why are you so angry?" Her canines ached. Desire tugged and pulled between them to her dismay. She should not, could not succumb to him.

"I am not angry." He shook his head like a creature surfacing in water, as though to clear his thoughts. The peach was still in his hand, and he gazed at it in apparent surprise. "Shall we sit?"

She took her seat again. He sat close, not close enough to touch, but near enough for her to pick up his scent. He raised the peach to his lips—he was *en sanglant,* unashamed, open to her—and bit into it. A little juice spilled on his lip and glistened at the side of his mouth.

She clenched her fists, willing herself not to lean forward and lick the gleaming drop. Instead she removed her gloves and took a peach along with the small knife that lay still on the china stand. The fruit in the palm of her hand, she cut into the yielding flesh, revealing its rich, hidden depths, easing out a crescent-shaped sliver from the dark, serrated pit. The taste was vivid, strong— never before had she so appreciated the Damned's theory of food as a sensual experience—a wild sweetness that spoke of summer and hazy, long, golden days. She took another piece.

Luke tossed his peach pit onto the china dish, where it lay with a few shreds of pulp attached to it in a small pool of juice. "I burn for you, Jane."

There was no denying it; he would read her mind. "And I for you. But there is no future in this."

"Your metamorphosis is so close. You feel it, do you not? Let me assist you." He took her hand in his, stroking the palm of her hand. "It is inevitable."

She snatched her hand back. "No. I must resist and resist you also. William and I have a bargain, that if I wager peace, he shall do nothing to hasten my metamorphosis and I shall pray that my human state remain unaltered."

"William said that? Consider you may be in too deep for his promises to carry any weight."

"I am already in too deep with you." She'd said it and blundered on, "I wish it were not so. All these years, Luke, I would so often think I saw you across a room or on a street, while I learned how to be mortal once more and earned my family's forgiveness."

"Their forgiveness! For the sacrifices you made!" He shook his head. "And I thought you'd be happy. I hoped you would be so. I expected you to be married and with a flock of children by now: that you'd have the only thing I could not give you."

"No. The only children I have are my books."

"So you write, still."

"Finally, yes. It has not been easy. I have felt that I was never sufficiently cured, and the ability to write again, and the desire to do so, took some years. And there were other indications that I was not completely mortal: when, for instance, I—" She stopped, blushing.

He looked at her with keen interest. "When you what?"

"It is nothing," she muttered in embarrassment. "I have never been able to speak of it."

"But you can now. Go on."

"Promise you will not laugh."

He laid a hand on his heart. "I promise."

"I received a proposal of marriage a few years after we—after our liaison—from a neighbor's son. He was a little younger than me, but it was a very good match for he was to inherit considerable property. My father was pleased, as were all my family."

"My congratulations," Luke said. "And what happened?"

"I broke off the engagement the next morning. You see . . . after I accepted the proposal, we were alone, and we . . ."

"Became amorous?"

"Precisely."

"You dined from him?" Luke gazed at her in astonishment.

"Oh, heavens, no. I was not *en sanglant* or anything of the sort. But it seemed only natural to . . . to bite his neck."

"I believe it is something mortals may do in the throes of passion." Luke, despite his promise, seemed to be having trouble keeping a straight face.

"Well, how was I to know? Besides, I wasn't in the throes of passion, as you so elegantly put it. I have only—" She stopped in embarrassment, unwilling to admit that she had experienced those throes only with Luke. Besides, doubtless he knew that already. "He seemed most alarmed, although I did not bite him very hard. He started to question me on my morals, and I was incensed that he should doubt me."

"Oh, of course. Fornication with the Damned does not count at all, as many respectable women could tell you."

"It is not amusing. It was mortifying for me, and naturally I had to end the engagement. His sisters, once my good friends, would not speak to me for some time after, and both families were very much disappointed. And I could not tell anyone, not even Cassandra."

"My dear Jane."

The heat in his eyes made her pull her gloves back on, yet she found herself doing so slowly, watching his face as she eased the kidskin over her bare wrists and arms, smoothing the soft surface to cling to her skin. He was *en sanglant* still, as beautiful as she had remembered for so long.

He stood. "I'll send for the carriage for you. I shall tolerate no rival, Jane."

"You mean Raphael? No, we both take good care of our souls. It is not to be."

"Ha. Not to be? Indeed." He was *en sanglant* again and his fierce lust flared around them. God help them all—only God would not, of course—if ever he and Raphael encountered each other while he felt this way. Raphael's carefully guarded state would inevitably change, and she would become responsible in part for his Damnation.

"And by the by, did Duval instruct you to engage me in bawdy talk to distract me during such serious negotiations?"

"You underestimate him, my dear. He is far more subtle than that. That was entirely my own doing."

"Call the carriage," she said, her breath short. "William has tried to trick me into a metamorphosis: I trust you do not do the same."

He walked to the door and spoke to the footman who stood outside and sauntered back toward her; she saw the intent in his eyes, but she would not retreat from him.

"Stay with me, Jane."

"No. William expects me."

"I meant for eternity, my dear Jane, not for the evening, as pleasant as that would be."

"I regret it is impossible."

"Ah, back to William, like the obedient fledgling you never were. Yes, you have changed indeed."

She stood with her back to the table, gripping the polished wood with her hand.

He took her hand and lifted it, peeling the glove down and over her elbow, pausing to view the blue veins at the crook of her arm; veins that lifted and swelled as her canines ached.

"Ah, you're so close," he murmured. "Your skin is like satin, Jane. I'd clothe you in satin, if I clothed you at all. I'd break strands of pearls to see them roll on your skin and warm. You smell like summer fruit, my love, ripe and sweet, and your heart beats so fast. Let me, Jane. I'll bite here, just a little." His breath scorched the skin of her arm. "You remember how it felt? That shock, and you can't decide whether it's pain or a wonderful violation, and then the tug and the shiver as you lose yourself." His lips trailed down her arm, following the slide of the kid glove, pausing again at the wrist. "Or here? Yes, here where your pulse is strongest, and all anyone will see is that I kiss your wrist, but you and I, we both know it's more. A close observer might wonder at the brightness of your eyes, and the way your lips part . . ."

He took her parted lips with his, fierce, sweet, and she was falling into his darkness and dazzle and glamour, as her canines scraped against his.

Oh God help me! It was only partly blasphemy. She drew back and smacked him with her fan, without much grace, on his ear.

"Ouch!" He stared at her, outrage warring with amusement, openly *en sanglant*.

"You're still quite the seducer." She gathered her disarranged gown around her shoulders.

"And you're still quite the prude." He smiled. "I love you, Jane Austen, and I've had years to perfect my seduction techniques, but it's rarely I've told any woman I loved her. And so my declaration of love is blunt and straightforward, for I can say it no other way."

She curtsied and looked him up and down, brazen and knowing. "It has been a pleasure to have this chat with you, Mr. Venning. No, do not stir yourself, for I see you are hardly fit to be seen. I wish you a good night, sir."

She left the room, as breathless as though she had run a mile, and collected her wits in the darkness of the hall, cool after the candle-filled dining room. He loved her still, but her elation faded already. Nothing could come of it. She must forget him and continue with her life, as gray and drab as that now appeared.

A footman emerged from a side door as the carriage approached, and Jane gave him a friendly nod as he opened the front door.

Raphael bowed and lowered the steps to the carriage.

"You stink of him," he said. His lips curled back into a snarl.

"Mind your own business, sir," Jane said.

"I'll ride outside."

She nodded and stepped into the carriage, and the snap of the ostrich feathers on her headdress against the doorway sent her into a fit of giggles.

He slammed the door shut on the train of her gown.

"And so?" William said. "I see you've toyed with Luke—or was it Raphael?—or both? But never mind. Were you successful?"

She walked to the fireplace in the book-lined room at the rear of the house that William had appropriated as his own, and where she had been invited upon her arrival.

"I don't know," she said. "He agreed, but I do not trust him."

She told him briefly of the meeting and the terms they had agreed upon, including the servitude for *les Sales*. William raised his eyebrows at that and whistled softly to himself. "That's punishment indeed. Some may choose destruction instead."

"It is an unkind situation. I pity them, for all they would kill me."

"I doubt you'd let creatures such as them injure you, even in your half-formed state." He paced, arms folded. "And you shook hands upon it?"

"Yes."

"You were gloved? He did not ask you to remove your glove?"

"No. Is that significant?"

"Maybe." He stared into the fireplace and kicked the logs.

"He said he will write to you tomorrow," Jane said. "It was all too easy."

"Doubtless he plans more mischief, yet you did more than we could. And Luke? What of him? Ah, don't look at me like that; I have no wish to become involved in your romantic tangles. Do you not weary of breaking each other's hearts? All I mean is, will he return?"

"He didn't say," Jane said. She tried not to think of the ardent light in Luke's eyes; now she felt tired once more and longed for her bed. William, however, was cheerful and energetic.

"Well, we will see. What will you now, Jane? Do you wish to return to your cottage, or will you accept a bed here tonight?"

"I'd best change my gown and go home. I'll write to my brother Edward tomorrow, and he'll send letters of introduction so you may meet the well-connected families of the county. And I suggest you have some sort of celebration with a roasted ox and much ale for the village, and they'll love you for it. So this is an end to it." She moved to the doorway.

"Don't be sad, Jane."

"But I am sad. You are my Creator and that cannot be changed. I shall never forget you, William. When I write, sometimes I stop and think, *I am writing about William,* or *He would say such a thing.*"

"And Luke also?"

"Oh, yes. But as you say, we've broken each other's hearts already, and there will be nothing more between us. There cannot be if I wish to save my soul."

As she walked to the door, he stopped her with a hand on her arm. "I have said I will let you go, and I shall keep my word. But allow me this: I must show there is peace between our houses by hosting a ball, and I must ask that the Austen household attend. You are my landlord's family, after all. Will you do it for me, Jane? We'll dance and drink wine and that will be an end to it, all politeness and civility?"

"Very well. I see it is my duty."

"I, too, have duties, and one is that I must tell you, in the little time that is left while we still talk so, that those who have taken the Cure often suffer, their lives shortened. I do not ask you to reconsider, merely to be aware that it is so."

"It means only that I must use my time wisely, and God's will shall be done." Blasphemous enough to talk of God with the Damned; even more blasphemous to say it in his arms, for he had gathered her in a chaste, tender embrace.

"Go," he said, and tears shone in his eyes. "We'll doubtless pass each other in the village—and, oh yes, I'll see you in church—and we'll be perfectly correct. I'll ask after my landlord, your brother Mr. Edward Knight, and we'll talk about the weather. I keep my bargain; I release you."

The next morning Jane came downstairs late, bracing herself for well-meaning comments on her poor looks and the deep shadows beneath her eyes. She had missed her early morning solitude with her writing desk and the pianoforte, and therefore her household duty of preparing breakfast. Doubtless there would be grumbling and complaints about her lying abed and neglecting her small share of the housekeeping. The dining room was deserted, but she followed the tumult of female voices to the kitchen.

"Look, Jane!" Cassandra, eyes bright, held a quartered peach in her cupped palms. "Such splendid fruit and out of season, too. I wonder from whose hothouse it came?"

Fruit was piled in a bowl, scattered on the table. Eliza, grinning widely, her mouth stained with purple grape juice, sliced a pineapple, pausing to lick her fingers.

Martha and Mrs. Austen, deep in discussion on whether they should bottle the grapes or make them into preserves, for there were too many even for the whole household to eat, looked at Jane with knowing smiles.

"The fruit came with a note addressed to us all," Anna said. She handed a folded piece of paper, sticky with peach juice, to Jane. "Surely not another admirer, Aunt Jane!"

Jane unfolded the note.

To the Austen household with the compliments of Luke Venning.

She turned it over. Nothing more. She crumpled the note in her hand and tossed it onto the fire.

Her family watched for her reaction. Whatever they might have expected, it was not that she would sit at the table, drop her face into her hands, and weep.

Chapter 16

"Would you like some tea?" Cassandra asked. "A dose of salts, perhaps?"

Jane, from her place on the sofa, shook her head and summoned a smile for her sister.

Apparently it resolved as a grimace, for Cassandra frowned. "My dear, do you not think you should rouse yourself? You have hardly eaten, you have not written in these past three days, other than your letter to Edward; this is not like you, to succumb so to melancholy."

"I regret if I cause you inconvenience," Jane replied.

"I should hate to see you develop the habit of low spirits in which our poor mother indulges herself." Cassandra paused. "May I inquire—you have been so open with me in the past—is this an affair of the heart that brings you so low? For you may confide in me."

"I'm not sure our mother indulges herself. I think it is in her nature. Possibly it is in mine, too." Jane sat up. "Where are Anna and Martha?"

"Martha has gone to visit her friend Mrs. Chapple."

"How nice for her."

Cassandra gave her a curious glance. "And I have sent Anna to help our mother. Anna was quite upset this morning after our walk."

Jane shifted on the sofa to see Anna and her mother in the garden, Anna with a smear of dirt on her face and a spade in her hand and Jacques the pug frisking around them. "She looks cheerful enough now."

"Fresh air and exercise are remarkably efficacious," Cassandra announced.

"I hate it when you try to sound like a sermon. What happened this morning?"

"We encountered Duval Richards, but he barely acknowledged us, just raised his hat and went on his way. I thought Anna would swoon, she turned so pale, and she cried all the way home."

"So he has tired of her."

"Poor little Anna," Cassandra said.

"She's seventeen. She'll recover, and I am glad Mr. Richards revealed his true character before she was entangled any further." Jane stood and strolled over to the piano, relieved that Duval had lost interest in her niece. It must indicate that he was sincere in ceasing hostilities with William, or so she assured herself, for she still had doubts about the success of her endeavor.

"Sometimes you are remarkably unfeeling. I was going to invite you to visit Miss Benn with me, but if all you will do is smile satirically and make hurtful remarks, you had best stay home."

"As you wish." Jane played a chord and a fragment of a tune on the piano. "If everyone is out or otherwise occupied, I shall practice."

The front doorbell rang and the kitchen door banged as one of the maids went to answer it.

Whoever it was did not seek admittance, for soon after, the front door closed, and Eliza, a letter in her hand, entered the drawing room.

"From the Great House, miss," she said. "My, that was a handsome footman!"

"Go back to the kitchen," Jane said.

"I was looking, that was all, miss," Eliza said, and retreated.

"Those girls." Cassandra shook her head. "This letter is addressed to our mother."

"Why would someone from the Great House write to our mother?" Jane said.

Cassandra shrugged. "It has to be a formal invitation."

Jane groaned. So this was the result of the appeal to her brother Edward to open the doors of Hampshire polite society to the Damned—doubtless her sister, niece, and Martha would be avid to attend.

"I cannot go," she said.

"Oh," Cassandra said, and then repeated the exclamation with a wealth of meaning. "Oh. You mean—Jane, forgive me, but is this the reason for your poor spirits? Has Mr. Fitzpatrick disappointed you once more? You said—"

"I can tell you no more," Jane said, but at that moment she saw Martha join her mother and niece in the garden, and Cassandra opened the window and waved at them, inviting them to come into the house.

Jane sat on the sofa again, bracing herself for the argument that would follow, the half-truths and evasions in which she would have to indulge, the hurt feelings of her family; and above all, that she had been foolish enough to agree to accept William's invitation to the Great House. How could she explain to her sister that her very soul was endangered every time she was near William, or any one of them?

"An invitation?" cried Mrs. Austen. She pried the wax seal from the letter with agonizing slowness. "Oh, goodness, girls, they are giving a ball at the Great House. Can you imagine what that will be like with their high standards of hospitality? Think how very grand our last evening was there!"

"I don't think we need attend," Jane said. "He is inviting us only to be kind, because we are the relatives of the owner of the house. I am sure James would not want Anna to go."

"But he says Edward particularly wishes us to attend, although Edward himself cannot be there. A shame, for I should have liked to have seen him and the children," Mrs. Austen said. "Well, Anna, you shall be the handsomest young lady there, even if they do invite the best society in the county, and we have but three days to prepare. You must all go to Alton tomorrow, my dears, and buy new trims and ribbons."

"Oh, indeed," Martha cried. "Jane, you must buy some new silk stockings."

"I can only imagine why," Jane said. From Martha's bright eyes and air of satisfied well-being it was obvious she had allowed Tom to dine on her once more, his earlier discourtesy forgotten.

"So you're feeling better, Jane," her mother said with a shrewd look. "Well, well. I suppose it is nothing to do with Mr. Fitzpatrick, or whoever it was who was kind enough to send the fruit? I did not realize Edward's hothouses at the Great House were so well stocked. Life in our little village is quite exciting these days."

"I liked it better before," Jane said. "I am finding it very difficult to write."

"You haven't even tried to write these last days. You've been lying around feeling sorry for yourself and feigning illness," Cassandra said.

"I have been unwell," Jane said.

"Now, girls, let us have no quarrels!" Mrs. Austen exclaimed. "I shall begin to think you are rivals for the same gentlemen if this bickering continues."

"You need have no fear of that," Jane said.

"Do—do you think Mr. Richards will be there?" Anna asked, blushing.

"If he is," Jane said, "you must look upon him coldly and flirt with other gentlemen, for he has been most discourteous. Have you not heard, Martha, from your friend at the Great Hall, that Richards is all but engaged to a young lady with a great deal of money?"

"I've heard nothing of the sort," Martha said, crushing Jane's invention. "And how did you hear about it?"

"Oh, I can't remember. From someone else there." As soon as she said the words, she regretted them, seeing the significant looks exchanged by the other ladies.

The next few days were spent in a flurry of preparation, alterations and improvements on gowns, the creation of headdresses, and speculation on who would attend among the people they knew. Jane tired of the activities soon enough and retired to the dining room to write, feeling a great sympathy for Mr. Bennet in a house full of silly women.

When her hand was too tired and stiff to write, she took long, solitary walks, carrying her pistols but not meeting any of *les Sales;* whether they were elsewhere or were safely downstairs at Prowtings wearing livery or caps with modest print gowns according to gender, she could not tell. Inevitably, if she paid no attention to the path she took, she would find herself walking in the direction of the Great House or Prowtings and, infuriated by her body's betrayal, turn away.

But the nights were even worse.

"*Jane, my Jane, how I've longed for you.*"

"*We should not.*" But he left fire everywhere he touched her, with knowing skilled fingers, his tongue and mouth—oh yes, he was en sanglant, *and willing her to become so, too. Fire and a drugged, drowsy sweetness that made her shiver with delight as they discovered each other again.*

"*You are so beautiful.*" *She touched his hair, his cheekbones, the elegance of bone and skin she loved so much. Her finger rested on his lips.* "*No, do not say I am. It is a lie. You'll not lie to me, Luke.*"

"*I'll lie with you.*" *His lip lifted and his aroused canines, as rare and hard as ivory, as fine and strong as silk, rubbed against her finger.* "*Now we shall be together forever, Jane. You'll be my Consort once more.*"

She could resist him no longer for he gave her worlds and time, a universe of experience and sensation when hours stretched and broke and re-formed to build again. They shared the glorious slide of skin and the touch of fang that was pain and pleasure and shock together, the slow swell and seep of blood, the scents of desire and fulfillment.

"No!" She sat up in bed, on fire still, her heart beating fast, canines sharp and aching.

She tossed the covers from her limbs and slipped to the floor, where the floorboards were a cold shock against her hot limbs, and buried her burning face in her hands.

On the opposite side of the room, Cassandra stirred and murmured something in her sleep. Would she awaken? Could Jane stop herself from confessing her craving for Luke, her horrifyingly sensual and vivid dreams?

And if you caused this, Luke, I hate you for it. No, do not reply. Only take heed and, I beg you, stay out of my dreams.

Elbows on the bed, she prayed as fervently as any Methodist to be spared, delivered, that her true release from the Damned might come about. She opened her eyes and gazed at the bed-chamber wall, expecting to see some sort of papish sign that her prayer was heard and her wish granted. But all that happened was an awareness of the cool cotton of her nightgown against her skin—far too much awareness, she reflected grimly—and at last the gradual slowing of her pulse and breath. Cautiously she explored her canines with her tongue and found them still sensitive but returning to their normal state.

How long, O Lord? Will You forget me forever?
How long will You hide your face from me?

How long before she was Jane Austen again, her own woman, cool and satirical and ironic; a gentlewoman, no longer young but accomplished and clever, a beloved and respected friend, daughter, sister, aunt?

Sleep would not come again tonight. She reached for her shawl and wrapped it around herself, sitting on the bed to pull on a pair of stockings. Her nightcap was buried somewhere in the sheets, but she could not yet bear to don her spinster's cap for the day. Anna was right; the cap was unflattering, but Jane had seen it as a proud statement of her status: *Yes, here I am, take me for what I am. I am past having to inconvenience myself for the game of husband hunting.*

Now she hated it, but village life had taught her the folly of changing the style of her cap, or making any other fundamental change in her dress. She would be exposed to vulgar speculation on her intentions—doubtless toward a gentleman—and there was little hope that Cassandra and Martha would defend her. More likely they would be the worst of the gossips.

She tiptoed downstairs and into the dining room, where she

roused the banked fire into life, quietly so the rattle of the poker would not disturb her mother sleeping in the room above. She lit a candle and reached for her writing desk.

This, at least, she could and must do.

At last the day of the ball arrived. A trap must be hired at the inn to take the ladies, and there was much concern over the possibility of rain that would splash mud onto their gowns. The arduous task of bathing was undertaken, with Anna, befitting her youth and beauty, allowed her very own tub of water, as was Mrs. Austen in deference to her age. Cassandra and Jane shared, as was their usual practice; Cassandra as the eldest bathed first, and Jane inherited the cooling water.

Both maids were put to work helping Mrs. Austen and Anna dress, while Cassandra and Jane fended for themselves. Cassandra looked on in astonishment as Jane retrieved her new silk stockings from their hiding place beneath her mattress.

"Well, what was I to do? Martha will borrow them, and my old pairs are so darned, hardly any of the originals remain."

"She goes out more than you do," Cassandra said, "but I really don't understand why she should borrow them without asking you, or indeed why she should need them on her visits to her friend Mrs. Chapple."

"I suppose she wants to impress her," Jane said, wriggling her foot into a stocking. "But she is certainly not impressing anyone tonight at my expense. Besides, we shall all be the poor spinster wallflowers, doing our best to impress upon the company that we are having as good a time as any of them. All of us except Anna."

Stockings on, gown tied, she picked up her cap with distaste.

"What's wrong?" Cassandra asked. She shifted the candle a little closer to the looking glass and pinched and twisted curls into position to lie in an orderly row across her forehead. Satisfied with her appearance, she placed her cap on her head.

"I don't think I want to wear this," Jane replied.

"But what else would you wear?" Cassandra, ever practical, replied. "It's a very proper cap for you to wear."

"Precisely. Very proper." Jane thought with regret of the ruined ostrich feathers of a few nights ago, which she had considered rather elegant, and sighed. "Do you ever get tired of being proper, Cassandra?"

"What a ridiculous question. Of course I do. But I daresay I shall never have the chance to be anything else."

"Maybe it's worse if you have had an unusual episode in your past, for you would then have to accustom yourself to everyday life again. But would not many say our experiences in Bath when the French invaded—"

"Oh, heavens! Is that the church clock striking the hour? We must hasten, Jane. Come, on with your cap." Cassandra sprang to her feet. "You have ink on your fingers still. Come here, let me scrub it off."

Jane subjected herself to a vigorous scrubbing that almost left her fingers raw and received Cassandra's muddled emotions of excitement, nervousness, and vague romantic longings.

The hired trap arrived, and the ladies clambered aboard. It was late for them to go out, although not so late it was dark, and more people than usual stood at their front doors to watch the gentry and the grand on their way to the Great House.

"This must be the most exciting thing that has happened in the village since Mr. Papillon's pigs got out last," Jane commented. "I am most gratified that we provide our neighbors with such good sport."

"Now, Jane, it is precisely that sort of remark which drives gentlemen away," Mrs. Austen said. "I trust you'll moderate your comments so that our dear Anna may not have her partners frightened off."

"A gentleman thwarted by so little would not fare well in anything beyond a dance," Jane replied, "but I am sure our brother would never forgive us if Anna were to fall in love again."

"I shall never fall in love again," Anna said, a pretty pink flushing her cheeks.

"Indeed. We must send you to a nunnery, then. You may spend your hours in contemplation in a gothic cloister. Possibly a silent order might be best, for—"

"Oh, stop talking nonsense, Jane." Cassandra pinched her wrist.

Jane fell silent. Her chatter served to cover the unsettling swirl of emotions in the trap—she seemed particularly susceptible this evening and could only blame it on anticipation of seeing William and Luke again. Since this ball was a celebration of peace between the two households, she knew with absolute certainty that Luke would attend.

She concentrated hard on not attending to the innermost thoughts of those around her: her mother's recollections of balls past, when her daughters were young and as eligible as they would ever be, and Mr. Austen's pride in them; Cassandra's romantic fancies of eligible gentlemen and many partners for Anna; Anna's excitement and plans to dance all night and turn the heads of handsome strangers; the driver's musing on whether his dinner would give him wind all night and how some strong ale at the Great House might cure him; and Martha— good heavens!

Jane trod on Martha's foot.

"What's the matter, Jane?" Martha said, her fond grin fading, but not as much as Jane would have liked.

"I beg your pardon." Martha's imaginings had an uncanny resemblance to Jane's dreams, with Tom taking the place of Luke, but with Martha, subjected to vigorous dining, taking a more passive role.

"The supper room will be quite splendid, according to Mrs. Chapple," Martha said.

"I expect you enjoy your long conversations with her," Jane said. "Indeed, I wonder what you find to talk about for so many hours."

"We exchange recipes," Martha said. "It takes some time to copy them."

"Of course."

"Oh, look how many people have come!" Cassandra exclaimed as they turned into the driveway of the Great House. "And carriages with coats of arms on the door—do you recognize any of them, Jane?"

Jane shook her head. As they watched, a party alighted from a carriage, and from the supreme beauty and elegance of the ladies and gentlemen (and the horses' unease), it was obvious to Jane they could only be more of the Damned. Beside her Martha, also watching, sighed softly.

"It is most unbecoming!" Jane kicked her friend's ankle.

Martha raised her eyebrows.

Jane, aware that she had revealed more about herself than she intended, busied herself with fan and gloves, and last-minute adjustments to Anna's headdress, a wreath of silk flowers for which everyone's bonnets had been ruthlessly plundered. Even so, their party looked exactly what they were: gentlewomen of little wealth or status. Jane hoped no one could tell there were at least two who had no claim to respectability.

As they alighted from the carriage Jane took Martha's arm. As Mrs. Austen and Cassandra entered the house before them, she murmured, "My dear, I must warn you—I regret that *those creatures* will know of your association with one of them and may consider you as their plaything, available to all."

Her pride in her discreet euphemisms was destroyed when Martha, with a wide grin, said, "Indeed? How very . . . interesting. What a delightful prospect for the evening! And Jane, you seem exceedingly well informed."

"My dear Jane!" William, standing in the hallway to greet his guests, stepped forward to take both her hands in his. "And Miss Martha. Well, Jane, how are you?" His concern and longing swept around her like a warm current; with all her heart she wanted to yield and become his fledgling once more. But she took her hands from his and dropped a polite curtsy, murmuring that she did very well, aware that her mother and Cassandra exchanged significant glances.

The ladies, bonnets and cloaks removed, made their way upstairs to the Great Gallery where they had danced before. Ahead of them, Elizabeth Papillon exclaimed about the beauty of the decorations, the gentility of the company, and the overall splendor of the evening. For splendid it was, the room draped with garlands of flowers and illuminated by Chinese lanterns and dozens of beeswax candles. A group of musicians Jane suspected came from London, for they were much smarter in appearance than the local waits, sat tuning their instruments.

Mr. Papillon, voicing concern that the lanterns might set the house afire, escorted his sister into the room. Jane and Cassandra exchanged a glance, both in silent agreement that they should sit as far away as possible from them without seeming entirely unfriendly. As they hesitated, Tom came to greet them, and led them to a group of comfortable chairs.

"And I'll claim the first dance with you, Miss Anna," he said, "for I am sure you will have partners aplenty this evening, and I should count myself a fool for not asking you."

"We are much obliged, sir," Mrs. Austen allowed with a regal nod of her head, and when he had gone, "Well, Anna, that is quite an honor, to be asked for the first dance in a company such as this, and by one of Mr. Fitzpatrick's friends."

"I daresay Mr. Fitzpatrick asked him to," she said. "It is mere politeness, ma'am." She sounded quite composed, but her fingers twisted and pleated the muslin of her gown as she glanced around the room.

Jane, aware that she, too, searched the crowd for a beloved face, took a glass of wine from one of the footmen. She should not have come; she should have claimed to be indisposed and stayed home. Let Anna dance a little, she reasoned, then they could leave, for doubtless Cassandra and the others might be overawed by the sophistication of the ball. She looked around for a place to put her empty wineglass, but another footman appeared, and she exchanged her empty glass for a full one.

"Jane," Cassandra whispered, "if you are thirsty, pray drink lemonade or tea. You know how you become when you drink too much wine."

"Drunk?" Jane said.

"No. Excessively satirical. It is not becoming."

"Indeed." She waved away a footman bearing glasses of lemonade. "I must disagree."

"Oh, thank goodness, here is that Mr. Venning and his friends, and I daresay he will ask you to dance."

"I daresay I shall refuse."

But she turned to watch their arrival.

Duval and William bowed and chatted with great affability. But William took Luke in his arms and kissed his cheek.

"Oh, I did not realize they were so—are they related, Jane?" Mrs. Austen asked. "You might almost think they were father and son, despite their closeness in age."

"No, ma'am. They have known each other for most of their lives, I believe." Maybe she had wagered peace after all, despite her misgivings, and William's, too. It was over, finally; this was the last time she need come to this house, at least during the occupancy of these particular tenants.

She turned her head aside so none of her family could see her tears.

"Miss Austen?" Luke bowed in front of them, hand held out, but Jane realized with a shock that he invited Cassandra to dance; it was quite proper that he should invite the elder sister to dance and equally expected that Cassandra, who never danced now, should refuse.

"Pray dance with my sister before she drinks all of Mr. Fitzpatrick's wine, sir."

"Miss Jane?"

"Mr. Venning." She took his offered hand. "I regret I shall dance no more."

He looked at her with pity and concern, a tenderness that nearly undid her. "Then you'll take a turn around the room with me?"

She stood and took his arm. As they walked, they caught fragments of conversation as one might catch small fish in a net trailed through water: a woman admonishing her daughter for appearing too forward; a quarrel between a couple, she querulous, he frowning; and, to Jane's delight, Duval and Margaret complaining about how difficult it was to get good help. Apparently *les Sales* proved indifferent servants.

Clarissa joined them and offered Jane her gloved hand. "I would rather embrace you, but I know you do not wish more contact than is necessary. I am most grieved that you will leave us again. But I shall speak no more of it."

"Do you return to William's household?" Jane asked.

"Of course. Margaret will stay with Duval, as will the others, but Luke and I were never intimate with them. Luke, you have very little to say for yourself tonight."

"I am feeling old," he replied.

"Old! Well, so you should."

The musicians played an opening chord and the dancers took their places, William partnered with another of the Damned Jane did not know, and Dorcas with Duval. "William's partner is of Duval's household," Clarissa said. "It is a gesture of peace between us. But what is your friend Miss Martha up to? She seems very popular." Then she laughed. "Ah, I know why. Do you think I should rescue her, Jane?"

Jane observed the cluster of the Damned around Martha. "I'm not sure she wants to be rescued, but if you would be so good, please make sure she is not in over her head."

Clarissa nodded and left them.

"I owe you an apology," Luke said, his voice strained. "Had I not lingered at Duval's and failed to fulfill the task William set me, there would have been no need for you to step in and endanger yourself."

"Why did you?"

He shrugged. "I wished to teach William a lesson, that I was not his creature to do his bidding."

"But he is your Creator."

"And naturally, a fledgling should be obedient to his Creator's wishes. You know a little how things are between us. I wished to make him uneasy."

"You certainly succeeded in that," Jane said.

They stood, arm in arm, watching the dancers, and Jane was pleased to see the respect and decorum that Tom showed toward Anna.

"She's a pretty girl," Luke said. "Almost as pretty as you were when first we met."

"Oh, nonsense, you flatterer. She is much prettier than ever I was. You're so old your memories are muddled; you must confuse me with another."

"Indeed not. I remember everything about you. I trust you'll think of me now and again," Luke said.

"Indeed. If ever I need a handsome rake or a witty, enigmatic gentleman in a book, my thoughts turn to you."

"I'm honored." He lifted her gloved hand and kissed her palm.

"I must return to my family. Your behavior will give rise to talk, and I fear I have drunk enough to become maudlin."

"Very well." He escorted her back to her mother and Cassandra and conversed politely with them of the size of room and the number of dancers.

He made his bow and left, and Jane watched him depart, as she had so many times before, it seemed. Had he not told her once that every conversation they ever had ended with a farewell, certain they would never meet again? This time she was certain of it; she would meet him only in her imagination.

Cassandra clutched her hand. "So tell me, Jane, did he make you an offer?"

"What?"

"He kissed your hand. We both remarked upon it."

"My dear," her mother said, "you need not be shy with us. You are a grown woman and surely you know your own mind."

"I do, ma'am, and there's an end to it, tonight. Nothing more between us. It's over."

She reached for another glass of wine.

"Pray do not hover," Jane said to her sister some hours later. "You remind me of a dragonfly."

"Oh, if only we had a gentleman," Cassandra said, looking

around the ballroom as though she were ready to pounce upon the nearest male and demand an escort.

"What on earth for? I have a headache. Gentlemen usually cause them." Jane pressed a glass of iced wine to her aching head. "I am quite capable of going downstairs on my own and having a footman send for the driver. No one will notice I have gone, and at my age surely I do not have any worries about my reputation. I have put in my appearance and stayed long enough to be civil."

"Yes, but there is drinking down there," Cassandra said.

"There's drinking up here, too, much of it by me. Never fear, I can look after myself." The pounding feet of the dancers formed a counterpoint to the thudding of her headache. She thought longingly of bed and rising early to write, of enjoying once more the calm routine she had craved for so many years.

"And I have no idea where Martha is," Cassandra continued.

"Oh, pray do not concern yourself. She's probably visiting Mrs. Chapple."

"I know it is hard," Cassandra said, pressing her sister's hand.

"What is hard?"

"That your friend has deserted you for another. It seems she wants to spend every hour she can with Mrs. Chapple, and I can see it distresses you. But may I advise you, Jane? Your sarcasm will only drive her further away. She knows you are a good friend and will turn to you again. Mrs. Chapple cannot supplant you in her affections, I am sure."

"I daresay you're right. Does Anna dance still?" She peered into the tossing mass of dancers.

"I hope she does not overtire herself," Cassandra said. "What energy the child has. She reminds me of you at seventeen."

"Ah, I, too, was young and silly and pretty once. I shall leave before I give way to any embarrassing display of sentiments. Pray give our hosts my thanks and apologies, for I have not seen them in some time."

She would not allow herself to dwell on what sort of activities might draw Dorcas and William away from a party in full swing. As she left the Gallery, stepping onto the crooked corridor that led to the staircase, she could tell the Damned took their pleasure nearby. Currents from the darkened part of the house spun around her, the pulse and spill of blood, desire, laughter—she forced them out of her mind and continued down the stairs.

A few lanterns stood in the flagstone hall, where a couple of footmen lounged on wooden settles, pots of ale in their hands. They jumped to their feet at her approach, the pots of ale placed out of sight on the floor, and she asked them to seek her cloak and bonnet and send for her driver.

A maid, somewhat rumpled and her face flushed with drink, led Jane to a side room where cloaks and bonnets hung from pegs or were laid upon a table. Jane had little trouble identifying her modest cloak and bonnet, but when she returned to the hall, Raphael stood there.

"Miss Austen, I fear your driver is somewhat the worse for drink." He bowed, very correct.

"In that case, sir—"

"In that case, Miss Austen, may I drive you home? It is the task assigned to me this evening, for outside they have strong ale and a whole ox roasting, and I fear there will be some aching heads tomorrow."

"That is most kind, sir." She dipped a small curtsy. Let them duel to the end with civility, then.

A footman opened the door and she stepped outside. The scent of roast meat was strong in the air, and the sounds of good-natured, if somewhat tipsy, revelry came from the side of the house. A fiddle squeaked with energy if not accuracy. She tipped her head back to gaze at the stars. A good night, clear and bright; a good night to be alive and know that life would continue now with no great disturbance or passion, for as long as her mortal span allowed.

The stamp of a horse's hoof on the gravel roused her from her reverie. Raphael stood waiting with a gig, and for the first time Jane felt at peace with him and offered him a friendly smile. "I beg your pardon; I contemplate the heavens."

He looked upward. "Yes, they change little. There is some comfort there."

"You have seen them change?"

"Stars die in their time." He held his hand out to assist her into the gig. "I trust you'll be warm enough."

"Oh, yes. It was a dreadful crush in there and the cool air is pleasant." What a relief to have a normal conversation with him, although she found she looked aside, simply because the sight of him was too much pain and regret mixed with the pleasure. She willed herself to gaze at his strong profile and wave of silvery hair as he touched the whip to the horse and turned the vehicle. She placed her hand on his; they were both decently gloved, and she was grateful for it. "I do not wish us to part with bitterness, for part we must. William has released me."

"Ah. As much as Creator and fledgling can be released."

"He will not pursue me. I shall visit the Great House no more while William is tenant. Tonight I have said my farewells." She removed her hand from his.

He nodded and flicked the whip to urge the horse into a trot.

"What shall you do, Raphael?"

"Continue with my scientific research and try to resist a metamorphosis as best I can."

"You and I are alike then. We both plan to be busy. But shall you stay with William?"

"I don't know." They were almost at the cottage now. "For that matter, I don't know if he intends to stay in Hampshire. He is becoming restless." He reined the horse in. "Would it be improper to ask if I may write to you, Miss Austen?"

"Not at all improper, but I think probably not advisable. I wish we could have met under other circumstances."

"I, too. But neither of us is willing to risk our soul, and quite rightly so, having escaped hellfire once." He hooked the reins aside and stepped down to assist her from the gig. "Ah, well, Luke and I would probably have torn each other's throats out over you. It's for the best."

"Truly?" she said with unseemly delight. "At my age?"

"Your false modesty does not become you, Miss Austen."

Inside the house, a bobbing light indicated that one of the maids, waiting up for their return, had come to open the door.

Jane took Raphael's hand, and the light fabric of her gown brushed lightly against him as she stepped down. "God be with you, Raphael."

She went inside the house quickly so he would not see her weep.

"I have a headache," she told Eliza. "Pray unlace me and let me sleep."

"Oh, what a shame. Were there many grand people there, miss? And did you dance? Miss Cassandra said she thought you might, but—"

"We'll tell you all about it tomorrow." And she was burdened more by the knowledge that she would never be able to tell anyone about this bittersweet night of farewells.

Chapter 17

Jane woke to the patter of rain on the eaves and the loud monotonous braying of one of the donkeys in the yard. She pulled the sheets over her head and feigned sleep as Cassandra stirred and stretched, the bed creaking.

"Oh," Cassandra said, a long sigh of sleepy reluctance. "Are you awake, Jane?"

She made a slight noise into the pillow.

"That donkey is such a noisy fellow." More rustling and creaking, and Jane knew Cassandra sat on the edge of her bed. "Are you feeling well this morning?"

"Quite well." Jane gave up the subterfuge of sleep. She turned to see Cassandra at the washstand, splashing water onto her face. "Did you stay long last night?"

"Not much longer than you, after we heard Anna had left with you. I must see how she does; poor thing, to become unwell at her first ball. I tapped on her door when we came home, but there was no answer and the room was quite dark, so I did not like to disturb her."

"I don't understand. Anna didn't come home with me."

There was a splash and a thud as Cassandra dropped the soap into the bowl and turned to her. "Why—one of the party—Mrs. Cole, I believe—told us she had left with you!"

Jane threw back the bedclothes, ran to the other end of the house, and flung open the door to Anna's bedchamber, revealing an empty room, the bed still neatly made. She turned and banged on Martha's bedchamber door, pushing it open to reveal Martha in a frilled bedcap blinking at her from the bed.

"Where's Anna?" Jane demanded.

"Why, she's in bed, poor girl. We agreed not to wake her. I am so glad you were able to bring her home—"

Jane turned and ran back to her room. Cassandra, in the act of flinging on a dressing gown, looked at her with alarm. "She did not—she is not there?"

"I thought maybe you had been misinformed, that the Papillons or some others we know brought her here. But her bed has not been slept in. I fear the worst."

Cassandra sank onto her bed. "What shall we do? I shall send for James—wait, Jane, what is it you do?"

For Jane had dropped to her knees to retrieve her weapons and men's clothes from beneath the bed. "Don't send for James," she said. She flung a pistol onto the bed and heard Cassandra's squeak of fear.

"But—" Cassandra turned her face aside, blushing, as Jane stripped off her nightgown. Her fingers splayed over her face, she gasped, "What—what are you doing, Jane? Surely those are not—Jane, that is wicked, it says in the Bible—"

"A pin, if you please." Jane, wearing drawers and in the act of binding her breasts, held out a hand.

"But—but why?" Cassandra handed her a pin, warm and moist with sweat. "Oh, I cannot—is that—where did you—"

"I'll explain later." Jane dropped the shirt over her head and sat to pull on her woolen stockings. Despite her fear, she wondered how Cassandra would react if Jane had the time or care to add that third, masculine stocking. Cassandra meanwhile shrank into the corner of her bed, hugging her knees, staring at Jane with horror and fear.

Neckcloth hastily knotted, coat on, feet thrust into boots, Jane loaded the pistols.

"How—how did you—" Cassandra whimpered.

"I shall be out for a while," Jane said. "Pray tell our mother and Martha that they must stay home. I hope I shall return with Anna and no harm done." She placed the pistols inside her coat and tied her hair back, before dropping the hat onto her head and running downstairs.

As luck would have it she met Jenny with a tray, bringing some clean plates back to the dining room. At the sight of her, the maid shrieked, and plates shattered on the floor. All would be explained later—there was no time to comfort the girl, who cowered among her broken crockery, screaming of robbers and rapists.

Jane ran outside and into one of Edward's tenants who helped with the outside work. He looked at her with alarm and grabbed for a pitchfork. "What are you about, sir? Sir, stop!"

Jane dodged away from him, amazed that for some reason he would address a robber or rapist as "sir"—it must be the clothes, she concluded—and reached for a bucket that she bowled at his legs, sending him tumbling to the ground. Sharp pain jolted through her canines as though her body, Damned and human, held memories of other fights, other dangerous situations. At the bottom of the garden she surprised herself by vaulting over the stile and laughed aloud at the sheer joy of it. And then the walk across the meadow, the grass wet and darkening her boots, the familiar, homely huddle of Prowtings ahead, smoke trickling from the windows. Off in the distance a few birds twittered, cowed by the rain, and a dog barked. It was a normal early morning in the village, a morning like hundreds of others, except today a peace had been destroyed, and Anna, her beloved niece, was a victim of that betrayal.

Honor demanded she approach Duval first—she had no doubt it was he—even though she might put herself in deadly danger. *Your honor as one of the Damned, you mean.* For certainly one of the respectable Austen ladies would not stride through the fields, dressed as a man, two loaded pistols inside her coat, thinking of honor and retribution. Pray God Anna was safe still, not violated or injured, or created against her will.

She approached the stone wall, now sleek and dark with rain, the plants clinging to the crevices as rich as green velvet and studded with raindrops. No one lurked behind it; she half expected to see one of *les Sales* lunge at her. Instead, a rabbit disturbed by her approach sat frozen, a dandelion dangling from its mouth, before dashing off into the shelter of longer grass.

The soles of her boots sounded quietly on the flagstones of the path. She had no doubt she was observed, although, because of the early hour, the house was shuttered and silent. She lifted and let fall the heavy iron knocker of the door, her other hand resting on one of the pistols.

Inside, someone stirred and the door opened. The footman who answered the door must be one of *les Sales,* for an air of misery and defeat hung around him. At the sight of her, he became *en sanglant,* as if to try and assert some sort of strength.

"I'll see your master, if you please," Jane said.

He nodded and stood aside to let her enter. She strode past him, not bothering to hide her weapons and pushing her hat into his hands.

"I apologize for the lack of grace among our staff." Duval's voice came from the staircase. "And you'll forgive me, I'm sure, for my state of undress. It is rather early, Miss Austen."

He descended the stairs slowly, the silk dressing gown he wore over his breeches and shirt billowing behind him like a gorgeous dark red cloud.

She waited, although every instinct she had urged her to attack. She was sure he knew it, for what else could cause him such amusement?

"I regret I'm disturbing you," Jane said.

"It is always a pleasure to see you. But let us go into the parlor. There should be a fire there."

The sullen footman opened a door, and Duval bowed, ushering Jane inside the parlor where so often she had spent happy hours in her calls to Prowtings.

"Dear me," Duval said, looking at the dirty, cold hearth. "Will you take some coffee, ma'am? I suppose it is too early in the morning for wine, or anything else stronger." A flash of canine as he spoke; a warning.

"No, sir. If you'll be good enough to send for my niece, I'll be on my way." She hooked her thumbs into the fall of her breeches, allowing her unbuttoned coat to swing clear and reveal the pistols.

"Your niece. And what makes you think she is here."

"Pray do not evade me, Duval."

"My, for a lady so determined to resist Damnation, you are certainly fierce." He took a step toward her.

"My niece, sir." She stood her ground. Even though she was armed, he had the strength and speed and ruthlessness of the Damned.

"Very well, she is here. But have you considered that she might be here of her own free will?"

"I have little interest in your methods of seduction, sir. She must come home with me." Oh, pray God Anna was not created. If this was merely a matter of Duval's casual lust, she and Cassandra and Martha could and would cover up any scandal and deny rumors. To all appearances, Anna's honor would remain unstained, with no child or disease to result from a liaison with the Damned.

"Have you considered she may not want to see you?"

Jane shrugged. "It is natural she should feel some shame, even if you cannot, sir."

"My dear Jane, I wonder how long it will be before your hand drops to that pistol—yes, you are barely aware of what you do—and you send me to hell."

"I wonder, too, and I do not believe I gave you permission to use my Christian name."

"I beg your pardon, ma'am." He bowed and left the room.

The familiar, ordinary sounds of a house coming to life in the morning broke the stillness: voices downstairs, the clatter and clangs of a kitchen stirring into wakefulness, footsteps in the hall and on the stairs. Someone was frying bacon, and outside, a man whistled.

She strolled to the window and unlatched the shutter, letting a shaft of early morning light into the room. The whistling man, carrying a scythe, passed by, leaving in the air a thin blue trace of smoke from his pipe.

The door to the room opened and Jane turned to see Anna, pale and dazed, clinging to Duval's arm. She wore a day gown that was slightly too large for her, doubtless borrowed from one of the inhabitants of the house. He escorted her to a chair, bowed, and left the room.

"Aunt Jane?" Anna blinked.

"Yes, it is I. How do you do, my dear?"

"Oh, well. Very well." A small, secret smile hovered around Anna's lips.

Jane took the chair next to hers. "We were somewhat concerned that you left with your friends."

"I beg your pardon," Anna said. "I thought they had sent word. Maybe they forgot. What time is it? I feel half asleep, and quite weak and foolish."

"You know why that is, do you not?" Jane said.

"Oh, too much dancing and excitement and staying up too late, and . . ." Anna blinked. "Mrs. Cole has been so very kind."

"And what of Duval?"

"He has been most gentlemanly. He . . ." Again Anna's thoughts drifted away.

Jane placed her hand on Anna's wrist. She stank of Duval, of blood—Jane tried to ignore her sudden pang of hunger—and her face held the sated, foolish look of pleasure of one who had been thoroughly dined upon. She removed her hand as she received Anna's half-forgotten memories, pleasure and wonder and confusion; this was all too intrusive.

Arousing, too. But she forced that unworthy thought from her mind and considered practical matters. If Jane were to persuade her to come home, Anna must be revived. But Duval might not oblige, and in that case Jane must and would carry her across the fields.

"Why are you wearing men's clothes, Aunt Jane? I know it is wicked and against all that the Bible says, but you look very handsome."

"Thank you, my dear. I try and look upon it as the sartorial equivalent of eating roast pork."

Anna gave a faint smile. "Would you like some tea, Aunt Jane?"

"I think not. You and I should get back to our cottage in time for breakfast, I think. We'll be there in a few minutes and drink our own tea. You may help me make toast."

Anna's expression of gentle amusement did not change. "I don't believe so, ma'am."

"But I thought making toast was an occupation to which you were most partial," Jane said. "And there is Martha's jam, remember."

"No."

Jane gazed at Anna, wondering how to reach her. She had no doubt Duval mastered her; her instinct was to grasp the young woman's shoulders and shake sense into her, though she doubted it would do any good. But she needed something to shock sense into her niece, to make her aware of the danger and impropriety of her situation.

"This is a very comfortable house," Jane said, keeping her voice gentle. "I am glad they have been kind to you. You remember its usual occupants, Mr. Prowting and Miss Lizzie Prowting, of course; they always ask after you. Now, that china shepherdess on the mantelpiece is one of Lizzie's favorites."

"It is pretty," Anna agreed.

Jane, with a silent apology to Lizzie Prowting, drew a pistol, cocked it, and aimed. The shot was tremendously loud in the room, echoing from the high ceiling.

Anna screamed and leaped out of the chair, fragments of china tumbling from her gown.

Jane, the pistol tucked into her coat again, grasped Anna's shoulders, and saw, with a guilty shock, that a splinter of porcelain as sharp as glass had pierced her niece's cheek. She made her voice firm and kind. "I am sorry to injure you, my dear. I did not intend that to happen. You must come home with me now!"

"You hurt me!" Anna whimpered, but her eyes were clearer. Some of that dazed, pleasured expression had faded.

"Come." Jane tugged at her arm but was far too aware of the trickle of blood on her niece's pale cheek, its slow bloom and slide toward her neck.

"Delicious, isn't she?" Duval said. He stood at the doorway, *en sanglant*. He too stared at Anna's blood.

"Don't touch her!" Jane moved to block his path.

His action was so fast she barely registered his blow until she landed with an ungainly thump a few yards away, the side of her face stinging and tender and one eye already swelling closed. She stood in time to see Anna in Duval's arms, his slow lick to cleanse the blood, his breath to close the wound.

"Well?" Duval said. "You are not needed here, Miss Austen."

Her teeth stung, and hunger stirred within her. "Anna," she said. "Oh, Anna, my dear, come home with me."

But Anna stood within Duval's arms, her head resting on his shoulder, a look of immense satisfaction and peace on her face, her eyes fluttering closed.

"Go," Duval said. "Go, or I shall create her as you watch."

"You would not dare," Jane said. "Besides, as Creator, you could not be her lover."

"Times are changing, my dear Miss Austen."

"Indeed. Once the word of the Damned was sacrosanct—you have changed that."

"But I have you to thank for that, ma'am. You see, your suggestion that I bring *les Sales* into my household was quite clever, but you forget that once our servants were our armies. It amused me to be the benevolent peacemaker for a while—a very short while, I admit." He looked at Anna in his arms. "I really don't know whether I should create her or keep her for entertainment. What do you think?"

Jane drew her other pistol. "Release her."

"You won't fire. You know I can move faster than you, and you wouldn't want to shoot your beloved niece. Your carelessness with your first shot would have scarred her beauty had I not healed her. You may thank me for that. Leave, Miss Austen."

"You are unmannerly, sir." She hoped her comment would wound him—after all, the Damned revered good manners—but Duval merely laughed.

"It's unmannerly to point a loaded pistol at your host, Miss Austen." He released Anna back into her chair and lunged at Jane. She saw him coming and fired, but her shot went wide. He pinned her to the floor, his face close to hers, and sent the pistol spinning away, smoke still rising from the barrel.

"You fear metamorphosis," he whispered. "You'd sacrifice your own niece to save your precious soul. Or maybe not. What say I hasten the process?"

She tried to twist away from him, but his strength and weight overwhelmed her; how soon before his scent and beauty seduced her and she succumbed to his power?

"Do we have a bargain? You or her, Jane?"

Chapter 18

Duval's breath was hot and compelling on her skin. "It won't hurt, Jane. You remember what it feels like. You may pretend you're a dried-up spinster, but I know your true nature. I want to help you, Jane. Cease your struggles. Become the creature you truly are."

How easy it would be to sink into his embrace; she tried to pray, but his laughter mocked and echoed in her mind. If she could not call to God, she could call to her Creator, but Duval thwarted her cry for help.

William's washed his hands of you, Jane. He can't hear you. He was never truly your Creator for he abandoned you once and does so again.

He laughed and scraped his canines down the length of her neck, touching his tongue to her hectic pulse, and she softened and stretched beneath him, ready to surrender. She trailed a languid hand down his body, reaching between them—

"Christ!" Duval choked out the blasphemy and rolled away from her, hands at his groin.

Jane leaped to her feet and retrieved her pistol. She probably wouldn't have time to reload, but she could use it as a weapon or a missile. "You forget I was taught to fight in an ungentlemanly way, Duval. Immortality is no protection against twisted cods." She reached out a hand to Anna. "Come with me, my dear."

"No, Aunt," Anna said. "Oh, poor Duval, what did you do to him?"

A half-dozen livery-clad men and a couple of women in print dresses and caps, one holding a broom and the other a ladle, rushed into the room and surrounded Jane, menacingly *en sanglant*. Despite the severity of the situation, the absurdity of the broom and ladle made Jane smile.

"I see it takes an injury to your private parts to make you summon your servants, something you could have done some time ago and saved yourself a great deal of pain and humiliation," she said to Duval, who lay huddled on the floor still, looking unwell.

He snarled at her in reply.

Les Sales gathered around Jane.

"Pray escort this woman out," Duval said.

"May we dine on her?" one of them asked.

"Not yet," Duval said. "If she returns to this house, you may drain her dry. Good morning, Miss Austen."

"Good morning, sir." Surrounded by *les Sales* and with one last despairing glance at Anna, who had slipped from her chair to kneel at Duval's side, Jane was escorted to the front door of the house.

The door banged shut behind her.

What now? As if in reply, she heard the thud of a horse's hooves approaching the house at a gallop, and she looked up to see William.

He reined in the horse. It sidled, froth at its bit, flanks wet with sweat. "Are you well? I knew you were in difficulties."

"Quite well if somewhat humiliated, although not so much as Duval. He has Anna."

"Damn him!"

"He is Damned," Jane said. "It is a pity you did not arrive sooner."

"The horse would not come willingly with me," William said. "Must you get into trouble so early in the morning? Pray do not roll your eyes at me so." He leaned from the saddle and gazed at her eye and forehead. "Did Duval do that? May I?"

His breath would heal her; it would also bring her closer to Damnation, and she had been compromised enough already by Duval.

She shook her head and leaned her face against the horse's neck, allowing herself comfort from the creature when she really yearned for William's touch. Its skin twitched a little at the contact, but the animal allowed her to stay. "He threatens to create her. If he does not create her, he will dishonor her further. She is his creature already, desperately in love with him, and ready to cast off her family. And he—"

"You need tell me no more, but I believe you have compromised yourself. You should have come to us first." William dismounted and pulled the reins over the horse's head to lead it.

"So I failed as your emissary," Jane said.

"Do not blame yourself," William said. "You did more than I expected or hoped and gave us a few days' respite. So, we're at war again, Duval and I."

"A plague upon both your houses," Jane said. "What of my niece? She is my concern now."

"I'll take you home. We shall rescue her, never fear."

"We?" Jane stopped.

William stopped also, and the horse began to tear at tufts of grass at the side of the road. "Jane, the doings of the Damned are no longer your concern, as you have made clear. We have a bargain, you and I. Let my household right this wrong."

"No! Forgive me for saying so, William, but I know well the

Damned are concerned only with their own. I will not see Anna become a casualty of your discord, nor the innocent people of the village, my brother's tenants, harmed. I must be with you on this. Her soul is at risk now, as is mine. Besides, honor demands my involvement."

"Your honor as one of the Damned?" William smiled.

"It sounds that way, does it not? Well, so be it. My honor as an aunt, as an Austen, as a woman. That is all."

They resumed walking. "What shall you tell your family?" William asked.

"The truth. I should have done so long ago. My father took my secret to his grave, and my sister and mother chose to forget what they had seen, just as so many wish to forget the dishonor England suffered then." She reached to pluck a handful of grass from the side of the road and offered it to the horse.

"Do you wish me to be there when you tell them?"

"No, I thank you. I must do it alone. And then I shall come to see you."

A few minutes more brought them to the Austen house, and they stopped outside the gate to the yard. William mounted the horse again and raised his hat. "I shall rouse the others. We outnumber Duval's household, or at least may match them, for we have some guests who stayed to dine." He smiled. "It was quite like happier times."

Jane pushed the gate open and walked across the yard to the kitchen door. She hesitated, not wanting to frighten the servants, and removed her hat. At least they would recognize her, even if scandalized by her men's clothes.

She pushed the door open, and the two maids, Jenny and Eliza, looked up from their work.

"It was you!" Jenny said. "Miss Jane, that is. Why, you gave me such a fright."

"Jane!" Martha came into the kitchen from the house. "Jane, you cannot dress like that; it's indecent. And we sent one of the men to the Great House to see if Anna—"

"She's not there. Where are Cassandra and my mother?"

"In the dining room. But Jane—"

"Come with me," Jane said. "I shall tell you everything. But my mother and sister must hear, too."

As they entered the dining room Jane's mother rose to her feet and regarded her with horror. "What are you about, Jane? Your face! Did you fall? We have no word of Anna, and you bring more shame on the family by dressing in men's clothes!"

Knowing she was to cause her family pain, Jane said, "I shall explain. But I beg of you, ma'am, sit."

"Will you take some tea, Jane?" Cassandra's eyes were downcast and red rimmed. She must have received the brunt of their mother's anger for both Anna's disappearance and Jane's shocking behavior.

Jane accepted a cup of tea but remained standing, too restless to sit, afraid for her family. How would they react at her news, at the resurrection of distressing memories? She would be cast out, she was certain, for after this they could not allow her to stay in the house. It did not matter that she had tried to rescue Anna; Jane's unwillingness to speak, to try and confide in her loving family, was the cause of her niece's ruin as much as Duval's lust. Duval, after all, acted only as his kind did.

She placed her cup and saucer on a small table nearby, her throat too constricted with grief and fear to allow her to swallow. She looked at the women in the room, dearest in the world to her, whom she was about to injure so terribly. "What I have to tell you will distress you and bring back unpleasant memories, and I am grieved that it should be so. But I must speak. You may remember some years ago that I was ill and we went to Bath—"

"What does this have to do with Anna? She must be our first concern." Cassandra's hands were knotted on her lap, her face flushed.

"I shall explain. It has everything to do with Anna. We went to Bath because I had been created one of the Damned—"

"Yes, yes," her mother interrupted. "And you took the Cure and all was well. We do not want to dwell, I am sure, upon those unpleasant times."

"You are right, ma'am. Yet it was the Damned who were our saviors then, in ridding us of the French invasion. I have never spoken much of those times for fear of causing you distress, but let me say merely that you saw me as one of the Damned and shrank from me and I do not blame you."

"But you're cured!" Cassandra insisted.

"Edward's tenants at the Great House are some of the Damned; so are Duval and his companions," Jane said.

"But what of Anna?" Mrs. Austen said, flushed with anger. "You spin a fantastic tale—now, miss, get to the point, if you will."

"I beg your pardon, ma'am. Pray bear with me." She took a deep breath. "Anna has become a pawn in the enmity between William and Duval. As you know, the Damned are out of favor, rejected by the Prince of Wales and polite society. There is a schism between those of the Damned, like William, who wish to live quietly, harming none, until things are forgotten, and others like Duval who resent the fall from favor and wish to retaliate. Duval has also taken in members of the Damned who, because of opposing views on the matter, were cast out from their households; you must know that the Damned cleave to one another. To be rejected from one's home is a deep disgrace and may lead to destruction. It was one of those cast-out creatures we call *les Sales* who attacked Martha and who makes our village unsafe."

"You knew this, yet you did not speak when Duval cast his sights upon Anna?" Mrs. Austen's lip curled.

"I have done what I could, but—"

"You have allowed us to associate with these creatures and not said a word!" Mrs. Austen said. "I shall certainly speak of this to Edward, letting his house to such tenants."

"It is not his fault, ma'am. I doubt he knew. But I did, and I am to blame for my niece's ruin. Now I must ask Mr. Fitzpatrick for help."

"And your own virtue?" Her mother's eyes were as hard as stone. "What of that? You have deceived us all these years. Are you Mr. Fitzpatrick's mistress?"

Blood rushed to Jane's face. "Mr. Fitzpatrick—William—created me. He is not my lover, for any amorous relationship between Creator and fledgling is deemed unnatural. Mr. Venning is—was—my Bearleader, the one who showed me the ways of the Damned. I became his Consort. It is a form of—of marriage among the Damned. I left him to return to you, my beloved family, and I never thought—"

"Jane!" Cassandra, hands at her mouth, stared at her.

"You refer, I assume, to a union without the blessing of the church or society." Mrs. Austen's voice was deceptively cool. Beneath, anger simmered. Jane feared her mother's anger and her sister's shame far more than any encounter with the Damned.

"I never thought I should meet him again, or that I would be judged for past sins by my family."

"You shame us!" Mrs. Austen stood and struck Jane on the cheek. "You have lied to us all these years! What would your father say?"

Shocked, Jane cupped a hand to her burning cheek. "My father, ma'am, knew nearly all of what happened in Bath. He did not know of my liaison with Luke, although he may have guessed it. He and I made the decision—which may well have been unwise—to not share my experiences with anyone, not even you, ma'am. What no one has known until recently is that, as much as I have wished to deny it, the symptoms of the Damned have never entirely left me. Being in proximity to the Damned, and with those whom once I loved, I fear again for my soul. And now I fear for Anna, for both her body and soul. I have asked William for help, for I tried and failed this morning to rescue her. But to return to William is to risk my own Damnation."

In the silence that fell, Cassandra stood and took Jane's hand. "My dear, I fear you are not well. We must put you to bed and we shall send for the doctor. You have always had a great imagination, and I fear that you are overexcited. You are sadly out of sorts to think such things might happen here! You have been unwell lately, and—"

Jane shook her sister's hand away. "You think I am mad? Don't you remember, Cassandra, how you saw me kill a man to save you? How I ripped into his throat and he died in front of us? You feared me then. I know you do not like to think of it. You, too, ma'am," she said to Mrs. Austen. "You were there. So was Papa. I started the course of the waters the next day and I suffered greatly, for the Cure is difficult and painful. The waters are like poison to the Damned. You—"

"She's right!" Martha said. "You should listen to her."

Mrs. Austen said, "I beg your pardon, Martha. I know you and Jane are great friends, but you should not let your partiality stand in the way. She is clearly unwell, and you do her no favor in supporting these preposterous and indecent claims."

Martha said, "Excuse me, ma'am. I have no knowledge of what happened in Bath, but she is right in all she says. I have become one of those who can identify the Damned, and I am particular friends with one of them at the Great House. I, too, knew the true nature of the inhabitants of the Great House and Prowtings, and Jane has tried to warn us about Duval."

"Mrs. Chapple is one of the Damned?" Cassandra said.

"No, my dear. I visit one of the gentlemen there." Martha blushed.

"What!" Mrs. Austen rose to her feet in outrage. "You, too, commit acts of impurity with one of those creatures? What would your father and mother say?"

Martha shrugged. "I doubt they'd like it much either, ma'am, and I daresay they're spinning in their graves. But I'm thankful it's not cards or drink or laudanum, and it makes me feel years younger."

"Yes, your complexion is much improved," Cassandra said, and fell silent at her mother's furious expression. "Jane, I—I am sorry. I am sorry you had to bear all of this alone. What shall we do?"

"You must wait here and pray both Anna and I return safely home," Jane said. She turned to her mother. "Ma'am, can you find it in your heart to forgive me?"

She flinched as Mrs. Austen approached her, wondering if her mother would strike her again. But her mother's voice was gentle and hesitant, tears standing in her eyes. "My dear, I shall pray for you. But will garlic help? I could dig up the garlic beds, although I fear mice may have eaten them—"

"Thank you, ma'am, but I regret that is merely rumor."

"Who did this to you?" Mrs. Austen touched Jane's bruised face with gentle fingers roughened by her work in the garden.

"Duval, ma'am. It will heal."

"I should like to hit him! How dare he!" Apparently having forgotten she herself had struck Jane minutes ago, Mrs. Austen gathered her daughter into her arms. "My poor child. My poor, brave child. Bring my granddaughter home, I beg you. And guard your soul against those wicked creatures."

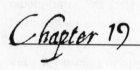

Chapter 19

She had tried to be calm and rational with her family, fearing hysteria or helpless weeping, and she thought she had succeeded, but at a cost to herself. As she left, she pulled the brim of her hat low over her face to hide the tears. She had not dwelled upon the dangers that might lie ahead, moved to pity at the sight of Cassandra's shocked incredulity. They had immense faith in her, her sense and courage, but would those qualities be enough? She wondered when she had stopped being the flighty one, the irresponsible youngest child, and suffered a sea change into becoming a responsible woman.

She wished she could undo these past couple of weeks, don her spinster's cap with pride, and settle herself in the dining room with pen and ink and paper, retreating into the worlds of her own creation. She touched her finger to her hat as she passed the Reverend Papillon, who, prayer book tucked beneath one arm, was doubtless off to perform good works among his (mostly) exasperated parishioners. Papillon raised his hat and looked at her in confusion, almost certainly finding her familiar but not able to identify the strange young gentleman.

She turned into the driveway of the Great House and saw a familiar figure walking toward her. She would know that arrogant, graceful strut anywhere, the tilt of his head, the angle of his hat, the way he swung the walking stick that contained a deadly blade; the features that all these years had haunted her dreams and assembled themselves into the faces of her fictional gentlemen, from the wicked to the virtuous, but never the foolish ones.

Yet she saw how grave his face was as she approached, his usual expression of detached irony replaced with an uncharacteristic seriousness.

He bowed. "I should not embrace you, as much as I should like to, for I see you are in some distress."

"I have spoken with my family."

"William said you would do so. And . . . ?"

"They were not particularly receptive. At first they thought I was mad, and despite my efforts, I think they have little conception of the danger Anna is in."

"And what of your danger?"

She shrugged. "Oh, they think me equal to the task, whatever the task might be. None so capable as Jane, you see. I suppose it comes with donning breeches."

"Did the breeches shock them?"

"More than anything, I think."

They had reached the front door of the Great House, and Luke led her into the Great Hall where the household had gathered. They stood in a silent semicircle around the great stone fireplace, their attention drawn to the box of mahogany and ivory that William held. When he saw her, he placed the box carefully on the mantelpiece and came to greet her.

"I must ask again: You are sure you wish to join us, Jane?"

"I am, sir."

"You are more at risk than any of us. You wish to remain mortal, yet you place yourself among us when passions run high and you are exceptionally vulnerable, ready to hurtle into a metamorphosis. Similarly, you are not so mortal that a graystone knife cannot cause you grievous harm. There is no dishonor in retiring from the fray."

"It would be a great dishonor to me if my niece came to harm, sir."

There was a murmur of approval from the assembled Damned, who certainly valued loyalty among family members.

"I shall fight, sir. You taught me well. But I shall have nothing to do with your knives."

"I should not expect it of you. You were with us at a time of great disorder, when we abandoned many of our proper traditions. Today you will see how these things are done." He smiled at her with great sweetness, but his kindness made her want to weep. This, she was planning to give up, these most perfect friendships with William and Luke, and with Clarissa who came to her side and affectionately tipped the hat from her head.

"What an ill-mannered young sprig you are," she said. "I am glad you are with us, Jane."

She drew Jane aside. William and Luke and Dorcas were deep in conversation, the box taken down from the mantelpiece. "You are not the only one who will not use graystone blades. I shall not. William and Luke must, because of their status among us. Do you want a knife—by that, I mean a regular weapon?"

"What will happen?" Jane asked.

"William has written a formal declaration of hostilities. Tom has delivered it, and we await the response."

"Why not attack them by surprise?" Jane looked at the group of the Damned. "We are equally matched in numbers."

"Because they are the Damned, too. It was different when we fought the French. Those were extraordinary times."

"And these are not?"

"Not yet," Clarissa said. She led Jane to a large wooden box, scarred and dented with a rope handle, and threw its lid open. Inside, knives and swords were piled.

Jane knelt to select a knife, balancing one and then another in her hand, running her thumb across blades. "So there is to be some sort of duel, and then we all fight?"

"More or less. We fight if the duel is inconclusive, and if we are lucky, the graystone knives will serve more as a display of strength than anything else. Proprieties must be observed."

"I see," Jane said, although she had little understanding. She slipped the knife she had chosen inside her boot and loaded her pistols.

The Damned clustered around the box of graystone knives murmured quietly in Greek, William asking each of them a question and receiving a response. Blasphemously, it reminded Jane of Holy Communion, except that instead of bread and wine, each received a knife safely stowed in a small leather sheath, which was strapped to the bearer's wrist on their outer clothing.

"They vow to use the graystone wisely and with respect," Clarissa said. "Each swears fealty to William. They will use the weapons only as a last resort, but chances are the fight between William and Duval will be enough."

"I'm amazed you trust him," Jane said. "He has broken his word once."

"I am concerned that Tom has not returned," Clarissa said, and Jane had the impression that she had spoken out of turn in mentioning Duval's betrayal. Clarissa crossed to the window. "Ah, here he is."

In a few minutes Tom had entered the room and bowed to William.

"The challenge has been accepted. In two hours, and it is to take place on the grounds here."

"Very well." William bowed. "What the devil took you so long?"

Tom smiled. "They offered refreshment. Duval has some remarkably pretty girls there—no, Jane, you need not look at me like that; your niece was not one of them. Duval keeps her to himself by all accounts."

Luke left William and Dorcas and came to Jane's side. "I see you are armed, Jane. When was the last time you fought hand to hand?"

"I regret I have had few opportunities recently, unless wrestling with a particularly tough dinner," Jane said.

"I very much doubt you'll need to fight, but a little practice would not come amiss." Luke unbuckled the leather strap that fastened the graystone knife onto his coat sleeve and laid it reverently aside. He removed his coat and Jane hers.

She gripped the knife, the worn wood smooth against her palm and fingers, the balance fine and true. Her feet took on a fighter's stance before she even realized what she did, light, ready to dart and shift.

The knife clattered onto the floor.

Luke raised his eyebrows as he withdrew a dagger similar to hers from inside his waistcoat. "I trust you won't throw your weapon away so readily."

She shook her head, one hand at her mouth, hoping the pain in her canines would subside. "I did not think that fighting you would cause this. A sudden pain—"

"Pardon my indelicacy, but are you *en sanglant*?"

"No. My teeth are merely sensitive. It takes me by surprise when I least expect it."

"It is to be expected. You and I fought together quite often as I recall. Among other things."

To cover her blush, she lunged for the knife, spun, and aimed low at his belly.

He laughed and pivoted with graceful economy of movement, so her blade whooshed past him.

"I'm rather fond of this waistcoat. I shall have to make sure you do it no damage."

He blocked her next few attacks with very little effort and a cool smile as though mildly entertained by her efforts. She, however, became out of breath and frustrated, until she realized his intent was to irritate her and make her lose her concentration. When he changed to an attack, she was ready, blocking his blow with a clash of blades, ducking and rolling to escape him, and almost succeeded in slashing his hamstrings behind the knee.

A small group of Damned who had gathered to watch offered a thin patter of applause.

"Better," he said.

Their blades met, clashed, slid, jarring her wrist and arm, and she landed with a sudden thump on the floor; damn him, he had caught her off balance and tripped her.

"Not bad," Luke said. "More?"

She looked up at him as he stood over her and considered kicking him, or even biting him—no, not that, and oh, her teeth ached again. She knew he would treat her less gently if they continued, and if he wounded her, she could accept no help or healing from him, for almost certainly his breath on her skin would catapult her into a metamorphosis. And that she could not risk, however much she desired his touch.

She shook her head. "I shall have to take my chances. I think you understand why."

"Of course." He offered her his hand with great courtesy.

She rose without his assistance, knowing she should not risk the touch of his bare hand upon hers, however much she might desire it. And yes, desire made her slow and clumsy as much as a dozen years of trying to forget, trying to behave as befitted a woman of her circumstances. Doubtless he knew how she felt, unless, in a gentlemanly manner, he declined to enter her mind.

She turned away to hide at least her face from him and stowed the weapon in her boot.

"Jane." His hand was on her shoulder, and even with its leather protection, the graystone knife at his cuff wafted a cold breeze against her neck. "I know this is difficult for you. Should you wish to—"

"I thank you for your concern. I have become somewhat irritated at being told that I do not know my own mind; I daresay it is no more than most women suffer, but I find it reprehensible."

"Of course." He bowed. "It is an honor to have you join us once more, Jane."

"You need not worry that I shall endanger anyone with my lack of strength or practice. I have learned some prudence over the years."

Luke bowed and excused himself, saying that he and William must talk some more.

"I expect they talk of a succession, should . . ." Clarissa, still clad in women's clothes, ran her thumb over the blade of one of the steel knives. "I must change into men's clothes. Will you and Dorcas come with me? We can dine—that is, we can take refreshment, if you like."

"Certainly." She doubted she would be able to eat, but she knew it was best to remove herself from Luke's disturbing presence. She went upstairs with the two women, and they passed some time drinking tea and admiring a new gown Dorcas had acquired, while Clarissa changed into coat and breeches.

"Will Luke succeed if . . . if things go badly with William?" Jane asked.

"Almost certainly. There has been friction between them, but a leader must by nature take a contrary path sometimes," Clarissa said. "It is likely that the fighting today will be more formality than anything else."

Dorcas said nothing, but Jane noticed her place her fingertips on the leather sheath that held her graystone knife, as though it could determine a good outcome to the fight.

Jane submitted herself to having her hair tied back, her coat and hat brushed, and her boots removed and handed to the footman who brought her a plate of cold meat and bread. Grumbling, Clarissa tied Jane's neckcloth, complaining that if she were not so prudish, Luke would do a far superior job. The footman returned the boots, now sporting a high sheen.

Clarissa, murmuring that she had another task for the footman, left the bedchamber with him, returning after a quarter hour with shining eyes and a general air of satisfaction that Jane recognized. The scent of a healthy young man hung around her.

"I suppose you did not leave any for me?" Dorcas inquired.

"I regret not. I recommend Peter."

"That *was* Peter."

"How can I tell? They all look the same in livery," Clarissa said.

"Or out of it, I daresay," Jane murmured.

"I suppose I shall have to go downstairs and find something for myself," Dorcas said after tugging the bellpull several times without receiving a response. "It's so difficult to find good help these days."

Jane nibbled at a piece of bread, knowing she should eat but lacking appetite. The possibility that the duel, or however the Damned wished to refer to it, might be more than a formality and escalate to real fighting and destruction weighed heavy upon her mind. What if she could not rescue Anna? And how would things change with her mother and sister and Martha now that they knew the truth about her?

A knock on the door interrupted her thoughts, and Clarissa bade whomever it was to enter.

Raphael stood in the doorway. "It is time, ladies."

"Do you join us, sir?" Jane asked.

"I must. He is my brother and my Creator. I suppose everyone has drummed the dangers of your actions into your ears?"

"Yes. I am mightily sick of it. I am well aware of the risks, as indeed you must be."

He bowed. "Come, then."

He led them downstairs and outside the house to one of the meadows dotted with ancient oak trees. William, with Luke close at hand, and the others stood beneath the spreading branches of one tree. Dorcas and Clarissa joined them, and Jane and Raphael stood a little apart, as though in agreement that they were not quite participants, but not merely onlookers.

Duval and his followers stood beneath another tree.

It was a fine late spring day, a slight breeze ruffling the new green leaves of the trees and rippling the grass of the meadow. Skylarks sang, invisible, above in a blue sky.

"They have chosen blades," Raphael said to Jane.

William and Duval, sure enough, drew rapiers and walked forward to meet between the two groups. They had removed their coats and thus the graystone knives each had strapped to the outside of their sleeves.

"How can immortals fight a duel to a conclusive end?" Jane asked as the combatants saluted.

"Whoever bloodies the other a third time in succession wins. It's rather like tennis." Raphael gave a tense smile. "They can hardly decapitate each other with those weapons."

Rather more like a chess match or a dance, as the two Damned stepped, parried, thrust. The onlookers applauded occasionally at particularly elegant moves, and then Duval's followers gave a shout as a spot of blood appeared and spread on William's arm. The pace quickened, William driving Duval back—his household broke apart to give the duelists more room, and then gathered again.

"Bravo!" Raphael said. "See, Jane, he caught Duval on the right thigh. So they're even now."

The fight intensified, the blades flashing in the sunlight, and with more intent now, the two of them moving this way or that. Most of the onlookers were *en sanglant,* aroused by the blood. It was so very different from the fighting Jane had learned, the ungentlemanly, informal attacks against a human enemy in skirmishes and ambushes.

Beside her, Raphael grimaced and raised a hand to his own mouth, a gesture Jane recognized.

William and Duval separated, rapiers pointing down.

"What's happening?" Jane asked.

"They've agreed to take a few minutes' rest," Raphael replied. "They exchanged a signal but a few seconds ago."

William returned to Luke's side. They spoke together briefly, and Luke breathed on the wound on William's arm to stanch it. A footman offered the two combatants wine, and William drained his glass and placed the empty vessel on the tray. This time Jane saw the small gesture he made to Duval to continue, and the duel resumed.

The sun lowered in the sky and still the fight continued, with an occasional break, the grass stamped flat and releasing its scent, along with that of vampire blood, upon the air.

"They're well matched," Raphael said. "Why the devil does he not use his superior strength? He has a longer reach than Duval, too. He may seek to tire him. Sometimes my brother is more subtle than wise."

"What will happen when darkness falls?" Jane asked.

"They will continue, although they will probably stop to dine. William will have to play host."

"That's ridiculous!" Jane said, made uneasy by the possibility that she would be beneath the roof of the Great House while the Damned took their pleasure.

Duval fell back, blood spreading upon his arm, and William lunged in to prick him on the thigh.

"Two cuts!" Raphael said. "Follow him, William, take him—"

But Duval recovered, rallied, and slashed at William's face, laying open his face to the bone. Blood spread and dripped onto his shirt.

"Not altogether gentlemanly," Raphael commented. "Now they become serious."

Duval stepped back and made a gesture with his free hand, but William shook his head, refusing a break, and now his fighting changed: still as graceful, but more deadly, with more speed. He drove Duval back and to the side.

Raphael grinned. "Ah, he attempts to position Duval facing the sun. Better, William." He grabbed Jane's arm and pulled her aside as the fighters neared them, close enough for them to hear the fast breathing, the pounding footfalls, and to see blood fly from William's cheek.

William's blade darted and flashed, raising two crimson splotches on Duval's shirt, on shoulder and upper arm.

Duval stepped back, missed his footing, and fell, his rapier dropping from his hand.

"Duval may concede," Raphael said.

William bowed and lowered his blade, waiting with the greatest courtesy for his opponent to rise.

Duval reached for his rapier and half rose, as though his ankle was wrenched. A low murmur issued from the onlookers. A wrench or sprain, for one of the Damned, was not something that could be cured instantaneously, the damage having taken place beneath the skin. Although it would heal faster than a similar injury to a mortal, this could mean that the fight, and therefore Anna's rescue, would be delayed.

William stepped back, his rapier pointed down, and bowed again. Had some sort of agreement passed between them?

Duval rose to one knee and sprang from his kneeling position at William. He was armed; even in the sunlight the small blade he wrenched from his boot was dull, deadly, the color of dust. He struck William's breast.

William took a step backward. His step faltered, and his rapier fell from his hand and rolled onto the grass. He sank to one knee, a hand at his breast, and Jane remembered the deadly chill, the weakness she had felt.

Luke rushed to his side and supported him.

"Treachery!" Raphael ran forward to join them, tears running down his face. "My brother!"

Duval stood, the small weapon in his hand, a triumphant smile upon his face.

For a moment the Damned were frozen in place, before weapons were drawn, blades that glittered in the sunlight. Jane did not look to see if any were also prepared to use their graystone knives. She drew a pistol, cocked it, her movements smooth as silk, her mind as detached as though she watched herself from a distance.

The Damned stood poised, as though awaiting an order, although William's household drew close around their fallen leader.

She aimed, pulled the trigger, and heard Duval's curse as the hand that held the graystone knife exploded in a flurry of blood and bone. He staggered, but recovered, and hurtled toward Jane, *en sanglant*.

She saw the murderous look in his eye and knew he intended to rip her throat out. Her hands shook as she pulled and cocked the second pistol, and then he was upon her, with the strength and fierceness of an ancient vampire at the height of his powers.

Pain ripped through her jaw.

The world shook in a dazzle of brightness.

The trigger—steel, a forge, brightness, fire, the hiss of red hot metal plunged into water—she threw off the sensations, aimed, and fired.

Duval fell back, a dark hole in his forehead, destroyed and sent to hell by Jane's hand.

Chapter 20

Jane dropped to her knees, her hands upon the grass, and the slow strength and quest of the roots of plants and trees flowed into her palms.

I am Damned.

"Take care!" Someone grabbed her shoulder, pulling her upright into a tumult of anger and blood and clashing blades. Clarissa, her face streaked with blood, grasped her arm and pulled her aside.

Jane stumbled, her limbs clumsy, senses overwhelmed. She reached for the knife in her boot, but the leather and the wood of the hilt came alive at her touch, a confusion of sensation. She drew her hand away.

"No, you must not fight," Clarissa said, and she turned to slash at one of Duval's followers who leaped at them. He retreated, blood welling from his arm, his coat ripped. "You are too new, too weak."

Dorcas joined Clarissa, the two of them fending off any of Duval's followers who approached. Jane sank to the ground again and wept, overcome with confusion and grief, while the sounds of battle died away.

"Jane." Luke's voice was quiet, his touch on her shoulder a comfort. "It is done. It is over. Come."

She stood and clung to him. She was *en sanglant,* her teeth sensitive and aching, and hungry. All she could smell was blood, Duval's, William's, sharp and fresh; and then the particular scent of Luke, dark and heady and arousing.

She raised her hand to her mouth in an attempt to get her teeth under control. "I am Damned."

"You must speak with William. There is little time."

William lay on Raphael's shoulder; Raphael covered with blood, and *en sanglant,* weeping.

She fell to her knees at William's side and took his hand, chill and heavy in hers. "I am sorry," she choked out.

"No, you should not apologize. I was never a true Creator to you and I am sorry for it."

"What shall I do now?" Tears ran down her cheeks.

"Luke is your Bearleader. My successor. He will do what is necessary now we have fought. I have asked for clemency for you."

"Why should I need clemency? But what of you? Is there nothing we can do?"

He smiled. "Dear Jane. Do not forget me. I know you wish to return your niece to her family, but stay here until I am gone. Yet first I must speak to my other fledglings alone."

She withdrew into the care of Clarissa and Dorcas who sat with her, grave and silent. They offered their wrists but she shook her head; she knew she should dine, as weak and shaken as she was, but she longed for Luke's blood.

Luke and Raphael looked up to glance at her at one point:

she could not see into their minds, but she knew they spoke of her. Her feelings of foreboding increased. Why should she need clemency?

One of Duval's followers joined them, kneeling by William's side.

"That is Charlotte. She is Duval's successor," Clarissa said.

Charlotte and Luke stood, bowed, and exchanged a formal kiss. A brief conversation followed, and Jane caught the name of her niece in their exchange.

"They will negotiate peace," Dorcas said. "But William has asked that Charlotte return your niece, and she has agreed."

"I cannot leave William," Jane said. "But I must fetch her from Prowtings."

The two women looked at each other, and Jane had the strong impression they held a private conversation.

"All in good time," Clarissa said. "She is in no danger now."

The two groups of the Damned stayed with their fallen leaders until sunset. Jane was summoned again to William's side. Jane was aware of a silent conversation that continued among the three men, as though they spoke in a far-off room, and she caught the occasional fragment of a word.

So absorbed had she been in her own grief and bewilderment at her state of Damnation, the fight to throw off random sensations and keep her mind clear, and her growing hunger, that she had barely noticed nightfall or the preparations for William and Duval.

Two funeral pyres now stood in the meadow, and footmen moved among the company with wine. Stanchions held torches, and flames were reflected in the eyes of the Damned, the darkness of the wine.

William stirred and spoke. "Burn the knives also. One should be kept for each household. That is all."

His hand slipped from Luke's.

Luke bent to breathe into his Creator's mouth, trying to bring him back, but raised his head, tears spilling from his eyes. "He is gone."

He stood and embraced Raphael and Jane. "You must take some sustenance, for you are both little better than new fledglings yet."

He called for wine and bit into his wrist, allowing a generous amount to fall into the glass.

Jane drank and passed the glass to Raphael. "When did it happen for you?"

He knew what she meant. "When I saw William fall. I wished to avenge him. I wish that task had not fallen upon you and that you do not have to suffer the consequences." Tears ran down his face.

"What consequences?" she said. "William said something to me of asking for clemency. Is that what he referred to?"

He shook his head. "It is too much to bear," he said. "He was my brother. My Creator. Now I shall lose everything I hold dear."

The household crowded around to lift William's body and carry it to the funeral pyre. Duval lay already on the other. The air was sharp with the scents of myrrh and other spices Jane did not recognize, and perfumed oil poured liberally over the wood.

Luke and Charlotte took flaming torches and set them to the wood. As the wood caught fire, the Damned crowded to unbuckle the graystone knives on their sleeves and throw them into the flames. Charlotte and Luke were the only ones who remained armed, and they each unbuckled their knives in a formal display.

The graystone sent great blue flames shooting from the heart of the fire, consuming the corpses and wood. Smoke obscured the stars and moon, for it was now night, yet as the flames subsided into a fiery glow Jane was surprised to see a lightening of the sky toward the east.

She approached Luke, who stood alone, hands clasped beneath his coattail. "It is almost dawn, sir."

He shook his head. "I never thought to see the sun rise on a day when he was not with me."

"I must fetch my niece and say farewell to my family."

"You will return to the Great House then. You will need to dine and you must be there, for there is a particular matter we must deal with."

"Of course." She longed to take his hand or embrace him, to offer comfort. Did she not grieve, too, for a Creator who had but recently acknowledged her? "What is this matter you speak of, Luke?"

He did not reply, but unbuttoned his coat, flung it away, and unfastened his cuff. He presented his wrist. "You will need strength for what you have to do with your niece. She must not remember too much of what has happened—do you understand?"

"I—" But she was not thinking of Anna, she was thinking of the luxury of his blood, taking his wrist in her hand and biting, penetrating his skin, taking him; an act of love and longing and need. His breath caught and his other hand caressed her head as she drank from him and tasted the sweetness and sadness his blood offered. But it was not the gesture of a lover, for he had withdrawn from her, engulfed in grief.

She cleaned and breathed the small wound closed, wishing for more, and feeling almost drunk with the power of his blood. She rebuttoned his cuff. "I shall return, sir."

"Yes," he said. "You must. Honor demands it." He leaned to kiss her forehead as he might that of a companion in battle.

She walked away from him as the night turned into day and the funeral pyres became gray ash. The Damned straggled back to the Great House, and a tentative piping from a bird brought the dawn chorus to life and awoke the day.

Prowtings was deserted when Jane arrived, no smoke from an early morning kitchen fire rising from the chimneys, and the front door unlocked. She pushed it open and called out, fearing that some of *les Sales* had been left to guard it.

Dining room and drawing room were empty, with the remains of dinner on the table. Jane took a glass and an open bottle of wine—it would be stale but serve the purpose well enough—and went upstairs.

After tapping upon several doors and finding the bedchambers deserted, she found one where a sleepy voice bid her enter.

Anna, pale and languorous, lay in a four-poster bed, in a room that clearly she had shared with Duval.

"Oh," she said, too weak to show much surprise, "it is you, Aunt Jane. I have been having such strange dreams. Terrible dreams."

Of course she would, poor child, having taken some of Duval's blood and thus finding herself linked to him.

"Good morning," Jane said as cheerily as she could. "I've come to get you out of bed."

"It is rather early, is it not? I feel so strange and tired."

"This will set you up tolerably well." Jane bit into her wrist and dribbled some blood into the glass, adding in some wine. She swirled the glass to mix it.

Anna blinked. "Duval would do that . . . Where is he, Aunt?"

Jane handed her the glass and looked into her niece's eyes. "I am glad you have had a tolerable stay with your new friends. It is time for you to return home now. You spent your time here with the other ladies walking in the garden and playing upon their pianoforte, and there was dancing in the evenings. Duval was a dreadful flirt, but you are not in love with him."

"Yes, Aunt." Anna took the glass from Jane and drank.

Jane kicked a few articles of clothing that must have belonged to Duval beneath the bed and collected Anna's garments together.

Anna had a little more energy now, and Jane helped her dress.

"Why is there a pair of gentleman's boots here?" Anna asked.

"Oh, the servants must have put them in this bedchamber by mistake. Apparently they were not very efficient." Jane tried to ignore the scents of blood and lust that lay heavy around the room. "Come, I need you to help with breakfast at home."

Anna gazed at her, a perplexed expression on her face. "I—there is so much I cannot remember. Were you not here earlier? I remember your asking me to come home and help with breakfast another time. Have I been unwell?"

"You're better now," Jane said.

"And why are you dressed like a gentleman? There is something else, now, too. What has happened to you?"

"I'll explain when we are home," Jane said.

During the short walk over the fields to the cottage, Anna darted quick, uncertain glances at Jane. Once, she stopped.

"Something terrible has happened to Duval." Jane was about to deny it, when Anna added, "And to you, too, Aunt. You are so very strange and pale."

"I shall explain all when we are home," Jane said. Home. She no longer had a home, not in any sense Anna would recognize.

They entered the cottage by the back door, and Jacques the pug flew out to greet Anna, barking wildly, although when he saw Jane, he growled and lurked protectively at his mistress's feet. Cassandra followed close behind. She looked as though she had been awake all night, and in tears.

"Anna! You are safe." She embraced her niece. "Come, my dear. We'll have tea in the parlor."

"Cassandra, I—"

But Cassandra looked at her fearfully. Now she knew, and when Jane followed her into the parlor, she saw her mother flinch away from her.

"I'll not harm you," Jane said.

"I wish I could believe you," Cassandra said. She put a protective arm around Anna. "Oh, tell me—the truth, I beg of you—that you did not use this child?"

What did they think she was? Was she not still their beloved Jane?—but she was changed now, rapidly becoming a stranger to them. She ignored her hurt and anger and answered Cassandra as calmly as she could. "I did not."

"Aunt Jane came to bring me home," Anna said. "They left me there alone, and I . . ." She shook her head. "I really cannot remember."

"You must see how I am changed," Jane said to her mother. "I have come to say farewell. Ma'am, I beg that you try to think well of me."

"I am shamed," Mrs. Austen said. "Our family is shamed that you should succumb to the lures of those wicked creatures, Jane!"

Her words struck Jane like daggers, but it was the vampire in her that made a cool and rational reply, even as she knew she would never see her mother again. "I assure you, ma'am, it was not my choice. I have prayed that this would not happen, but circumstances were against me. I would have given anything—anything!—to have remained mortal." *Anything except my writing, which I may have lost now, too.*

"I wish I could believe you," her mother said.

"What—what happens now?" Cassandra said.

"You offer me a cup of tea," Jane said.

"Oh, I beg your pardon. Yes, of course." Cassandra handed her a cup that rattled upon the saucer, spilling tea.

"I don't understand," Anna said, glancing at her aunts and grandmother in turn. "What have you done, Aunt Jane?"

"My dear," Jane said, "I have become one of the Damned and must shortly take my leave of you."

"But—but you can't be!" Anna cried. "Aunt Cassandra, ma'am, tell her she may not go!"

"I regret it is so," Jane said. She put her half-drunk cup of tea down and buried her face in her hands. She would lose them all, lose Anna; never see Anna become the extraordinary woman she could be and not see her other nieces and nephews grow up. And she would lose Cassandra, beloved Cassandra.

She looked up and saw them staring at her, confused, fearful, angry. "Pity me," she said. "Have pity on me. William is dead. My Creator is dead."

"You will be lost to us," Mrs. Austen said. "And do you intend to resume your liaison with Mr. Venning?"

"I wonder it concerns you at all, ma'am, since you consider me a thoroughly depraved creature by my own choice. I do assure you I have an eternity in which to break the Ten Commandments should I wish, but I believe in that particular matter it is the gentleman's decision." She thought again of Luke, remote in his grief; time would tell, she supposed, and time was all, everything, she had. Forever stretched ahead of her, barren, hopeless.

"We shall never see you again?" Cassandra asked.

"It is probably for the best." She held out her hand and Cassandra took it; she wished she had not, receiving a wild storm of anger and misery from her sister. "My dear, there are some manuscripts I have been working on; you must do with them as you see fit, and also the one the publisher holds to ransom. I have little enough else to give you. You and Anna may have my jewelry and my music. My worldly goods are few, I fear. And Martha—where is she?"

But as she spoke, Martha rushed into the room and flung herself into Jane's arms. "I shall never forget you, my dearest friend!"

"Nor I you. Pray have my silk stockings; you regard them as yours, anyway, and my books."

"What happened at the Great House last night?" Martha said. "They say there were great blue flames shooting into the sky and the villagers thought it something from the Book of Revelation."

"They were almost right. William is gone. And so is Duval."

"Oh, Jane!" Martha produced a handkerchief and dabbed at the tears on Jane's cheeks.

"Where has Duval gone?" Anna said.

"He has gone to a warmer climate."

"It is no laughing matter!" Mrs. Austen said.

"Ma'am, either I laugh or I weep. You are impervious to my tears, yet I must not laugh; what do you expect of me?" Jane stood. "But you have little enough time to dwell on the matter for I must leave. Think well of me, if you can, ma'am. I beg you to remember only happier times. Cassandra, will you kiss me good-bye?"

Cassandra gave her a quick, shamed kiss.

Anna embraced Jane. "You're so cold, Aunt. Will I truly never see you again?"

"I fear not." She kissed her niece's sweet delicate cheek. "Pray give your father my love."

Anna burst into tears and ran from the room.

"I'll come to see you." Martha gathered her in a fierce embrace. "I shall tell you how everyone does. Dear Jane, this need not be so final as you think."

"It must be. I shall lose the human qualities that make me

your daughter, sister, friend. Pray do not seek me out, but remember me, I beg of you. Forgive me, dearest friend."

She cast one last, agonized glance at her mother and gently pushed Martha away. She stood for a moment in the ordinary, comfortable drawing room she would never see again: the music she had copied stood on the instrument, and the volume of Cowper from which they had read aloud only a few nights ago lay on a small table. On the sofa someone's sewing lay in a tumbled heap, a project she would never see completed. Cassandra sat weeping, with Martha standing bewildered in the middle of the room.

Her mother looked resolutely away, her face like stone.

Jane let herself out of the front door of the cottage, pulling her hat low over her face once more, and set off for the Great House. Thus she had left the house the last time, thinking that nothing could be as painful as the revelation of her true nature to her family.

She could not reach out to Luke. She suspected he was immersed in a grief for William so deep she had no understanding of it, for to her William had been an imperfect Creator for a brief time. What comfort could she offer Luke?

The funeral pyres smoldered still in the meadow, a group of her brother Edward's tenants standing on the driveway and speculating what those great bonfires could mean, with the blue flames that had illuminated the trees almost as bright as day. They took no notice of her as she passed.

As she approached the Great House her uneasiness intensified. What was expected of her now, and why, as William lay dying, had he negotiated clemency for her? She had so much to learn among the Damned, and although once she had been one of them and Luke's Consort, now Luke's status had changed; everything was different.

The front door opened as she approached. Inside, Luke waited.

He bowed. "Your niece is well, I trust?"

"Thank you, yes. She is—she is safe now." She could not say the words *at home* or *with my family;* the wounds were still too fresh.

She stepped toward him. "How do you do, Luke?"

"Well enough, ma'am, I thank you."

Two members of the Damned emerged from the doorway that led to the Great Hall; she recognized them as Charlotte's followers.

"We ask that you give up your weapons," Luke said.

For heaven's sake; what damage could she possibly do any of them with a pair of unloaded pistols and a knife? And why was Luke so formal and distant with her? She handed over the weapons to the other two vampires.

"You must come with us," one of them said.

"Why?" She turned to Luke. "Forgive me, but will you not tell me what is the matter? Of what am I accused?"

Luke took her hands. His touch was gentle but held a hint of steel. "Jane, you are to go on trial for the destruction of Duval."

"What! After he killed William?"

"There were protocols that should have been observed. They were not."

No use to argue that she had no knowledge of protocol or rules, that Luke should have warned her. He was in her mind, finally, now, speaking of love and regret and sorrow. But he said aloud to her, so the others might hear, "I must do this, Jane, however much it goes against my heart, to establish a lasting peace. There has been too much destruction and sorrow."

"I understand, sir." *You act as a leader, not a lover.*

Precisely. I am sorry for it.

"I, too," she said aloud and let herself be led away.

Chapter 21

"I have to stay in here all day?" Jane said, outraged.

"Luke thought you would be comfortable here," one of her captors said.

He fell silent as her fangs extended. She looked around the bedchamber, which was quite pretty and cheerful with its chintz curtains and matching bed hangings, and saw it as a dungeon, a prison, for she would be alone.

"What am I supposed to do here?"

The two members of the Damned looked at each other, uneasy. "We can send in a footman if you—"

"Or there's some books," the other one said. "And wine."

"Thank you. I wish for nothing." They were trying their best, after all. She was not yet far advanced enough in her metamorphosis that the idea of a footman presenting himself to her did not fill her with embarrassment. She wasn't even sure if she hungered, for all was unfamiliar to her now; she could not distinguish appetite from her general feeling of disorder. Although she hated to admit it, she needed her Bearleader; she wanted his presence, his scent, the soothing tones of his voice, even though he was the one who had ordered her imprisonment and trial.

All of this produced a restlessness, a compulsion to move. She paced, peering out of the windows to see if the daylight faded, for she longed for soft, voluptuous darkness that would enfold her like a lover's arms. But the sun shone with resolute cheer, slanting through the windows and setting dust motes afloat in the air.

She glanced at the door. Was it locked?

She strode across the carpeted floor and forced herself not to try the door handle, for to do so would be an admission of weakness. Besides, whether it was locked or not was immaterial; she could scent the two who had brought her to the bedchamber standing guard outside and hear a soft rumble of voices. A flirtatious female voice joined in with a giggle, a pulse beating fast with excitement and anticipation.

Her jailers were about to dine.

Jane pressed her back against the door, shoulder blades against the painted wood, and clasped her hands in front of her so she would not be tempted to fling open or break down the door. On the other side cotton slithered against skin, layers of fabric slid and bunched, buttons were eased undone. A coat landed on the floor with a thud.

The woman gave a gasp of desire and fear mixed, her scent becoming ripe and luxurious. One of the men murmured softly to her. He was pushing her hair aside, a fragrant curtain, as he sought her neck.

And the other—his boots creaked as he knelt before her to dine on that most favored and intimate location at her thigh.

Jane closed her eyes. This was obscene, terrifying—for would not she become as they? What if they opened the door and invited her to join? She doubted she would hesitate.

The small punch of fangs against skin released the delicious scent of blood made heady by arousal, and the woman cried out, the sound of someone who experienced great delight or a surprising pain. Her nails scratched on the plaster wall; she sought purchase as her legs weakened with shock and pleasure.

The one who knelt at her feet laughed and took her weight with arms and shoulder, releasing a gust of her scent, and then resumed his dining. All was pleasure and gratification, a dark brilliance of blood and completion.

Jane rushed across the room to the washstand. She grasped the ewer with unsteady hands, poured water into the bowl, and plunged her face into its cool depths. She straightened and made the mistake of viewing her reflection, or what was left of it, in the mirror that stood atop the washstand; nothing but a blurred, ragged hint of her image.

She moaned aloud with horror and need, and sank to her knees, water dripping onto her shirt, her face in her hands, and wept.

When next she looked up, the light had changed, becoming softer and dimmer, and the glow from the windows was muted. She got to her feet and removed her coat, shirt, and neckcloth, and this time washed her face with the herb-scented soap in a china dish on the washstand. She rolled the soap in her hands, watching bubbles form and burst; she could take as long as she wanted to wash her face, or to do anything else she wished, for did not eternity stretch before her?

The door clicked open as she patted her face dry. It was Luke—she knew before even she saw him—but her delight was dimmed by what the remnants of her humanity recognized as betrayal. Her next reaction, that of a respectable spinster, was that she was half naked, but she would not let him see her shame; she could not bear mockery from him. Her physical metamorphosis might well be complete, but Miss Jane Austen had not yet cast aside her human emotions.

He bowed and opened a drawer in a dresser, and another, and produced a clean shirt and neckcloth for her. "I trust you have been well looked after?"

"I asked to be left alone and your jailers obliged."

He nodded and tossed a clean pair of drawers and a pair of stockings onto the bed. "I can send for hot water if you wish to bathe."

She shook her head. "Thank you, but what I really wish is to know what is going on and what heinous crime I have committed."

He crossed to the table where a decanter of wine and two glasses stood. Pouring wine, he said, "You killed Duval. It was not your place to do so, nor were your weapons proper."

"And ignorance, of course, is no protection against the law of the Damned."

He nodded and handed her a glass of wine. "My preference would be to treat it as the indiscretion of a young fledgling, for if you had not killed Duval, certainly I, or one of my choosing, would have done so. But Charlotte thinks otherwise, and as the leader of this household I understand her wish to abide by the letter of the law. We have had misrule; now we wish for peace and order."

"So what happens?"

He stood with his back to her, looking out of the window, and she slipped the clean shirt over her head.

"Take off your boots," he said without turning.

"I beg your pardon?"

"They need to be polished." He nodded toward a bootjack in the corner of the room. "There will be a trial. You need to look your best, for witnesses will attest to your character. I of course cannot oblige, for I am too close to you. I am sorry for it. I have spent the day talking to others who will testify on your behalf."

"And if I am found guilty?"

"The knife or exile."

She realized then the full horror of being cast out; she would have nowhere to go, no friends, no connections, no family among either the Austens or the Damned. "So I contemplate a slow descent to hell or a fast one?"

"I would do anything in the world to prevent either," he said. "Anything, that is, but compromise the honor of this household and the possibility of peace." He took her boots and carried them to the door. The simple act of putting boots outside for a servant to collect, polish, and return made the situation even more bizarre, like some hideous parody of everyday life.

"When will this take place?"

"Tonight. Before we dine." He gazed out of the window again, his frame expressing unease. "You will need to keep up your strength. I fear for you, so recently created once more. We must proceed with caution."

"Indeed. You have a nice plump servant in mind for me?" Despite her sarcastic tone, she became *en sanglant* and raised her hand to her mouth.

"Indeed no. I was suggesting nothing of the sort. In your relatively inexperienced condition, you'd probably reduce that nice plump servant to a weakened shell and still hunger for more. You need someone who can temper your hunger and help you curb your passions. If you will have me, Jane, I think it might be best."

"Best for whom?" Her fangs shot forth once more. This time she did not bother to hide them, and when he turned back to her, she saw he was also roused. "It is most good of you, sir, to offer."

"Good of me! I think not." He advanced upon her, beautiful, dangerous, as desirable as she remembered. "The leader in me insists that justice be done, but I—your Bearleader, your Consort, your lover—I want you, Jane. I want you with me forever."

She stepped back. "You may offer me eternity, but in this case it is not yours to grant."

"Then I offer you what I can in this moment. My blood. My love." He sank to his knees before her and, with a burst of shame, she thought of the vampire outside her bedchamber offering and taking pleasure.

He pressed the side of his face against her knee. "I know. The poor girl could barely stand after, but I do not think she had any regrets."

"You knew?" Of course he did, just as she had known. "I trust you did not arrange that charming episode to take place outside the bedchamber door to whet my appetite?"

"And did it whet your appetite? I see it did, from the brightness of your eyes. You hunger, Jane. Do not deny yourself. Do not deny me." He tipped his head up to gaze at her, *en sanglant*.

"I should refuse you. I do not think you have entirely forgiven me for leaving you."

He laughed. "And you want my forgiveness? Now?"

"No. Not now." The past came rushing back as she reached for his neckcloth and tugged it loose, revealing the perfect column of his throat, and then the present overwhelmed her memories.

"First you are my dinner, then my lover, and now my valet," Jane said.

"Pray hold your tongue. This is serious business." Luke knotted her cravat and stepped back to admire his work. "Now turn. I must brush your coat. I wish you and I were going out to hunt the French, Jane, instead of what we must do."

"I, too." She sighed. "Luke, if I am found innocent, what then?"

He looked away. "You were—are—my Consort."

"You do not sound entirely comfortable with the idea."

"We shall talk later."

"I suppose I should think we have all of eternity to squabble and patch up our differences," she said.

He did not reply but straightened her waistcoat and gave her an approving nod. "We gather in the Great Hall. Let us go."

They went downstairs and into the room, which was occupied by a great number of the Damned. Other households in the area must have heard of the duel and its outcome and come to see the spectacle, a thought that did not cheer Jane particularly. There were even some of *les Sales,* their desperation temporarily soothed by Luke's hospitality, identifiable by their poor clothing.

The rest of the Damned were dressed for the evening, the men in coats and knee breeches, and the women in graceful gowns and flashing jewels.

"It is not merely vulgar curiosity that so many are gathered," Luke said, probing her mind to her annoyance. "This is something of importance to all, that we get this matter settled and are able to live at peace."

Jane held her head high and was glad for her clean linen and polished boots. She might be considered a criminal, but she would not act as one. Memories of the shameful episode concerning her Aunt Leigh-Perrott flooded her mind; the whispers and evasion, the well-meaning attempts of the Austens to pretend one of their family had never been accused of theft, stood trial, and risked transportation. Far worse prospects than Botany Bay lay ahead for Jane if things went wrong.

Luke led her to Charlotte, who stood at the great fireplace, wineglass in hand. She was dressed with great elegance in an ivory gown trimmed with ermine, a large paste comb in her dark hair.

Charlotte nodded at Jane with little interest and addressed Luke. "We should proceed."

She tapped the wineglass she held with a heavy, bejeweled ring, and the room fell silent at the insistent high chime that resulted. Charlotte sat in a heavy chair by the fireplace, and Luke, after giving Jane an encouraging smile, took his place among the other Damned. Some stood; some sat in chairs clustered together. Jane was not offered a chair.

Charlotte spoke. Jane had never seen a woman address a room so, particularly a room where both men and women gathered, or with such assurance; she reminded herself that she, too, must be prepared to speak rationally and clearly when the time came.

"This is Jane. Though recently created, she was one of us before having taken the Cure. She stands before us accused of destroying one of our kind, Duval, with improper weapons and with no authority. The penalty will be the knife or banishment. Jane, you may speak."

Jane took a deep breath. "I am aware that ignorance is no defense, so I shall not dwell upon my lack of knowledge of laws and customs. I was one of the Damned for only a short time when the French invaded, and I believe I acquitted myself well then. My second metamorphosis took place as William, my Creator, was killed. You may ask yourself what any of you would have done in such circumstances. I gave Duval the justice he deserved for his treachery, and I do not regret it."

There was a short silence. Charlotte said, "Thank you. Who will speak on Jane's behalf?"

"I shall." Clarissa pushed her way through the crowd and dropped Charlotte a slight curtsy. "My name is Clarissa Venning. I knew Jane in Bath when she was first created one of the Damned. She fought bravely against the French and was captured but did not betray us. I regret that she left us for her mortal family. She had the promise of great powers, but she was taught little of etiquette or correct behavior in those times; you may remember how things were. We all thought most highly of her, ma'am."

"Thank you." Charlotte sounded dispassionate, almost bored. "Is there another character witness?"

"If I may, ma'am." Raphael came forward. He bowed to them, and Jane noticed Charlotte frown slightly. "I too have undergone a second metamorphosis following the Cure. We shared the same Creator. Had she not acted as she did, I would have taken the responsibility. Jane is—"

"You need continue no more," Charlotte said. "I believe you work on a new cure, a most unnatural and abhorrent practice. It is also clear to me that you desire this woman, and as such your evidence is not trustworthy."

"Very well, ma'am." Raphael bowed deeply to Jane and made a shallow, mocking bow to Charlotte.

At the side of the room Luke became *en sanglant,* and Raphael returned his snarl.

Tom offered a brief and graceful endorsement of Jane's virtues, which Charlotte dismissed with a casual wave of her hand and the comment that he did not know Jane at all as one of the Damned.

"Your family, Jane Austen. What of them?" Charlotte asked. "From whom are you descended?"

"My father was a clergyman, the descendant of a respectable family that has lived in these parts for some generations. I have brothers in the law and the Navy and—"

"Middling folk." The contempt showed on Charlotte's face. It was a matter of pride among the Damned that most of them, or so they claimed, were descendants of great and noble families, even royalty. She addressed the room again. "Before I pass sentence, is there anyone else who wishes to speak on this woman's behalf?"

"I do, ma'am."

The redheaded woman strode to the front of the room, her gauzy green gown flowing behind her. She ignored Jane and curtsied to Charlotte.

Jane glanced at Luke, but he met her gaze with indifference.

So she was doomed by her birth and the woman who had betrayed her once before. Luke's attempts to find a character witness had failed, and there was little he could do now. She forced herself to stand upright and keep her expression calm.

Chapter 22

Charlotte looked at Margaret, eyebrows raised. She must surely know the history of Luke and Margaret, and how Jane had been Margaret's rival.

"Proceed." Charlotte fingered the heavy jewels at her throat.

"I am Margaret. I met Jane in Bath in '97. She was there to take the Cure and so was I, for I had left the Damned and my former Consort, Luke. After twenty years, my mortal husband wished for a reunion and an heir, and I thought that was what I wanted. Jane took me to Luke, for she wished to fight the French, as did I, and I feared I should not survive the Cure and that my death as a mortal was close. But Luke, though he revived me and accepted me back into the household, no longer loved me. He loved her. She fought bravely against the French to whom I betrayed her."

A small gasp ran around the room.

"I was discovered. William asked Jane to make the judgment, and she chose that I should be banished. She thought it more merciful than the knife."

Charlotte nodded. "So she did you a great wrong."

"Not at all, ma'am, if you refer to that judgment. Some survive banishment, and I did not become *sale*. I was fortunate. As to the rest, I learned a bitter lesson, that I could not pursue one who loved me no more. I suffered enough that I knew I would never betray one of my own kind again, particularly over a gentleman." She glanced across the room at Luke, and they exchanged the ironic, rueful smiles of former lovers who knew each other too well. "But that is nothing to do with this court. She is an honorable woman, ma'am. She longed to return to her mortal family, which she did at great cost, for in so doing she lost Luke's love as surely as I did. Has there not been sorrow enough, already, ma'am? I beg you, despite her inferior birth and her ignorance, proclaim her innocent."

"Very well." Charlotte gazed out over the room. "What say you? Guilty or not guilty?"

Jane supposed the Damned might retire for their decision; she hoped they might do so, for she found it agonizing to watch their expressions and small gestures and to catch snatches of silent conversation.

Luke did not speak. She did not expect him to, for he must remain impartial.

To banish one of her kind over a love affair gone sour . . . No, sir, I assure you it was more than that . . . You did not fight against the French, you have no notion of what it was like . . . You accuse me of cowardice?

Charlotte sent a warning glance at this particular group, who stood, backs stiff, *en sanglant,* ready to fight.

I put little store by Margaret's testimony. Consider she left her Consort . . . Indeed, she reveals her own poor character with her story. I am surprised she was not hanged as a traitor . . . Jane spoke well if briefly. She made no excuses, and remember she has experienced a recent metamorphosis. We should exercise leniency . . .

She was not accustomed to following several complicated silent conversations and realized the futility of trying to interpret what she heard. Instead she closed her mind to the hubbub and resolved to show bravery at the verdict. Had she not once narrowly escaped the guillotine? She had proved her courage once and could do so again.

One of the Damned she did not know stepped forward and announced, "Not guilty."

A burst of applause ran around the room, and Jane bowed like an actor upon the stage, remembering with a pang of nostalgia the family theatricals of her childhood.

"Very well." Charlotte stood and turned to Luke, running a carelessly seductive hand down his sleeve. "Well, now that is over, sir, we must talk. We must decide on the disposition of *les Sales,* whose houses they should go to, and—"

"Another day, ma'am," Luke said to Charlotte, brushing her hand away. To Jane he murmured, "Do you think you could try to look less murderous? You know there is no woman for me but you."

She forced a smile, curtsied to Charlotte, and approached Margaret. "I wish to thank you. Your testimony was entirely unexpected."

"I wronged you once. Now that the score is even we may go back to being enemies." Margaret gave her a friendly smile—at least, Jane thought it was friendly. "How amusing to see Raphael and Luke snarling over you."

"Is it?" Jane said.

But their conversation was interrupted by others who came to shake or kiss Jane's hand and welcome her back to the company of the Damned. Someone thrust a glass of wine into her hand. A little apart from the others, Luke and Raphael, wary and *en sanglant,* watched each other like a pair of animals about to fight.

But that's what they were—certainly not human, and even two gentlemen vying for the hand of the same lady might well behave in similar fashion, although their teeth would remain firmly under control. What, she wondered, was the correct etiquette for such a situation?

Tom touched her arm. "I'd kiss you, Jane, but I think Luke would tear out my throat, even if it was truly a gesture of relief or brotherly affection. I regret my testimony did so little to help."

"Thank you for trying." Jane grasped his hand and shook it. "Do you know—did Luke ask Margaret to speak on my behalf?"

"I don't believe so."

"What will Luke and Raphael do? Will they have a duel?"

"Pray try not to sound so avid, my dear." Tom smiled. "A little bloodletting, perhaps—why, you may see for yourself."

For Luke and Raphael now circled, coats tossed aside and fists aloft, as Jane had seen her brothers fight. But it was clear their fangs would be used also, for Raphael aimed a blow at Luke's face and backed away, his knuckles slashed and blood dripping on the floor. Jane found herself *en sanglant,* as were several of the Damned near her, and they gathered in a crowd around the two fighting men.

Luke snarled and attacked, his fist connecting with Raphael's ribs.

They appeared to be in deadly earnest, but the watching Damned cheered and laughed and placed bets. Many of the women were *en sanglant,* eyes bright and greedy.

"My dear, you must stop the fight," Charlotte murmured in Jane's ear. "You must let the favored gentleman know your preferences."

"How?"

A cheer arose as Raphael slashed Luke's collarbone with his fangs, dangerously close to the neck.

Jane removed her coat and laid it on a chair. Squaring her shoulders, she strode forward and forced the two men apart, at some risk to herself from exposed fangs and flying fists. She rather wished she had a bucket of water to throw over them as one might break up a fight between two dogs. For a brief moment the three of them struggled, both men cursing at the interruption. Raphael's fist shot over her shoulder and landed on Luke's nose.

A footman, holding a tray of wineglasses, paused nearby to watch the fight, his eyes widening at the spilled blood. Jane twisted away, grabbed the tray, and tipped the contents over Raphael and Luke.

"You fool! Do you think I'll still want you with a nose that's squashed flat?" It was her turn to snarl now as she pushed Luke against the wall.

"What are you—" Luke fell silent as she pressed her hips and thighs against him to hold him still and placed her forefingers against his broken nose. She winced as she heard the crunch of damaged cartilage returning to its rightful place. So did he. "Ouch! Who taught you to do that?"

She regarded her handiwork, his nose bloody and swollen but restored to its natural shape. "I saw it done once in Bath."

He shook wine from his hair. "Very effective if inelegant."

"What was I supposed to do?"

"Kiss me."

"Kiss you while you were fighting? I would have been lucky to keep my own nose intact."

"No. Kiss me now."

"I'll taste Raphael's blood on your mouth."

He snarled and then laughed. "So, a little perversity will not harm you, my dear."

She did not put her lips to his immediately. She spent some time cleaning and breathing on his wounds to close and heal them, paying particular attention to the gash at his collarbone for the opportunity it gave her to breathe carelessly on his neck. She apologized extravagantly and at length; he growled with lust.

She blew on his nose to aid in healing, which made him laugh, but his grip at her waist told her he was becoming impatient. The nudge of her lips against his became her capitulation, a heady, prolonged kiss where she tasted both Raphael's and Luke's blood, a deliciously wicked mingling of flavors.

"I think," he said finally, "we should declare formally that we are Consorts."

"I did not think we were not Consorts."

"Ah. A formal declaration is old-fashioned, and during the invasion many of our customs were abandoned. A mutual agreement then was enough, and besides, we were middling sort of Damned. But now, as William's successor, I must consider my honor and yours, too."

"Very well. You know this time I shall not leave."

"Indeed." He looked away, and a shadow passed between them. "You don't believe me?"

He shrugged and laughed. "It is nothing. See, we have kissed so long everyone has become bored at the spectacle and gone in to dine. Shall we join them?"

She would rather they dined alone, but she knew his position as leader demanded he play host. She slipped her hand into the crook of his elbow, and they proceeded out of the Great Hall and upstairs to the Gallery, where the footmen not only served delicacies but provided themselves as such; and a group of visitors from London eagerly awaited the attentions of the Damned.

Luke greeted these new mortal guests with great affability, pleased that the Prince of Wales's rejection of the Damned had not been adopted by all society, and gossiped with them of the activities of the *ton*. The Gallery was lit by only a few candles, and in the pools of darkness, on satin and velvet sofas, the Damned dined. Soon enough, Luke took Jane's hand and drew her into the darkness and the pleasures that awaited them there.

She had forgotten the casual squalor of a morning among the Damned, the discarded garments and spilled wine, the mortals made crapulous and wobbly from too much wine and the loss of blood. Luke was gone, which did not worry her particularly as she knew he slept little.

She peered out of the nearest window. Morning? It was closer to afternoon, from the quality of the light. A gentleman, half dressed and yawning, dried blood on his neck and shirt, held a glass of wine out with a shaking hand.

"Ma'am, if you could be so kind?"

She bit into her wrist and let a drop of blood fall into his glass. Someone else must have revived the footmen, for they moved quietly among the sleeping Damned and their guests, clearing up glasses and plates and cleaning. Jane smiled as a footman lifted the dangling leg of a woman, propping her foot against his hip so he could sweep beneath a sofa.

Yawning, she left the Gallery and sought out the bedchamber where she had been imprisoned the day before. A maidservant looked up from laying a fire and scrambled to her feet. She was from a local family, one of those who were attached to Edward's estate. She struggled to remember the girl's name. Rebecca, that was it, shortened to Becky.

"Beg your pardon sir—Miss Austen, that is. Why, I didn't . . ." Her voice faded away.

"Can you find me a gown to wear, Becky?"

"Of course, miss. I believe Mrs. Kettering's maid may help." She stared at Jane. "I'd never have thought . . . I'll fetch her."

She wiped her hands on her apron and ran out of the room. This was something Jane had not anticipated, that every day would bring a reminder of the life she had left, that the staff, particularly the lower staff of the house, would include people whose families she knew and who would know her. She suspected that as her metamorphosis developed she would lose the yearning for her family; meanwhile, every day in this house would remind her of what she could no longer have.

Becky returned shortly, carrying a collection of gowns, undergarments, and shoes chosen by Maria, Mrs. Kettering's maid. Jane watched as Maria scolded Becky, pushing her aside to lay gowns flat on the bed and smooth out creases, exclaiming at her clumsiness.

"These are all too grand," Jane said. "I should like a simple day dress and a cap."

"A cap! I don't even know if we have such a thing, ma'am. Becky, fetch Miss Jane some hot water, if you will." She sorted through the gowns, laying some in the linen press. "Those you shall have for evening until Mr. Venning buys you some new." She gave them a covetous glance, anticipating likely ownership of the gowns after Jane had ordered new ones.

Jane sighed. How Martha and Cassandra would have enjoyed this! She wished she could take more pleasure in the process, but decided a cotton gown, far smarter than anything she had owned, and a matching spencer were suitable.

"What do you want with the spencer, miss?" Maria asked.

"I want to take a walk."

Maria shrugged as though Jane had admitted to some inexplicable eccentricity but grudgingly allowed her a scarf to tie around her head in an improvised turban.

The borrowed stays were not a good fit, designed for another woman, and the shoes slightly too large, but after washing and dressing, Jane prepared to go outside. Edward had great plans for the gardens, she knew, and she wanted to see how work progressed. But here she was again, thinking of the Austen family of which she was no longer a part, filled with regret. This would not do.

She lingered among the rosebushes that were showing plenty of buds and bent to see if they yet held a scent.

"Jane?"

She whirled around. Raphael stood there, wearing a greatcoat and hat.

"I have come to bid you farewell," he said.

"You are leaving? For long?"

He patted his waistcoat pocket. "I am leaving this household. Luke has written me letters of introduction. I had long intended to meet with men of science in England, and now William is dead I have little to hold me here."

"I'm sorry. I shall miss you."

"I shall miss you, Jane, but I cannot stay. This house holds too many memories."

"It does for me, too."

"Ask Luke to take you elsewhere. They—or rather, we, the Damned—rarely stay long in one place."

"Yes, I think that would be best." She hesitated. "Thank you for speaking for me yesterday, and I am sorry if I offended you, Raphael."

"You didn't. We cannot choose whom we love. You and he were Consorts, once, after all. I lost the fight, and that's an end to it." He smiled and held out a gloved hand. "Shall we shake hands and depart friends?"

"With all my heart." She took his hand. "Raphael, I do not wish to pry, but will you take your cure?"

He shook his head. "I have work to do yet. I wish you well, Jane."

He turned her hand in his and kissed her palm. The brief touch of his lips told her more than he could say aloud of his sorrow, disappointment, and anger, and of the bitter relief of leaving her. She gasped and would have spoken, but already he strode away from her.

She had not treated him well. But if she had given rein to her desire and flung them both into a metamorphosis, would they not have savagely resented each other for it? She shook her head. As one of the Damned she must learn not to linger over what might have been.

She walked on, enjoying the pulsing life of the world around her, the energy of plants and of tiny creeping things. This is what she had now, this perception and capacity for amazement. She would like to write about . . .

She stopped. She would like to write about this? But what was she thinking? She was one of the Damned. She could not write anymore.

She bent to pluck a rosebud, running it through her fingers, and laughed as it pricked her. Her blood welled crimson and powerful. She breathed on the tiny wound to close it, and the rose unfolded its petals, miraculous, displaying its fragile golden heart with a gust of sweet scent, a taste of the summer to come. Of many summers to come, too many to count. Jane would live to see this rosebush withered to dust and the Great House a deserted ruin.

But she could not dwell on such things, for now she must accept the pleasure of the moment.

She tucked the rose into the pin that held her fichu closed and smiled as she recalled Maria's amazement that one of the Damned would want such a thing; did not the ladies of the Damned flaunt the display of bosom and throat? But Jane had insisted, claiming she did not want to freckle, although she doubted she could.

After a while she strolled back into the house, wondering

where Luke was, or any of them, for she had seen only servants busy about their work this morning. The small book-lined room at the rear of the house that had been William's particular haunt was empty now. She had hoped to find Luke there.

Possibly she needed to dine again, even though it was some hours from darkness. She trudged up the stairs, but outside the bedchamber was alerted by a soft whimper. This was really too bad, that she was destined always to be on the other side of this particular doorway while others took their pleasure.

She pushed the door open and stopped in horror at what she saw.

"Will you not join us, my love?" Luke smiled at her from the bed, where he held a half-naked woman in his arms, Becky, the maidservant from earlier that day.

Luke could see Jane was *en sanglant,* and, to her mortification, was probably amused at her embarrassment and jealousy. "She's quite sweet and tender. A lovely scent, too, like lilies."

"Get her out!" Jane shrieked. She bounded to the bed and dragged Becky away from Luke.

Becky, a goose-feather duster still in her hand, fell onto the floor with a soft thud, a silly lopsided grin on her face. "Sorry, miss."

Jane turned to Luke. "I thought you loved me!"

"So I do, which is why I allowed you to deplete me last night. Forgive me if I seek merely to replenish the stock, so to speak."

"And is your state of undress absolutely necessary?"

He propped himself up on one elbow and scratched his chest. "What is the matter, Jane?"

Jane glanced at the girl at her feet. "I trust you do not expect me to revive her."

"Of course not." Luke sighed and got out of bed. In response to Jane's scowl, he donned shirt and breeches and poured a glass of wine.

Becky, propped up against the side of the bed, watched Luke drip his blood into the wine and licked her lips.

"Pray fasten your gown!" Jane said. "I have no wish to view your bosom."

"*He* said it was a very fine one," the girl replied. But she made an effort to make herself decent once more and, having drunk the wine, straightened her skirts and rose. "Do you want me to finish dusting, sir?"

"Absolutely not!" Jane said.

"He said he'd give me a sixpence, miss."

Luke reached into his breeches pocket and removed a handful of change. He handed her a coin, and with a toss of her head, apron tied once more and the feather duster tucked into its waistband, Becky strutted out of the room.

"You gave her half a crown!" Jane said, outraged.

"I didn't have a sixpence. I was not about to engage in vulgar bickering over coinage." He sat on the bed to pull on his stockings. "I assure you I did not mean to injure you, and I am somewhat surprised you should be so distressed. I am aware your metamorphosis is imperfect at present, but we are the Damned, Jane. This is what we do."

"Pray do not preach at me!" She had been *en sanglant* the whole time since seeing Luke and Becky coupled, and she raised her hand to her mouth to retract her aching teeth.

"You'll become accustomed to it, Jane."

She nodded, aware that he was probably right.

"And probably the best thing you could do is summon one of our footmen and rid yourself of these fancies."

"Fancies? You do me wrong, to take my feelings so lightly."

He looked up from pulling on a boot. "Your feelings? But they are remnants of your mortal life. What you have just witnessed is not inconstancy or infidelity."

"But it feels like it." She became *en sanglant* again, embarrassingly so.

"You will feel differently in a few days when your metamorphosis is complete." He reached for his other boot. "You must dine often and lightly."

She sat beside him on the bed, not from any amorous intention but because she was weak and defeated. "What shall I do, Luke?"

"What do you mean, my love?"

"To occupy myself."

"Ah. Well, we have the best of society—that is, country society—some excellent dining, and there will be cards and dancing, too."

"And conversation?"

"Conversation? I suppose so, if you wish." He leaned to kiss her lips and neck. "I regret we have no war at present if you wish for more excitement."

"It's not enough."

"Not enough?" He reached for his coat. "Would you like to take a ride? We'll have the horses prepared so they'll tolerate us. I don't know if we have a habit in the house, but you could dress in your men's clothes if you like."

"I don't mean at this moment. I mean it is not enough to sustain me for—for a longer time."

"What would you like?" He shrugged his coat on and knelt at her feet, taking her hands in his. "I will give you whatever you want, Jane. Anything. I love you. Pearls as big as pigeon's eggs, cloth of gold, jewels, houses. We'll go abroad. You'd like Italy, or I hear the Americas are interesting."

She smiled and shook her head, knowing suddenly what she missed above all. "Ah, my tastes are more modest than that. Give me paper, Luke. Paper and ink and pens, and above all, solitude. I want to write."

Chapter 23

"So what is it about?" Luke said, a hip propped on the table where she worked in a small room in an older part of the house.

She tapped the thick stack of paper into shape, the work of the past few days. "It's about me, or someone very like me. She is a woman of modest means who is created and goes to live with strangers."

He shook his head. "You'll never get it published, not while the Damned are so out of favor. Am I in it?"

"Yes. You're always in my books. So is William."

"Will—will you read it to me? Before we dine?" He looked shy at making such a request. She was touched by his uncertainty, proud that she had introduced a new pleasure to someone of such vast and ancient sensual experience. Her canines popped out in vulgar readiness.

"I beg your pardon." She righted her teeth. "Luke, when I was Damned before, I could not write. Why is it different this time?"

"I don't know. We know little of those who undergo a second metamorphosis. Possibly more of your human qualities remain this time, since you are older in human years and your character and abilities more fully formed than at the age of twenty-one. By the by, have you dined today?"

"Not yet. I've been busy. I shall."

"Jane, my love." He picked up her inky hand and kissed it. "You delay your full metamorphosis, and I long to make you my Consort. Pray try. You'd like some tea, would you not?"

"Oh, Luke." She leaned back in her chair and laughed. They both knew that he offered her not only tea but the one who would bring it, one of the house's handsome footmen. "I'm afraid I'm not thirsty."

He laughed. "You are impossible, Jane. Do you fear that you will lose the ability to write entirely if you complete your metamorphosis? On my honor, I doubt it will happen. You're so close, a hairsbreadth away." He sighed and closed his thoughts abruptly from her.

"What's wrong?"

"A passing sorrow, that is all. Let us speak of more cheerful matters. Your new gowns should arrive today, and the other ladies are most excited to see them. Shall I mend your pen for you?"

"If you wish." She stroked his cheek. "Pray be careful. The knife is exceedingly sharp."

As usual, the pen slipped, and between kisses she licked the blood from his finger. She had never loved him more, but she pushed him out of the room to continue writing undisturbed.

Writing as one of the Damned was quite wonderful. She had enormous stamina—her hand never tired, and she filled sheet after sheet, thrilled by the speed of her writing and the surprising twists of her imagination. Yet she missed the slow revelation, the thoughtfulness that used to accompany her writing, the knowledge that she worked toward a certain resolution and balance. This was more like riding in a carriage drawn by runaway horses.

"Ma'am?" A servant knocked at the door.

She sighed. Luke had ordered her tea—and more, if she wished it. She bade the footman enter and watched him with growing appetite. He was good to look upon—Clarissa and Dorcas had chosen the footmen, who were all tall and dark-haired, with as much care as a gentleman might choose a matching team of horses. Their livery was cut to show off their long, handsome legs and broad shoulders.

And they all had delicious smiles.

She looked at her manuscript again and then at the footman, who, caught balancing the tray on one hip while unfolding a small table, smiled at her with a flash of white teeth and blue eyes. She struggled to remember his name. Simon, that was it.

"Simon."

"Yes, ma'am?"

She lost her nerve entirely. "Pray leave the kettle on the hearth. I'll make the tea."

"Very well, ma'am."

She continued to watch as he leaned to place the kettle next to the coals where it would keep warm. He was so handsome and his scent was equally pleasurable, and she wished she was not so nice, or squeamish, or, as Luke would say, such a clergyman's daughter.

He straightened and caught her gaze and her unmistakable condition of *en sanglant*. "Will there be anything more, ma'am?"

She sighed. "I suppose Mr. Venning instructed you."

"He did, ma'am, and I'm willing." He gave a cheerful grin. "Throat or wrist or—"

"Throat. No, wrist. No—I've changed my mind." She stood. "No, wait."

"My, it's hot in this room, ma'am." It wasn't, but she loved him for saying it, and for unbuttoning his coat. "But then I suppose your kind run cold."

"Well, no, our skin is cold to the touch but . . . and . . ." Her voice faded away into a growl of lust.

He folded the coat and laid it on the sofa, the act of a man trained to take care of his uniform, and began on his waistcoat buttons. "Throat or wrist, whenever you're ready, ma'am."

"Lock the door, if you please." She didn't want any other of the Damned coming in to observe; no, she didn't want any of the Damned trying to share her pleasure. And she particularly didn't want Luke coming in and advising her on how best to go about the business.

The waistcoat was folded and laid atop the coat. He was down to shirtsleeves now, and as he turned to lock the door she observed the fabric was slightly damp, clinging to his magnificent shoulders.

He pulled his neckcloth off in one splendid swoop of linen and unbuttoned his shirt placket with the other hand. "Where will you have me, ma'am?"

"Sit on the sofa."

Alarm flared in his eyes; no wonder, she trod toward him like a beast attacking its prey, and as she passed the table, her gown brushed against the pile of paper and set it fluttering to the floor. No matter. His pulse beat fast at his neck, and he leaned his head back obediently as he had been taught, offering himself to her, his arms spread wide on the back of the sofa.

He groaned as she settled on his strong thighs and touched her tongue to the blue vein that arose on his neck in response to her.

She wanted this, to be strong and an equal partner to Luke. But she wanted this for herself, for a taste of youth and beauty, for the sweet, simple act of taking blood without complications, without sadness, without regret.

* * *

She made tea while Simon sat, pale and smiling, on the sofa, embarrassed to sit in her presence but not able to stand without swaying.

"I trust I didn't take too much," she said, a little anxious. After all, the poor boy had to wait at table in a little while, and she didn't want him to swoon.

"No, ma'am. You were most eager, that's all; it quite took me by surprise." He gazed at her with admiration. "Let me make the tea, ma'am."

"Nonsense." She gave the teapot a brisk stir. She felt quite splendid, strong and energetic, and hoped there would be dancing tonight. The Damned enjoyed dancing for all their lack of musical taste, for as Luke had once explained, the rhythm of the music was akin to the pounding of a human pulse.

She poured him a glass of wine and dripped a little of her blood in it to revive him. To her relief the color came back into his face as he sipped.

"If you don't mind me saying so, ma'am, you look most handsome."

"Thank you," she murmured, not much inclined to make conversation, for her mind was drifting back to her writing.

"More so than when I first came into the room."

"Do I? It must be your blood. I enjoyed it very much." She turned to gaze at the mirror over the mantelpiece and not even her usual, fuzzy blur of a reflection showed.

She put her teacup down with a crash on the table and jumped to her feet in alarm. Her writing. Oh, let her still be able to write, for now she was sure her metamorphosis was complete. She rushed to the scatter of papers on the floor and began to gather them.

Simon, his coat half buttoned, knelt at her side. "May I help you, ma'am? Is everything well?"

She snatched pages from his hand and put them back in order.

With a great gust of relief she read over what she had just written. Yes, it still made sense; she knew she could immerse herself in the novel (for she supposed that was what it was) once again, and in fact, invigorated and confident, knew what should happen next.

"Oh, thank you!" she cried and kissed Simon, who blushed with pleasure. "I am most grateful and all is well; all is very well indeed."

Later that day she went upstairs to find the bedchamber in chaos. A half-dozen footmen hauled water to fill a tin tub, the air thick with steam. A new gown lay on the bed and Maria stood by, ferociously ordering the footmen how to do their job; Dorcas and Clarissa presided over an arsenal of rouge, curling irons, hair ornaments, ribbons, and silk flowers laid atop a dresser.

"What on earth is happening?" Jane asked.

"Mr. Venning sends his regards, ma'am, and requests that you become ready."

"You're to officially become his Consort tonight," Clarissa said. "Jane, your hands are like a schoolboy's—we shall have to scrub away that ink."

"What will happen?" Jane asked. She remembered Cassandra scrubbing at her inky hands and pushed the painful thought away.

"Oh, it's a simple enough ceremony," Dorcas said, turning Jane so she could unfasten her gown. "You both swear fealty to each other and drink a glass of wine."

"Dear Jane!" Clarissa embraced her.

"What's the matter?" Jane asked. "You become sentimental. What troubles you?"

Clarissa shook her head and blew her nose. "Oh, you know, for us it is like a wedding. I wish William were here to see it."

"I wish I'd had more time to prepare," Jane said with some anxiety.

"We'll make the best of a bad job, ma'am," Maria said. "Although you look well today."

"Who was it?" Dorcas asked. She sniffed at Jane's skin. "Ah. Simon. Such a pretty boy. Yes, you are in excellent looks. Luke will be much relieved, for he has been dragging himself around like a horse on its way to the knacker's yard."

"May I not see the gown?" Jane asked. "I have not had a new gown in so long."

"No, you must wash. There will be other gowns."

"Something troubles you, Clarissa," Jane said as she lowered herself into the hot water, and Clarissa's mind snapped closed to her. "I beg your pardon. I do not mean to pry."

"It's nothing," Clarissa said. "Try to think of me as a sentimental bridesmaid."

Jane was not convinced. "What are you not telling me? Is a public consummation of our union expected, or must I fight a duel with the hundreds of women who believe they have a claim to Luke?"

"Vulgar girl," Clarissa said, and poured water over Jane's head.

It seemed like hours later that she was released, very clean, painted, primped, curled, and wearing a gown that, with her new stays, fit like a glove and revealed most of her bosom. Jewels and silk flowers were woven into her hair. If she could have seen her reflection, she doubted whether she would have recognized herself. The footmen, come to empty the bath of its water, cast her admiring looks, and Simon a wink.

"Hands, ma'am." Maria dropped blobs of cream onto her hands, scrubbed almost raw in the attempts to remove the ink.

Both Clarissa and Dorcas were uncharacteristically silent and distant as they finally made their way to the Great Hall where the ceremony would take place. Jane had expected that they might receive company that night, but it was the household only that were present, Tom and Luke awaiting them. She found it reassuring that a large crowd of onlookers might be considered vulgar, just as most considered a wedding to be a private, family affair.

She ran into Luke's arms, feeling like a girl—yes, surely her metamorphosis was complete for her to feel so young and strong and confident. Yet he, too, had an air of reserve about him, despite his obvious pleasure at seeing her in her finery.

"I shall never forget this night," he said, bowing to kiss her hand.

"Why should you?"

He looked extraordinarily handsome, dressed in simple black coat and breeches but with a waistcoat of elaborate embroidery, his tawny hair in fashionable disarray.

Two glasses of red wine stood on a small table next to a book with an ancient, battered leather cover bound with clasps.

"This is what we shall read," Luke said. He opened the book with great care. "Are you able to read this script? It is from several centuries ago and written by hand. Then we each vow fealty to each other and drink wine."

"Very well," Jane said. The ceremony seemed ludicrously simple to her, yet the reverence with which Luke handled the book impressed her.

"So we shall begin." He opened the book and read. As Jane listened to the cadence of the archaic words she understood why this ritual, for all its simplicity, was so important to Luke. He had inherited William's position at a difficult time in the history of the Damned; the emergence of *les Sales* and the threat of civil war made it essential that now the traditions of the Damned be honored.

He smiled and handed the book to Jane.

She read: *"I swear fealty to this man, Luke. I will be with him until the heavens fall, the seas dry, and all on earth be destroyed. I will be with him through fire and ice and storm. I swear by blood and by love that I will be a faithful Consort."*

He took the book from her hands and laid it on the table.

He handed her a glass of wine. "Drink, my love."

She raised the glass of wine to her lips, the wine so dark that it almost looked like blood, but she tasted the transformed grapes and oak and other stranger, and more complex, flavors.

He drained his glass and threw it to the floor, and she followed his example, for glasses used for such serious purpose could never be used again.

"So." He took her hands. "We are truly Consorts forever now."

He leaned to kiss her, and his touch held desire and sadness and profound loss.

"What's wrong, Luke?" But she had trouble saying the words, for things were changing and she clutched at him in terror. "Help me . . ."

"I promised William," he said, and before she spun away in darkness, she saw the tears spill from his eyes.

Chapter 24

Outside a donkey brayed.

Jane groaned and pushed her head beneath the pillow. She didn't want to wake just yet; she wanted to return to that wonderful oblivion and peace, and soon enough Cassandra would wake and chatter like a magpie and the day would begin.

But why was Cassandra making that strange squeaking sound? And the warm heaviness at her feet—one of the cats must be visiting from the kitchen. "Go away," she said sleepily.

But the creature snuffed and huffed and squeaked again and lurched up the bed, and something warm and wet and smelly brought her to a full awakening.

She opened her eyes to meet the bulbous gaze of Jacques the pug busily licking her face in bright sunlight in the bedchamber at Chawton.

"Good Lord! You're awake, Jane!"

She blinked and turned to see her brother James at her bedside, papers spilling from his hand onto the floor. "Thank God. How do you do, my dear?" But he bounded to his feet and bellowed down the stairs, "Ma'am, Cassandra, Martha, Anna, Edward, Henry, she is awake!"

"I most certainly am now, you shout so loud," she said, trying to make sense of why she was here and feeling so weak and strange.

But the rest of the family came thundering up the stairs to embrace her with cries of joy and tears and overwhelm her with their presence, filling every available space in the bedchamber, until Martha very sensibly suggested that possibly Jane, after lying in a swoon for so long, would tire easily and told everyone to depart.

"How long have I been here?" Jane asked. She clung to Martha's arm, her legs weak, as she got out of bed.

"Four days. We feared you would not awake. We have prayed."

"Is that why my brothers are here?" Moving from bed to chair had exhausted her.

"We thought you were dying. And . . ." Martha washed Jane's face as tenderly as she might an infant's. "Edward has some business at the Great House now his tenants are gone."

"His tenants?" Jane repeated. She closed her eyes as Martha brushed her hair.

"Oh, yes, just a day or so ago. The village was quite surprised. Come, drink some of this wine and water, my dear."

"I am sorry. I feel so very stupid. I cannot remember anything." She let Martha help her back into bed.

The next couple of days passed in a blur of sleeping and awakening to find her mother or sister or Martha at the bedside and urging her to take some tea, or wine, or soup. Quite often they cried; Jane wasn't sure why, for she became stronger and knew she recovered, but she wept too and knew something terrible had happened.

But they also talked of goings-on in the village; how one of Mr. Papillon's pigs had escaped and devoured Goody Walters's vegetables, and she had chased the greedy animal through the village with a spade, threatening to butcher it. And Mr. Prowting and his daughter had returned from London where she had had a dress made there almost as fine as the one Jane had worn on her return. "But much more modestly cut," Cassandra had added. "I have sewn in a panel at the neckline for you, Jane. I think it is quite pretty."

"Thank you," Jane said, wondering which gown Cassandra spoke of, for she owned no gowns that could possibly be described as fine or cut in an indecent fashion.

Her family didn't mention a piece of news that must have had the village agog: that the younger Miss Austen, wearing a gown with virtually no bodice, had been brought back from the Great House on a cart, near to death.

On the afternoon of the third day of her recovery she opened her eyes to find the bedchamber full of her brothers engaged in a lively literary discussion.

"No one will like this heroine," James declared. "She's wicked and unwomanly. What Jane needs to write is a good, virtuous girl, the sort of girl we can admire. This Fanny . . ." he shook his head.

"My Fanny?" Jane said. "Fanny Price?"

"Yes! And the Crawfords—are they really brother and sister?—this book will be a scandal," Edward said.

"But this," Henry said. He ruffled through the papers. "I have never read anything of this nature in my life. How did you do this, Jane? *She sat in a blaze of oppressive heat, in a cloud of moving dust, and her eyes could only wander from the walls, marked by her father's head, to the table cut and notched by her brothers, where stood the tea-board never thoroughly cleaned, the cups and saucers* wiped in streaks, the milk a mixture of motes floating in thin blue, and the bread and butter growing every minute more greasy than even Rebecca's hands had first produced it.'" He frowned and said to his brothers, "Do you not see? It is as though Fanny's thoughts transform the objects, or they become her thoughts; they explain her feelings."

"I don't know," Jane said, but her eyes filled with tears. "I don't even remember writing that."

"Now, come, Jane." James handed her a handkerchief. "We don't mean to hurt your feelings, but we could not resist reading your new novel. But it is rather . . . shocking. This scene near the beginning with the gate . . . well, it is not the sort of thing a lady should be expected to write."

"Aunt Jane, I have brought you some tea." Anna squeezed into the bedchamber, a cup and saucer in her hand. "And Papa, Aunt Cassandra says that your sister is not strong enough for your teasing and noise and you and my uncles are all to go downstairs."

When her father and uncles had gone downstairs, Anna reached into her pocket. "Aunt, when the men brought you from the Great House, they brought also this letter."

"Thank you, my dear." The tea was wonderful, hot and soothing; she didn't think she had ever drunk anything so delicious in her life.

But she had.

And the letter held a scent as powerful and evocative as the details of that slovenly house in—yes, it was in Portsmouth, she remembered now. The Prices' house. She feared her teeth might become sensitive, although she couldn't understand why that might happen, but no sudden toothache or discomfort erupted.

"I have a secret." Anna leaned forward. "I shall be a writer, too."

"It should keep you out of trouble," Jane said.

"Should it? I don't think it kept you out of trouble."

"Beloved, impudent girl." She leaned to kiss her niece. All she felt was the touch of her lips on Anna's smooth skin; she received no startling embarrassing revelations, or thoughts she would regret discovering. "I should read this letter alone, my dear."

When Anna had gone back downstairs, Jane laid the tea aside and broke the seal on the letter. She unfolded it and began to read.

At first she wept as she read and remembered, and then a few sentences later she laughed for sheer joy. She folded the letter carefully and slid it beneath the sheets; then, for the first time without assistance from Cassandra or Martha, she got out of bed.

She put on a dressing gown and stockings and slippers, and, finally, her spinster's cap, her hair twisted up beneath it. She took a deep breath and turned to the small mirror on the dressing table the two sisters shared.

She smiled at her reflection and then gathered up the sheaf of papers that constituted her latest novel. She would put it aside for a while, for she knew this was unlike anything else she was likely to write, and she would have some work to do.

Moving slowly, for she was still not back to her former strength, she made her way downstairs to the dining room and her writing slope. There was work to be done in the time she had left.

Chapter 25

Reading, Berks, 1839

"There's a gentleman to see you, Mrs. Lefroy."

Anna looked up from her writing desk. "I told you I should not be disturbed, Sally. What gentleman?"

Her maid held out a card. "He's in the parlor, ma'am."

"There isn't a fire there. Will you show him in here?" She looked at the card that now bore Sally's greasy thumbprint. "Please bring us some tea."

Mr. Luke Venning.

The name certainly sounded familiar. Had not Aunt Jane had a suitor of that name? She vaguely remembered a ball at the Great House in Chawton when she had been quite young, sixteen or so, and her aunt Cassandra whispering that maybe tonight dear Jane would receive an offer. She, Anna, had been fairly scandalized that a woman of her aunt's age—some years younger than she herself was now—might consider love or matrimony. Nothing had ever come of it, though. But what an odd spring that had been!

"Mr. Venning, ma'am." Her maid showed in a gentleman.

Anna stood and curtsied, and then, abandoning vanity, grabbed her spectacles from the desk.

The gentleman bowed. "Maybe you don't recognize me, Miss Anna. I beg your pardon, Mrs. Lefroy."

He was exceptionally handsome, lithe, not tall, but well made and graceful. A little too pale, perhaps, but his gray eyes sparked with life.

"Yes," she said and sat down abruptly. "Yes, I do recognize you. Will you not sit down?" Then, foolishly, "You haven't changed a bit."

He smiled. "Well, that is to be expected. You know what I am?"

"Yes, of course I do. You're one of the—the Damned. Only naturally we delicate ladies are not expected to know that word, let alone recognize you."

"Indeed. Society has become sadly polite."

"I trust you are well, Mr. Venning? Oh, that's ridiculous. Of course you are well."

"I am very well, thank you. And you?"

"Oh, well enough. I have become a sort of Mr. and Mrs. Bennet combined with six daughters to marry off. I am a writer now, like my aunt Jane. I even tried to finish her last book, *Sanditon*—I suppose you have read her books?"

"Indeed, yes. She read *Sanditon* aloud to me; it made me laugh."

"Oh! Do you know how she intended to continue it?" She leaned forward eagerly, the writer in her on full alert, before she realized that Aunt Jane couldn't possibly have read this aloud to Mr. Venning. He and his companions had left Chawton long before. What was he about?

"I have some explaining to do," Mr. Venning said, but at that moment Sally came in with the tea tray and a swish of petticoats

Anna was fairly sure was directed at him—her hands were also reasonably clean, which made Anna very suspicious.

"Please don't eat my maid!" she burst out when the girl had left. "She's all I can afford and not much use as it is."

"I have dined today, ma'am," he said with gravity but a twinkle in his eye.

"That was a very odd time in 1810," Anna said. She poured tea, the homely, familiar gesture giving her a certainty from which she could venture into dangerous areas. "There is so much I don't remember. Occasionally I dream about . . . about one of the gentlemen who I believe stayed at Prowtings for a time."

"Duval?"

"Yes. Please don't tell me what happened. Sometimes it's best not to know."

"Very well. I shall say only that your aunt Jane saved you from ruin and destruction at great cost to herself." He sipped his tea. How odd to be drinking tea in her study with one of the Damned!

"I owe her much," Anna said.

"And I, too." He reached into his coat and withdrew a packet wrapped in a scrap of faded silk. "These are letters we wrote to each other. You should have them. I am going to the Americas shortly and who knows what may happen there."

She stared at him and reached for the letters, but drew her hand back, alarmed at what she might discover. He laid them on the sofa next to her.

"When Aunt Jane was ill—it was around the time you left Chawton—she received a letter. Was it from you?"

He nodded and reached for the bundle of letters. He unwrapped the silk and handed one to her. She remembered giving that letter to her aunt, who sat pale and handsome in bed, having apparently returned from the brink of death.

She unfolded it, her hands trembling.

"William was her Creator and mine," he said. "Raphael was his brother and fledgling and somewhat in love with Jane."

Beloved Jane,

I have deceived you greatly except about that which is most important—my eternal love for you. Yes, you took the cure that Raphael invented at William's request, made as he lay dying. He said he had failed you before and would not fail you again, for he made a bargain with you that you should not become one of the Damned.

This was the only way. I regret that I had to deceive you so, for I feared that you would refuse the cure for love of me. I trust this is not merely arrogance on my part.

Forgive me, dearest Jane.

I shall love you forever as much as you wish and however you wish. It is your decision, but know that I yearn for you and will do so for all eternity.

Luke

"And what happened then?" Anna asked. "She—she began a liaison with you?"

"We were sworn Consorts," Luke replied. "It is a form of marriage among us. She sent me a reply to the address I included in that letter, and we remained lovers. I don't like what she did with *Mansfield Park,* however—I suspect that in her first draft, which she wrote at the Great House, Fanny was one of the Damned."

"Impossible!" Anna cried.

He shrugged. "It is so. She sent me my letters when she lay

dying at Winchester; I did not see her, but I stood vigil outside that house on College Street and I knew the exact moment her soul fled. I hope she knew I was nearby."

"I miss her so much," Anna said.

"I, too." He stood. "Sadly, eternity for my beloved Jane was only seven more years. You may do what you wish with the letters, Miss Anna. I wish you all health and happiness."

"Thank you," she said, dazed and troubled. On a sudden impulse, she stood and kissed his cheek. "Thank you, and I wish you well."

After he had left, she sat and stared at the bundle of letters for some time before ordering a fresh pot of tea—an extravagant gesture for a widow with six daughters, but she suspected she would need the sustenance—and began to read.

Halfway through she poured herself an even more extravagant glass of brandy, normally reserved for medicinal uses only.

Two hours later she scribbled a frantic letter to her aunt Cassandra and sent it and the letters to Chawton.

Chawton Cottage, a week later

The two women sat on the sofa in the drawing room, the bundle of letters between them.

"I always wondered about those visits to London," Aunt Cassandra said. "She'd come back looking very bright-eyed, not like someone who'd been poring over proofs day after day. I daresay your uncle Frank knew, too."

"And she never mentioned anything to you?" Anna said.

"Jane was very good at keeping secrets." Aunt Cassandra's mouth snapped shut in a firm line.

So was Aunt Cassandra, Anna decided. "Well, Aunt, since you have many of Jane's letters, would you like these, too?"

"I'm not sure. What will happen to them after I die? I wouldn't want these letters falling into the wrong hands, and in her letters to us she was often quite rude about people we knew. After all, Jane's books are still being read. I hear they're quite popular. What if people wanted to know more about her, as if she were someone like Sir Walter Scott?"

Cassandra reached for the bundle of letters. "There was something I wanted to ask you about, my dear, since you have experience of married life. I marked them with a slip of paper . . . ah, yes, here they are. What does this particular phrase mean? And this?"

Anna's cheeks heated. "Oh. That's, um, something married people do, Aunt."

"I thought so. And of course everyone knows how depraved the Damned are." Cassandra stood and hobbled to the sideboard. "Let's have a glass of wine."

Oddly enough, Aunt Cassandra seemed quite proud of her younger sister's scandalous activities. She waved away Anna's offer of help with the decanter, although her fingers were knobbed and frail with age, and poured them both a glass of wine.

"Don't you think the world might want to know that she found love, as her heroines did?" Anna asked.

"Her heroines were mostly silly girls," Cassandra said. "Except for Anne Elliot who had the sense to marry a sailor."

"But so did Mrs. Price. Do you know, Aunt Cassandra, Mr. Venning told me she originally wrote Fanny to be a vampire?"

"Oh, nonsense. I always wondered about the Crawfords, though." She placed her glass on the table. "Thank you for coming to see me, my dear. Next time, bring the children."

* * *

After Anna had left, Cassandra sat alone in the growing darkness. At her age it was more than likely that she'd fall asleep, and she should really call for the maid to light the lamp. But for the moment the darkness was friendly and comforting.

She looked at the bundle of letters, those surprising, joyful, indecent letters.

Why couldn't you have told me, Jane? You were the sun of my life, the gilder of every pleasure, the soother of every sorrow; I had not a thought concealed from you, but you concealed this from me.

Cassandra rose, bracing herself for the creaks and odd aches and pains that accompanied every movement these days; really, had it not been for the matter of her immortal soul, Jane had been a fool to settle for this rather than eternal youth and beauty. Once she had danced all night and walked for miles, talking and laughing with Jane. Now crossing the drawing room was a great and painful undertaking.

She poured herself another glass of wine and with great care made her way back to the sofa and grasped the bundle of letters. Then the next few steps to the fireplace.

She set the wineglass on the mantelpiece and threw the bundle onto the fire, reaching for the poker to encourage the glowing fire into a blaze.

She raised the glass in a toast, the flames reflected in the deep red of the wine. "To Jane, my dearest Jane, who found true love after all."

Afterword

Although *Jane Austen: Blood Persuasion* and my earlier book about Jane Austen as a vampire, *Jane and the Damned* (Harper-Collins, 2010) are works of fiction, I feel it's useful to include some background information about the Damned in England.

The history of the Damned in England lacks documentation and suffers frequent distortion and exaggeration. By the late Georgian period, the Damned were fairly well established, thanks to their association with the Prince of Wales, later the Prince Regent. They lived openly in the most fashionable circles as leaders of society, notable for their debauchery and lewd behavior, both of which were celebrated with appropriate shocked horror and lurid detail in newspapers, broadside ballads, and gossip magazines.

We know that the Damned had been in England since at least the medieval period, although they were regarded as exotic and untrustworthy outsiders and generally kept their activities quiet. It is from this period and other times when the Damned had to assimilate that most of the legends arose: for instance, that they could not tolerate daylight, garlic, or crossing water.

Afterword

They were active in England in Queen Elizabeth I's reign and celebrated as exotics, along with Native Americans and Africans, at her court; she certainly found male members of the Damned attractive, and it is quite possible that the Virgin Queen took lovers from among their ranks. Although they continued to be in evidence at the Stuart court (James I also enjoyed the company of handsome male vampires), it is suspected that many of them left England during the Interregnum to return with Charles II, one or more of whose mistresses may well have been vampires. Samuel Pepys makes frequent references in his diaries to the allure of female members of the Damned and fantasized about them during sermons in church.

Many vampires moved to England during the Inquisition in Europe, but one of the most well-known waves of immigration was during the French Reign of Terror, when members of the Damned were executed, immortality being no match for the guillotine. Ironically, in the early days of the French Revolution, the Damned thrived, leading the freethinking, atheist sentiments of the period.

Thus England, by eighteenth-century standards a well-regulated, rational, and tolerant nation, became something of a haven for the Damned, explaining their sudden emergence from the vampire closet. That the Damned lived openly in late Georgian society is obvious from the extensive collection of publications informing mortals, particularly women, on the etiquette of dining with the Damned, when guests might well provide both dinner and after-dinner entertainment.

The popularity of the Damned reached its height after their acts of heroism in leading the resistance against the French during the 1797 invasion, in which Jane Austen, then in Bath to take the waters as a cure against vampirism, found herself involved (see *Jane and the Damned*).

Earlier in the year an unsuccessful and well-documented French invasion had taken place in Fishguard, Wales, after bad weather had thwarted the original plan of landing and taking the major port of Bristol. The invasion was easily routed by the local militia and the populace, including a forty-eight-year-old female cobbler, Jemima Nicholas, who, legend has it, captured single-handed twelve French soldiers. In an ironic twist worthy of a Gilbert and Sullivan operetta, captured French officers escaped a few months later in the yacht of the English commander.

The November invasion was more successful, thanks to a brilliantly conceived plan tempered with a good deal of luck, in which the French in one coordinated effort took major port cities, rallied the common people, and marched inland to London. The Royal Family went into hiding, the volunteer English militia proved inadequate against the highly disciplined French army, and the English found themselves helpless, demoralized, and deeply shamed by the first invasion of their country in more than seven centuries.

Happily the occupation lasted only a couple of weeks, but the task of piecing together the actual events has challenged historians ever since. First, very little source material remains. The French destroyed many of their records of the invasion, given that it was of such short duration and reflected so poorly on their nation's military reputation. Given the level of collaboration with the enemy among all strata of English society, families sought to cover up any dubious activity, burning firsthand accounts and other records, and pretending that those two weeks in November held nothing out of the ordinary. In addition, the French seized England's many local news presses and the Royal Mail system, cutting off communications nationwide.

But the main reason for the cover-up was that the resistance to the invasion was led by the most unlikely heroes and heroines in England, the Damned.

Over the next few years, the Prince of Wales turned his back on his former friends, banning them from the court in 1810. The Damned, scattered over the country, quarreled on how they should conduct themselves—whether they should attempt to live openly or hide. Open conflict broke out, and households disbanded. Some, like Duval's household, sought revenge against humankind, not endearing them to humans they encountered. Others, like William's, planned to live quietly until they were once again accepted by polite society. The middle and lower classes, who might have been sympathetic to the plight of the Damned, also received the brunt of a long and ruinous war, massive inflation, and a series of poor harvests; finding themselves in the cross fire of civil war among the Damned was the last straw. Legislation was passed during the Regency period restricting the activity of the Damned and depriving them of property and political power.

Once again, the Damned retreated from public view. We can only speculate what became of them, although many, like Luke Venning, crossed the Atlantic, attracted by the challenges of the Americas. As the Georgian period morphed into the Victorian, it became unthinkable that the Damned had, in effect, once ruled society and saved England, and thus the rewriting of history began in earnest.

Janet Mullany © 2011

A Glossary of the Damned

en sanglant: to be aroused; to have one's canines extend. Involuntary and uncontrolled *en sanglant* is considered vulgar and ill-bred.

to dine: to feed upon mortals, who consider it a high honor and greatly pleasurable.

Bearleader: a combination chaperone/mentor who teaches the young **fledgling** correct etiquette and manners. The Bearleader is generally, but not always, the **Creator** of the fledgling vampire; the one who turned (created) him or her.

les Sales: literally, the dirty or unclean ones—cast out and feral members of the Damned. It's a French word, so the *a* is pronounced like the *a* in *father.*

Janet Mullany

Raised in England on a diet of Georgette Heyer and Jane Austen, **JANET MULLANY** has worked as an archaeologist, a classical music radio announcer, a performing arts administrator, a bookseller, and a proofreader/editor for a small press. Her first book, *Dedication* (2005), the only Signet Regency with two bondage scenes, was followed by the award-winning *The Rules of Gentility* (HarperCollins, 2007). She has written three more Regency chicklits for Little Black Dress (Headline, UK) as well as contemporary erotic romance for Harlequin Spice. She lives near Washington, D.C., where she is hard at work thinking up new and terrible things to do to Jane Austen.

BOOKS BY
JANET MULLANY

JANE AUSTEN: BLOOD PERSUASION
A Novel
ISBN: 978-0-06-195831-1 (paperback)

When your neighbors interrupt your writing it's bad enough. When they're vampires, it's a bloody mess.

In 1810, Jane Austen is in the midst of penning her greatest masterpieces when old Undead friends become new neighbors and raise hell in her tranquil village.

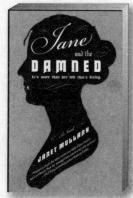

JANE AND THE DAMNED
A Novel
ISBN: 978-0-06-195830-4 (paperback)

When aspiring novelist Jane Austen becomes one of the Damned—the beautiful, sexy vampires of Georgian England—she regards her transformation as a gift. But as an immortal, Jane will have to decide whether eternal life is too high a price to pay for the loss of what means most to her as a mortal.

THE RULES OF GENTILITY
A Novel
ISBN: 978-0-06-122983-1 (paperback)

"I consider the pursuit of bonnets and a husband fairly alike—I do not want to acquire an item that will wear out, or bore me after a brief acquaintance, and we must suit each other very well."

A most unusual and engaging novel about Miss Wellesley-Clegg, a young woman living in Regency London who struggles to find the perfect man—and the perfect bonnet.